MW01701713

Obsessable: The Making of Savannah St. Clair

A "Who I Am" Trilogy

L.D. Jackson

Soul Dope Publishing, L.L.C.

Soul Dope

Obsessable: The Making of Savannah St. Clair is a work of fiction. Names, characters, places, and incidents either are the product of the author's imagination or are used fictitiously. Any resemblance to actual persons, living or dead, events, or locales is entirely coincidental.

Published in the United States by Soul Dope Publishing, L.L.C.

ISBN: 979-8-9890851-0-1
eBook ISBN: 979-8-9890851-1-8

Front Cover design: DLR Designs
Back Cover & Spine design: Andrade Hendricks

Printed in the United States of America

Dedication

To Mark.

The Reason for Everything.

Acknowledgement

Crafting "*Obsessable: The Making of Savannah St. Clair*" has been a remarkable journey, ignited by the incredible support, encouragement, and contributions of numerous individuals. While naming each of you would be a challenge, please know that your presence and involvement have deeply enriched this endeavor and I love you for doing what you do best.

To my family, whose boundless love and understanding sustained me throughout this creative endeavor, I extend my heartfelt appreciation. Your belief in me never wavered, and for that, I am truly blessed.

A special thank you to my friends, who provided both inspiration and solace during the moments of self-doubt. Your presence in my life has been a constant reminder of the power of genuine connections.

I extend my gratitude to the dedicated editors and beta readers who meticulously combed through the manuscript, offering invaluable insights and help in shaping this story into its final form. Your meticulous attention to detail and constructive feedback have been instrumental in bringing *Obsessable* to life.

To the reviewers who took the time to engage with the novel and share their thoughts, thank you for your thoughtful analysis and candid opinions. Your perspectives have enriched the journey of *Obsessable* in ways I couldn't have imagined.

Last but not least, a heartfelt thanks to the readers who have embarked on this literary voyage with me. Your enthusiasm for storytelling is what fuels my passion, and I am humbled by the opportunity to share my work with you.

With immense gratitude,
L.D. Jackson

Prologue

Revenge is a dish best served cold."

commonly attributed to Pierre Choderios de Laclos

Some days leave an impact so strong on us that it changes our lives forever. When I opened the door and saw my assailant standing there, I knew my life would never be the same. I should have killed her the last time she assaulted me, but I let her get away. *How did she find out where I lived?* I thought. There she was, my ex-wife, unashamedly holding a bottle of chilled Dom Perignon. The ink barely dried on the divorce papers, but here she was, trying to start more shit. "*Bitch,"* I cursed in my head.

"What the fuck do you want?" I asked. The nerve of this slut was to be at my door, oblivious that her life was in danger. She should have backed up but didn't. She stood there fearless, wearing a smirk.

"I came to celebrate!" she said, holding the bottle high, grinning like a million-dollar jackpot winner.

"Ain't no damn celebrating I want to do with you," I said as I moved to close the door, but she stepped forward and blocked it. Now I'm not one of those guys that beat up women, but she was about to feel my vengeance for the treacherous shit she did. The betrayal was so poisonous that no antidote could cure it.

"*How could you go and fuck someone, and you're my wife? Of all the muthafuckah's on the planet, you pick my best friend? And to top it off, you do it in my bed? Nasty, no-good, ho.*" These spiteful thoughts ran through my mind while she just stood there, smiling.

A chill engulfed me; my jaw tightened. The frosty, early evening air mirrored my mood. Her amused hazel eyes were fixed on me. She must have thought that I was bluffing, but I wasn't! Granted, I've done bogus deeds too, but I never fucked her friends or brought anyone into our bed. *Trifling ass, lower than a snake's belly.* Rage paced like a caged animal in my head. Should I risk murder charges or close the door? I questioned myself. The former was the option I savored, happy to rot on death row. But no, not for this cunt. She wasn't worth it.

"Remove yourself from my home before I hurt you," I said in a low and lethal voice. I tried to close the door, but she held her ground, immovable.

"Whatever reckless game you're playing, you need to stop," I said, pushing my 6 feet 200 pounds frame against the door, trying to free her arm, but she fought me. *It was time to change tactics.*

"I've got to go," I said, adjusting the damp towel around my waist from my shower, and continued, "My new girl is waiting for me." The sagacious smile she wore abandoned her. It was replaced with a look of deep sadness, carving a river through my eyes and heart. "*Damn.*"

"*What?*" Her eyes locked on mine, searching for the truth. Tears etched contours of pain down her face as she shook her head from side to side. Beneath my anger, an ugly, raw wound, long covered, was exposed. The agony was palpable, not just for what she'd done to me but for what I'd done to her. Too many nights, she'd cried while I'd done things she never deserved. I tried to focus on the way she had wronged me. It seemed easier than admitting my mistakes, but now as she stood weeping, I wanted to apologize. I played a role in the demise of our marriage. "*Don't fall for her bullshit; you will regret it,*" the words blared like an oncoming train in my head. I stood there, powerless to close the door to my home or heart. I lifted her chin and caressed her face. Her tears slowed as if she understood what I felt but couldn't say.

As if I was seeing her for the first time, I realized how much she had changed. She was always gorgeous, but now she appeared more exceptionally so. She could be a model for MAC Cosmetics. Her long cinnamon hair, which she normally wore in a bun, cascaded provocatively over her caramel shoulders. A flowing mane with streaks of gold. Her eyes radiated a seductive gleam. Gone was the innocent eighteen-year-old I married six years ago.

She parted her luscious red lips, and I yearned to kiss them. High-voltage lust danced over my wet skin, electrocuting me with desire. Her black trench coat fell open. I had once considered her plump, but now I could see the butter spread in all the right places. Her full breasts peeked out from her tresses, nipples like chocolate drops. My mouth watered. An expensive red garter was cut high enough to expose clean-shaven delight. Long legs encased in thigh-high red silk stockings, with sexy red stilettos. A delectable package of sensuality. The combination would make a man come without touching himself.

The irony struck me. This woman was a thousand times sexier than all the women I'd slept with. I wouldn't have gone elsewhere if she had given me this before. *But why the enchantress now?* There was only one reason: Jared. We'd met in sixth grade and were as close as brothers. Up until the day I found him in bed with my wife. My enmity swelled with the memory, and I didn't care how good she looked. She rolled the icy bottle over my chest, weakening me. It was time for her to go, for I knew that if she stayed a little longer, I wouldn't be able to control my burning desire. The shift in my mood change didn't escape her eye.

"I have a gift for you!" She spoke.

I took her wrist, pushed her backward, and said, "I don't want it!"

"Are you sure?" She lowered her eyes, inviting me to gaze upon her body. She rolled a hard nipple, and I salivated with desire. My manhood jumped like a greyhound in the starting chute. My towel fell to the floor. I felt engulfed in a fiery furnace, flames lapping at my groin. Urgency consumed me as I pulled her in. I slammed her against the door. We were all over each other, tongues and hands lustily exploring. We covered each other with moist, hot, passionate kisses. I moaned as she rubbed her tits against my chest. I wrestled with her coat; the champagne hit the floor. I grasped her bottom and lifted as she wrapped those fine legs around me. The anticipation of being inside her juiced me, my member pulsating fully erect. "Oh my god!" Gripping tight, I impaled her. She was so wet it made my body shudder from head to toe, and her warm and soft vaginal muscles immersed me. She begged me to take her, and I moved in and out of her with long, deliberate strokes. Her vulva, fully engorged now, retained the allure of a petaled rose. She was so delicious that I wanted to cry with each thrust. Then the vision of Jared returned. I buried my face in her hair, trying to erase it, but it held on like a viper poised to suck my life out. A porn movie of the two looped through my mind in high definition with Dolby Sound. It embittered and stimulated me.

"You bitch!" My thrusting was fueled by envy. Every fiber of my being was enraged, but that didn't stop me. I rammed harder. "Fuck, I hate you!" I uttered.

"Sorry, baby," she said, but I didn't believe her. She had purposefully done it to break my heart. Suddenly, she uncoiled her legs, startling me and upsetting my rhythm. Smiling seductively, she turned me around and backed me into the door. She moved down my body with her tongue, leaving a trail of gentle bites and kisses. A desperate frenzy took over. *Was she going down on me?* I thought. She had never done it before. *Oh god, please do it.* My engorged penis bounced. She licked the head and took me in her mouth, lips and tongue working me. She deep-throated me so skillfully I didn't dare avert my gaze. My knees buckled. She had me on a wild roller coaster, and I held on for the ride. Pausing for a moment, she popped the cork on the Dom and poured it over my member. She sucked me as champagne dribbled from her mouth. My ecstasy mounted. I yelled as the floodgates opened, and I released a waterfall of whiteness. She caught every drop, sucking me dry like a pro.

"You bitch!" I said as I slid to the floor, drained of power.

She smiled disingenuously, "Checkmate."

We got it on for the next two hours like rabbits on meth. We made love in every room of my new place. She took over my body, making me her personal acolyte. I enjoyed every second as we christened my furniture, floors, stairs, and kitchen counters, leaving her scent on everything. It wasn't how I planned to spend my Saturday night. I had friends, including a woman I had just met, waiting for me at High 5ive Rooftop Bar, but now I didn't care if I ever touched another woman again. We lay on the kitchen floor, wasted, our bodies entangled amongst shards of a shattered bowl of strawberries. I dipped fruit in the cream between her legs and dined. Aftershocks coursed through me. The only thing I could think of was, *how could I live without her now?* This vixen wanted me back. *Could we start over?* I asked myself. *Could I trust her again?*

Before Jared, she had always been faithful and loyal in every way. No man could have had a better wife except for sex. She had put that dog to rest today and was now lying content in my arms. But how could I love her again? She had broken my heart. Women don't understand that it isn't personal when a man bangs another woman; it doesn't mean anything. Like a carpenter who uses a hammer or a plumber who uses a snake, a man uses his dick as a tool to get a job done, nothing else. He cleans up and goes home to the wife he loves. But when a woman does it, she causes irreparable harm, for she castrates his ego and carves out his heart with a jagged razor leaving the guts of his soul spilled on the ground. But what we'd shared today seemed so right. I lifted her head, and she kissed my face. She read my thoughts and moved atop me like a lioness to dominate her prey. She took my mind off the past. Before, I was her high-powered Ducati Superbike. Now she handled me like a classic Duesenberg, slow and easy.

"Michael," she breathed in my mouth, between sultry pirouettes over my lips. Her call of my name was pure, a longing. It made me realize the forgiveness I owed her. I touched her face and peered into her beautiful eyes. The emotions cascading through me were so intense that my body trembled. I wanted to possess her again, this woman who once held my future securely. Then I did something unexpected. *I cried.* I let go for what seemed like eons, expelling the agony and pain of loss and reveling in the joy of finding her again. But still, I couldn't forget. She knew better, and he did, too. *Better.* That's what tortured me, stripped me bare. She needed to set the record straight.

"Did he fuck you better than me?" I gazed into her eyes, certain those orbs were hiding something. She was silent for a moment, and I felt the pressure in my head elevate. I swore that if she didn't answer correctly, I would bash her skull and take that murder charge.

"Baby, no one has ever done me better than you!" Her reply didn't assuage my doubt, and she knew it. She kissed my forehead and then my lips. Her eager tongue slipped into my mouth. It was warm and pungent with my seed. "Come with me," she said, pulling me to my feet. Her half-naked, sexy body swayed before me as she picked up her coat. Strutting down the hall to my bedroom, she glanced back. I sensed a setup, a wrecking ball hurtling towards me. Sweetly she smiled, an astute sorceress, and I drank her poison.

Following her into my bedroom, my sanctuary was now her temple. I was her supplicant. She put on a D'Angelo CD, "*How Does It Feel.*" It was our song on our honeymoon in Carmel, the night I first made love to her. It made me smile. She danced slowly to me and reached for my hand, leading me to my bed, where I swore she would never be again. At her silent behest, I lay on my back. My shaft bounced back to life. Her touch hypnotized me. She slipped her hose from the holder and was ready to make out again. It amazed me because she never initiated sex. She didn't act like she enjoyed it but tolerated it because she wanted little ones. Twins. She had an obsession since she and her twin sister were separated early.

In almost six years together, she hadn't gotten pregnant. She bound my ankles to the brass bed with her stockings, and a hundred alarms went off in my head. But the sight of her voluptuous caramel mounds and her tantalizing cherry silenced all caution. With a belt from her trench coat, she climbed onto me, sliding up my thigh, sweetness nearing my cock. I wanted her to mount it. And she did. My hard inches plunged into her warmth. I watched as she rode me, lips glistening. *Damn, how she worked those hips.* She stopped as I neared another climax, poised to go over the edge.

We made eye contact as she moved up my chest and tied my wrists to the headboard, her deliciousness inches from my face. I strained to put my mouth on her. She gave me what I wanted; sat roughly on my face. I tongued her swollen clit and then sucked it in. Brazenly, she rode me to another orgasm. She slid off and took my shaft into her mouth. "So, baby," she said, rolling her tongue around my head. Clearly not focused on her words: her mouth held me spellbound. "Is this what you wanted from all those women you fucked?"

Her syrupy and acerbic words hurled me back to the day she'd found me out. From the first day I laid eyes on Monica, I knew I should ignore her, but I didn't for one reason, her natural 44DD tits. A month into my bump-and-grind sessions with her, I canceled a date on her birthday. Of course, she was pissed, but I talked some sugary bullshit, and she let me back in. Well, the next week, she used my words to finesse my talk against me, and I checked her. The next time I called, she answered the phone, "Mrs. Michael Wilson." I cussed her out and never called back. One night as I left another woman's house, she was sitting on the hood of my BMW M8 Coupe. I blew it.

"Oh, so you think you can screw me and lie to me?" she screamed, "you messed over the wrong one, but I can show you better than I can tell you." I went on with my life without thinking about her. Until she arranged a special "service" for me. It was Sunday morning, and my father's All Saints Progressive Baptist church was packed with over three thousand people. My father, Pastor Ephraim Wilson, was into his sermon when an usher handed me a note. He signaled a couple of rows back. It was Monica, seated with at least seven women beside her that I had sex with. My shock multiplied: Tammy. I dated her many months ago but hurled her to the curb after she said she was pregnant. A baby rested in her arms. I coolly read the paper. "What happens when the hunter gets captured by the game?"

"Damn!" I slid out of the pew. I wanted to quietly get them out of the sanctuary before they embarrassed me. I bent down and whispered to Monica, "Baby, I missed you. Can we talk?" An explosion ensued. "Playa', you got me twisted!" The service came to a halt. My father stopped preaching and quickly surveyed the situation. With a nod, his aides took control and ejected them. But not before Monica made her case for all to hear. I returned to my seat beside my wife but didn't look at her. I just sat there tight-jawed with a phony smile on my face. My father talked briefly about "desperate, lost souls." The chorus of amen was boisterous, but I knew nosy members were already on social media. My father quickly moved on. By the end of his sermon, everyone was on their feet except for my wife. My mother, Marguerite Wilson, whisked her out. When I got home, my quiet wife vanished. The woman who replaced her was ferocious. This savage yelled, cursed, and threw things. The baby was the clincher. "How could you?" I tried to calm her and told her it was all lies.

"You think I'm stupid?" She got in my face. "I know what you're doing!" When she finished her tirade, I told her I would do whatever I wanted. The banshees' eyes glazed over. She went to the kitchen, grabbed the biggest knife, and charged me. I dodged her, then beat her unmercifully. I stayed away for a week. I wanted to make my point: never challenge me again.

"Answer my question, Michael. Is this what you wanted?" Her words jolted me back to the present. *What could I say? The truth? Yes. I craved coitus. I did unexplainable things for the nookie.* I searched her eyes, hoping to find some sympathy and see the woman who always had my back, no matter what. The one I'd known I would marry from the second I'd seen her. An angel that glowed lit from the inside. Within six months, we'd tied the knot. I'd never meant to devastate her this way.

"What happened to you?" I asked.

"You happened to me," she retorted.

"What, Dr. Frankenstein, don't you recognize your handiwork?" She inquired, and I said nothing.

"Do you realize how much I trusted you? With all the horrible things men have done to me." Tears flowed down her face. "I opened my heart and put my confidence in you." Venomous words. "Why? Because you promised you wouldn't hurt me." This struck me hard. "My whole life, from childhood, I could never trust a man, not one!"

I knew only a little about the horrors of her life. Her parents had abandoned her at birth. There was some kind of family tragedy when she was 6. Her strict aunt got guardianship. Three years into our marriage, there'd been a suicide attempt on her twenty-first birthday. The hospital recommended psychological evaluation, mandatory counseling, and pills. Several months later, she'd zipped back into her "good girl" persona.

She sat on the bed near my side. "I didn't ask you for much, did I?"

She'd asked for only one thing; give her a happy home with happy children. For the first time, the full extent of the damage was registered in my mind that I'd never even apologized for.

"When I heard that woman in the church that morning, all of my hopes died," I could feel contempt in her voice as she continued, "Since that day, I've wanted to cause you the same devastation."

Without a doubt, she'd accomplished what she set out to do.

"I think pain should be multiplied, she exclaimed. "You increased my grief exponentially." Dread rose in me as I wondered where this was headed. “Did it hurt when you walked in, and Jared was inside me?"

"Get out of my house now!" I wailed, struggling to break free of my restraints. They didn't budge. *How did I let this cunt tie me up?*

"When you asked earlier if he did me better than you, I lied,” she informed.

The sight of her and him together flooded my mind again and transported me back to the day of their betrayal. It had been months since the Monica incident. I thought we’d moved past it. Happily, she sent me to work with a great breakfast and a big kiss. Several hours later, she called my secretary, saying the house was on fire. I tried to call her, but it went to voicemail. I feared the worst. As I turned down Campus Drive in our prestigious neighborhood of Oakland Hills, I expected to see fire trucks. Instead, Jared's black Escalade was parked in the driveway. I figured he must have put it out. It never occurred to me that it was he who burned hot.

I stepped into the Twilight Zone and moved up the staircase to the master suite. I was bewildered when I walked in and heard her screams of enjoyment. My mind denied it, even as I stood at the door. She looked at me while begging Jared to ram harder. He was so into it that he didn't recognize I was there.

In a murderous fury, I rushed at them. She moved aside. He and I fought like two wild bulls. We were both bloodied when I slipped, and he got away. I turned my wrath on her, but she stood unafraid. A revolver in her hand. She managed to put on a sweatshirt and jeans. The suitcase by the door said everything. "Tomorrow, divorce papers will be served," she picked up the bag, “Sign and return them to my attorney. If you don't oblige, you won't live to regret it!" I did exactly as she said. I also sent that bed to the dump and moved out of that house.

"So, did you enjoy eating me?" I didn't remark.

She continued, "Well, I visited Jared earlier and fucked him. His cum is delicious, don't you think?"

I spat at her, "You scandalous bitch!" I should have known better than to let her in.

"But wait, you haven't heard the best part," she intoned.

I tried to block her out, but it didn’t work. "Since early in our marriage, your daddy’s been constantly trying to get into my panties!" Her words froze me. She wouldn't. "After I left Jared, I went to see Pastor Wilson and gave him the best fucking of his life." No one could be this devious. “He didn’t tell you? He’s the one who's been taking care of me since I left your sorry ass." The wrecking ball hit and totaled me.

“I will kill you,” I said. She threw her head back and roared with laughter.

"I left my bra under your momma’s pillow too." She leaned into my face. "Serves her right for the way she treated me!"

"My mother never did anything to you!" I said as I imagined my mother's discovery.

"Clueless fucker." She hit me so hard that I was sure she had broken my jaw. A cold deadness moved into her eyes as she stood over me. She kicked me hard in the nuts. The room spun. I couldn’t stop coughing. The pain was excruciating. I would murder her, no doubt.

"That’s for the baby." She climbed off the bed and reached into her jacket pocket. Pulled out a slip of paper. "Let me tell you if you wonder what this is all about." Leaning over me, she spat calculated words. "I would’ve forgiven the infidelity and maybe even the baby." Tears flowed, and she defiantly wiped them away.

"Do you remember our specific conversation that morning before your groupies came to church?" Her face was red with fury as she waited to see if I remembered. "I was helping you put on your suit jacket, and you asked me why I was so happy." She paused, smiling momentarily as if the memory evoked was joyful. But just as quickly, the anger reappeared.

"I told you I'd made reservations at The Top of the Mark in San Francisco for a couple of days for a romantic getaway?" It came flooding back. I'd never seen her so excited.

"Memory jogged, right? I had planned our stay to give you some great news. But you remember how you stomped me brutally before you left?" Her words cut me deep.

No! My mind screamed as I closed my eyes. I knew what she would say. "I had to call your mother for help. She drove me to a doctor in Sacramento. A friend of hers. Not that I could get care. Nope, but so that no police report would be filed against her beloved son for feticide." I was numb. The facts of my actions sunk in.

"Right. I was ten weeks pregnant. You killed my babies!" Now I understand everything. "Yep, it was twins!" she said, holding a sonogram test and throwing it at me. For the next hour, I lay powerless as she destroyed every one of my possessions. Beyonce's *"Sorry"* blared on repeat. Now I regret moving to such a remote part of Upper Rockridge. I didn't live near my neighbors. No one would hear the carnage and call for help. This crazy psycho destroyed my whole life. When she entered with a huge blade, I began to shake. "I was nothing but faithful to you," she fumed. She entered my closet and shredded everything. An angry litany flowed from her mouth, leaving the room again.

When the door to the garage opened, I began to cry. Not my Beamer! I heard my prized possession being pulverized. "You ruthless bitch!" Yes, I harmed her, but I didn't deserve this. She returned, berserk and out of breath. She reached inside her coat and pulled a .38 revolver from the pocket. Sheer terror seized me as I'd seen her break down before.

"Were you saying something?" she said, grabbing my shaft hard. Pressed the weapon into it. A groan escaped from my lips.

"Please, God, please," I whispered, afraid to move.

"Oh, now you want to call on him...you weren't calling on the Lord to help you keep this in your pants," she taunted.

"What I did here," gesturing at the room, "is what you did here," pointing to her heart. With a wicked look on her face, she spun the chamber. I was distraught. "I've got two bullets inside. One for each of my twins!" When she placed the revolver to my head, I cried and begged.

"Please, God," I uttered.

"Save your prayers; he never answered any of mine. So, fuck him and fuck you!"

"I'm sorry for everything I did to crush you," I said through blurry eyes.

"Oh, sorry, huh," she said, shaking her head. "Too late." She moved the gun from my temple and placed it in my mouth. The metallic taste was a harbinger of the bullet that was coming to separate my brain from my head. Light years seemed to pass in silence as sweat rolled down my face and mingled with my tears. She smiled and pulled the trigger. Click. A loud yowl escaped as my body shook with terror.

"Give me a chance to make this right," I begged.

"My babies will decide," she said. Again, she spun the chamber and put it back in my mouth. She pulled the trigger again. Click. I could tell she really wanted me to die. I sobbed frantically.

"Well, I guess they chose you to live." Disappointed, she stood. I dared to take a breath. My heart pranced with uneasy euphoria. With all the carnage today, at least I was still alive! As if to assure me this hadn't been a game, she opened the chamber, and two bullets fell on my chest. I was ecstatic as she walked away. She put her coat on and stuck the gun in her pocket. This insanity was coming to an end. *Thank you, Jesus*!

"The only reason my children gave you a life sentence instead of death is that you will be tormented for many years." Her eyes narrowed as she glanced at me. She stood there, lost in contemplation. "But I put this on everything," she patted the pocket where the gun rested. "If you give me a reason, I will gladly end you and your entire family." Then she was gone. I strained to hear the sound of the door closing. As time passed, I recounted everything; I found it unbelievable. I'd made it through. I tried to pull my restraints free, but there was no slack. I had no idea how I would get free, but I was grateful to be alive. Angrily, my mind started planning how I would get even. "Crazy...bitch...I... will...kill...you!" I yelled.

She poked her head back in, and my heart jumped straight out of my chest. "You said what?"

I cursed myself as she entered the room with a large can of lighter fluid. Goddammit! "You're right, I'm crazy," laughing as she doused my room.

"Too crazy to let someone like you live. You've been given the sentence you gave my babies." She took out a lighter and a piece of paper. "Our marriage certificate," she said, lighting up the paper. “Here’s to letting death do us part since you didn’t want to keep your part of the vows.”

“Please...please don’t!” I screamed, to no avail. I fought against my restraints. She threw the burning paper in the air, and I watched in horror as it floated to the floor in slow motion and caught the carpet on fire.

“Bitch, come untie me!” I yelled angrily as I twisted, trying to free myself.

“That’s Ms. Savannah St. Clair Bitch, to you! Enjoy your trip to hell,” and then she was gone. At that moment, I knew for sure she’d lost her fucking mind, and I was certain mine would never be the same again.

Chapter One

"One's own self is well hidden from one's own self: of all mines of treasures, one's own is the last to be dug up."

—Friedrich Nietzsche

Savannah stared up at the lofty, exquisite behemoth of a skyscraper. It stood on 57th Street and Park Avenue, in the heart of Manhattan. The search for her twin sister, Elisha, and revenge on her aunt Tina, who separated them over eighteen years ago, had led her here. She'd intended to come here six years ago. What stopped her? Michael's bullshit promises, that's what. Her plan had been to flee her Aunt Essie's asylum in Oakland the day she turned eighteen. The day before her birthday, she met Michael, and everything changed.

The white sun was reflected in the windows of the buildings. It gave the illusion of a joyous yuletide in the city. It was getting even more frigid in the festive winter wonderland. The chilled December air told the real story. It blared a warning: a cold-hearted woman, Savannah St. Clair, had arrived in the Big Apple. Although the streets were alive with trumpeting angels, ringing Christmas music, and trees with millions of lights sparkled, none of it could change her focus. Maybe, once upon a time, many years ago, it would have.

As a child, Savannah wanted nothing more for Christmas than to experience this. Tina Preston was her mother's sister and one of the most beautiful women she had ever seen. Her milk chocolate skin, flawless makeup, and impeccable designer clothes were stunning. She lived and worked in New York City. She was a high-fashion model who, during her downtime, often visited Los Angeles bearing lots of gifts, especially at Christmas time. Savannah, her twin Elisha, and their brother David, who was one year older, were always glad to see their aunt. She doted on them, even though their grandmother, Barbara Ann Preston, who they affectionately called Nana, tried to discourage it. Not only did Tina lavish gifts and attention on the kids, but she also helped her mother financially. Nana was the kids' only caregiver, and the extra cash was a great help. The kids' parents, Lolita and Gary St. Clair had abandoned them at birth, choosing to live as junkies on the streets of Los Angeles.

Lolita, as Tina told it, had once been a beautiful, promising athlete on her way to college before she met Gary, a street-savvy, fast-dealing French boy from the Upper East Side in Manhattan, who had been sent to Los

Angeles by his parents, to live with an aunt, to keep him out of trouble. It hadn't worked. Savannah loved to snuggle with her twin in her Nana's lap listening to Tina regale them with stories of Christmas in New York. Joyously, Savannah would wave her hand, begging to visit. She wanted to see everything, especially FAO Schwarz, where most of their toys came from. Tina had promised that one day she would bring them to visit. That hadn't happened.

Nana and David died in a car accident when the twins were five. A horrific tragedy that still haunted Savannah. She thought they would move with their aunt to New York afterward. It didn't happen. Instead, Tina and another aunt, Essie Wallin, came to town and located their mother, Lolita. Their mother promised to get off drugs, and the twins were forced to live with her. She was still in the throes of her addiction, and the twins' lives quickly went from heaven with Nana to a nightmare. That was just the beginning of the horrors. On the twins' sixth birthday, something unimaginable happened. Afterward, Tina, who was there for the birthday celebration, took Elisha and left Savannah to live with Essie. It would prove the cruelest of hell.

Like everyone else, Tina had failed her. She had never visited or called in eighteen years to check on Savannah or let her speak to her sister. Savannah would never again be that wide-eyed child wishing to experience the city at Christmas. The only dream she harbored now was to exact long-overdue revenge on Tina and reunite with her sister, the person she loved and missed most in the world. A Santa with a list and a bag of presents over his shoulder stood a few feet from her. His mocking grin seemed to grow wider. He was a liar. She'd done everything to be on the "nice," not "naughty" list. None of her good deeds had mattered. Santa had stopped visiting the year her Nana died. All of it was a colossal tale of fuckery. She approached him and violently slapped the list out of his hand.

"You lying bastard," spitting in his face. Most people passed by, ignoring her. Some shook their heads, while others stopped and recorded the scene with their cell phones. Savannah didn't care about any of them. This was deeply personal. She picked up the list. Just as she thought, the paper was blank. She pulled a few of the presents from the bag. They were empty, just like God's promises. Nana was a Christian who had taught Savannah to always believe in God, prayer, and the power of love. Nana would say, "God loves you, baby. He is faithful to his promises and will never forsake you." She had believed her grandmother too. But with each calamity, God's silence and failure to act only caused more heartbreak. She wiped away her tears every time, clinging to hope, giving God another chance to redeem himself. It never happened. Her damaged soul held rooms of evidence as proof.

Savannah dropped her head and wallowed in pity thick like quicksand, pulling her down into an untenable place. Even now, it seems so unfair. She only wanted to love the same person for all time and give birth to beautiful, healthy babies. Wrapping her arms around her stomach, the sadness wouldn't let go. Her babies would've been about 8 months old now. She should've been preparing bottles, changing diapers, and smelling the scent of baby powder. Instead, she had empty arms and a hollow heart. She needed to let go of the past and continue her mission. She wiped away the tears, resolute in her determination to seek revenge. Nana had been so wrong about so much.

Contrary to what Nana said, the meek didn't inherit the earth. They were beaten to death with two-by-fours. Those who mourned didn't find comfort; they got more shit taken away. And the peacemakers? They got violently fucked in the ass. Raw? Yes, but it was the ugly-ass gospel preached from the pulpit of life.

The cold wind whipped at Savannah, and she shivered, throwing Santa's blank list to the ground. Yep, she would be as naughty as she wanted to and dare him or anyone else to say anything. That went for God, too. His way had only gotten her screwed in the ass with no Vaseline. Now she would be the one with the twelve-inch dildo in her hand. Reaching into her pocket, Savannah pulled out a piece of wrinkled paper. Like Santa, she had a list, but hers was not blank. She didn't need to check it twice, either. Everyone on it was etched in her memory, and soon she would be carved in theirs, too. On the paper was the name of Tina's company, Preston Enterprises, Suite 2107. Now she would discover why her aunt had taken her twin sister and left her behind in the most horrendous part of the underworld.

Tina exuberantly took a deep breath as she climbed into the cab. She placed her hand on her chest. Unbelievable. Had she just signed a multi-million-dollar deal for her modeling agency? "Damn, right, I did!" The driver glanced in the rearview mirror. Arrogantly, she stared back at him. No cabbie could ruin this day for her.

"Where to, ma'am?" he asked, feigning politeness. She rattled off the restaurant's name and pulled out her cell phone.

"Hello, my gorgeous wife," Tina masked her excitement.

"Hello to you too, baby!" Mya sang sexily. "How did it go?"

It felt delicious to get this huge win overall. Tina knew the anticipation would be driving Mya and her other friends crazy. She was silent for a while. "Do you have a bottle of champagne on the table?"

"You know we do. The gang's all here; all we need is you." Someone snatched the phone from Mya.

"Right, get yourself down here," Deshay said. Mya grabbed the phone back.

"I'm about 20 minutes away." Tina glanced out at the traffic.

"I signed the deal! We got it!" Tina could hear the applause.

Most of the restaurant patrons were probably staring at her United Nations family. They could be a wild bunch. It mattered very little what others thought about her wife or her friends. They were the center of her universe: they made all her challenges as a smaller agency against world leaders in New York City worth it. Everyone at that table played a major part in her life. Mya, her Latin bombshell who'd always been her port in the storm. They'd married in

Vermont after being in a committed relationship for five years. Kimeya, an Asian American with legendary versatility in front of the camera. Chelsea's cool, blue-eyed, blonde-haired beauty epitomized European style. There was Deshay, her gorgeous, keep it real, African American, ride or die. Then there was Tanzi, her BFF, the one she depended on the most, especially in business. She was the master planner and visionary of the group. Tanzi, a full-blooded African from Kenya, was both captivating and intelligent. Tina owed most of her firm's success to her legal prowess and connections. Tanzi was one of New York's top corporate and trial attorneys.

Everyone there, except for Tanzi, had worked together as models from their teens. No matter what they went through, they were true friends. A rarity in life, especially in this city. They were the top models at Preston Enterprises, along with a stable of notable, exotic women. The five-year contract with one of the largest media houses was proof. All those years of hard work had paid off. "See you soon." Tina ended the call and stared out the window.

A sudden, rueful thought took hold and snatched away the one thing she needed to hold onto: her happiness. Paranoia about the past and the things she had done? Despicable, unmentionable things. Things not one of her closest friends or even her wife knew anything about. The memories were always there, dogging her, always a step behind. But now, she had love, money, friends, and prestige. It was real; she held it all in her hands.

"It couldn't slip away again," she whispered. Yes, it could! A voice deep within her, born of experience, screamed.

"Good afternoon, Preston Enterprises." It was the cheerful voice of Cindy, Tina's secretary.

"Hey Cindy, we did it!" Tina laughed, listening as Cindy shrieked with delight. It was a victory for everyone. "We are so proud of you, Tina; *you* did it!" "We all did. Please let everyone know and tell them to take the rest of the day off! I'm going to the restaurant to meet the gang, so I'm AWOL!"

"I totally understand, and you deserve it. Before you go, I need to tell you about a visitor earlier. She said she'd been referred to you," Cindy exclaimed.

"That can wait until tomorrow," Tina tried to interject.

"Well, I need to let you know something. She wanted to wait for you, but I told her you would be out most of the day."

"And?" Tina intoned.

"Well, Mya called, and I told her I had made reservations for your group at Casa de Reyes, and before I hung up, she headed out."

"Don't worry about it. Now go home," she said and hung up.

Tina stepped inside Empellon's restaurant, took off her Versace sunglasses, and greeted the hostess with a warm smile. Savannah watched intently from the bar area. She might not have noticed her without the smile, which revealed her huge dimples and those straight, white teeth. Her aunt had changed a lot. Once a gorgeous woman, now she was a lean, wannabe version of a man. Her hair was cut short; she wore an exquisitely tailored navy pants suit with a white dress shirt. None of it could hide the fact that she was still a woman. As she headed towards a group of women, her joyful stride upset Savannah. They all stood, kissed, and hugged like one big, happy family.

Palpable anger rose from Savannah's stomach and coursed throughout her body, causing such intense heat she could have set the seat on fire. Savannah shook herself free from the deep pang that threatened to suffocate her and watched instead with calculated animus as Tina and her friends toasted with champagne, laughed, and talked. How dare Tina have so much when everything had been taken from her? And where was her sister?

"Enjoy your big moment, bitch." She let them get comfortable, then picked their flesh apart like a vulture.

"Tell us all the details, baby." Mya leaned in to kiss Tina discreetly on the cheek.

"Well, let's just say our firm opened a major door with this one. But I've been talking business all day and am ready to celebrate." Tina sipped her bubbly as Mya tempted her with crab nachos.

"Aw, ain't that cute!" Deshay chimed. Tina shook her head at her tipsy friend.

"Well, I know you're tired of talkin' business, Tee, but I want to give you your props." Deshay poured herself more champagne and then passed the bottle.

"We're all very proud of you, Tina. To Preston Enterprise," Kimya said as they raised their glasses. "To us!"

Tina lifted her glass as they all took sips of champagne. Her eyes watered as she fought back the emotions flooding her soul. She took them in one by one, so grateful for her friends. This open show of love and friendship touched her deeply.

"Alright!" Tina broke the awkward moment. "Enough about me; what's going on with my girls?"

"Well, I'm glad you asked. I haven't had my usual weekly counseling session," Kimeya joked.

Everyone at the table laughed. It was well known within the group that Tina thrived on being everyone's confidant.

"And who is it this week?" Mya rolled her eyes.

"Fernando!" Kimeya batted her long eyelashes.

"You are so fickle!" Mya took another sip of her drink.

"Mya's right. Last week you were making wedding plans with Akio," Tina pointed the finger at her.

"I can't help it if I like to keep my options open," Kimeya threw a chip at Tina, then one at Mya. "Variety is the spice of life!"

"And AIDS is the MSG that will kill you, too," Tina said.

"Like I said," Mya replied, dipping a nacho in guacamole, "you are confused."

"What's up with all this hating?" Chelsea said, "maybe she wants to explore her options before settling down." "Spoken like the true whore that you are," Mya said, smiling at Chelsea.

"You're just jealous because your ass is on lockdown with Tina!" Deshay said, gyrating her hips. "All you get is the same old bump and grind every other week!" Chelsea high-fived Deshay.

"Tell her, Shay!"

"When you've got the hottest woman ever created, there is no need to be jealous." Tina passionately kissed Mya. Mya blew a kiss at Deshay.

"You'll need to stop," Tanzi chided. "You sound like guests on Jerry Springer.

"Well, let's talk about me now!" Deshay lifted both of her arms up.

"Ummm, we don't want details about your romp with Ruben! But did you use a condom this time?" Kimeya said nonchalantly, taking a sip of her margarita. "I love your badass kids, but you don't need any more."

Deshay stood, pointing the finger at her. "Bitch, you need to keep my kids out of your fuckin' mouth!"

"Deshay, sit your drunk self-down." Tanzi reached for her arm and forcibly pulled her back in her chair.

"Keep playin' with me, and they're goin' to put your picture on the back of a milk carton!" Deshay slung her words at Kimeya.

"You already have three different babies and ten different babies' daddies." Kimeya did her best, Maury Povich accent: "Thomas, you are not the father!"

"That shit ain't funny," Deshay snorted as they all laughed.

"Look, ho's, don't let me read your pussy whipped asses." Deshay rolled her eyes at the group.

"They need some dick!" Chelsea exclaimed. Several patrons at the next table glared at them.

"Ain't shit a dick can do for me," Tina said, glaring at Chelsea.

"What kind of place is this?" an Adam Sandler look-alike yelled from the table beside theirs, grabbing everyone's attention.

"This is supposed to be a fine eating establishment, but it's really a goddamn Lesbo hangout!" Blue Eyes said, taking a swig from his beer as he and Adam Sandler look-alike burst into laughter.

"We ought to make them suck our dicks; that will teach them," the Adam Sandler look-alike said, smacking the table.

"What the fuck did he say?" Kimeya fumed as she and Tina angrily stood up. Tanzi motioned them both to sit down.

"Don't," Tanzi winked at Tina. "Let me have the pleasure." She stood confidently. They had been through this before. Usually, people rolled their eyes, and Tanzi was the first to ignore them. However, this was a special celebration for Tina, and she deserved it. Tanzi's chair scooted loudly against the floor as she reached into her suit pocket. She pulled a business card from the case and approached the men's table.

Tanzi slammed her card on the table, jarring the crystal glasses. Blue Eyes' beer tipped over and spilled into his lap. He jumped up, cursing. The restaurant, which had been loud, suddenly quieted. Tanzi frowned. She was comfortable commanding attention; adept at getting her point across. News outlets routinely covered the large settlements she got for her clients. Major law firms would settle rather than face her in court.

"Listen," she said, looking at one, then the other with menace. "If I hear one more word from you, I will be on the phone in a heartbeat with the County District Attorney seeking a warrant for your arrest for violating the Administrative Code of the City of New York Section 8-602 that makes it unlawful to harass or make threats of violence against individuals based upon sexual identity."

Blue Eyes read the card, then looked back at her. It was clear he knew who she was. He sobered quickly. "Besides criminal charges, I'll bring a $10-million-dollar harassment suit against you under the city's Human Rights Law before you have time to pay your tip!"

Tanzi said, patting her card. "Do you understand me?" Tanzi glared at them.

"Yes," Blue Eyes' face reddened.

"Good." Tanzi returned to her friends. She grabbed her champagne and took a long swallow while the others patted her on the back and gave each other high fives.

"Now, suck on that, bitch," Chelsea said to the Adam Sandler look-alike as he and Blue Eyes threw money on the table and left.

As Savannah eyed Tina's group, the bartender sat another bourbon neat before her. A gift from another hungry man who thought he could get lucky with a $15 drink. From the second she'd walked into the bar area, swaying her curvy hips suggestively, eyes followed her. She understood the power of her allure and wielded it like an enchantress. Whatever she wanted, a man would give it without question.

Before Michael's bitch outing him in church, she'd never considered using men. Savannah took a swig of the fiery whiskey and did a quick calculation: she had about twenty-five grand left of the money she extorted from Michael's father. In New York, that wouldn't last long. After she dealt with Tina, she'd find a few wealthy benefactors and implement her next plans.

As she stood and downed the rest of her bourbon, she saw a man who resembled Michael at the bar's end, smiling. By now, somebody must have discovered his charred remains. The Wilson clan, their church, and the Bay Area knew the carnage she'd left in her wake. Not only had she left her bra under Marguerite's pillow, but she also left an incriminating package of pictures and other details documenting Pastor Ephraim Wilson's kingdom relationships with members of his congregation, including his long affair with the wife of his assistant pastor.

She delivered the same package to a writer at The Oakland Tribune. She could hear the collapse of the House of Wilson. The thought made her smile. Served them right for everything they had taken from her. Smoothing her dress, she puffed out her chest. *That, ladies, is how you get revenge!*

Now it was Tina's turn. She'd closely watched her and her groupies like a lioness stalking its prey. The tall, Black woman was Tina's power. The Latin woman, on the other hand, had her heart. She would take them both.

"Now, let's see how you feel when everything you have is gone."

Tanzi was staring at something across the room. Everyone's heads turned to see where she was looking.

"Hello, Auntie Tina," a gorgeous woman said cheerfully.

Immediately, Tanzi was captivated and didn't know why. The woman looked coyly at each of them. Tanzi's first impression was that the woman's look didn't match the clothes. She wore a tight, sleeveless red dress with a neckline that plunged to her navel. Her huge breasts pushed against the material, two prisoners begging to be released. Her hair draped wildly around her shoulders. Tanzi felt flushed. She didn't date anyone, not men, and especially not women. She rarely had sexual thoughts. She doubtless wasn't gay, so why the attraction?

"Auntie Tina?" Deshay was puzzled. "I thought you were an only child?"

“I’m her niece, Savannah,” the woman remarked, pulling a chair from the next table and sliding between Tina and Mya. Mya had to move over; the woman was so close she practically sat in her lap. All were speechless for the first time that evening, staring at the provocative intruder. Tanzi observed how oddly Tina looked at the woman, a mix of familiarity and puzzlement. Tina stood and mumbled apologetically. “Excuse us,” sliding her chair back.

“Don’t leave your party on my account, Auntie.” The woman reached for some nachos on Tina’s plate, staring at Tanzi.

“You’re the shit today, am I right?” the woman said, reaching for Mya’s half-empty flute. She downed the golden liquid in one swallow. They all looked from Tina to the woman as she leaned into the table, lasciviously gazed into Tanzi’s eyes, and smiled.

Chapter Two

"There is no coming to heaven with dry eyes."

—Thomas Fuller

Leaving her friends to enjoy the party arranged for her, Tina grabbed Savannah's hand and hailed a cab to sort this matter out in private.

"Shit!" Tina said to herself, glancing out the taxi window. She did not need this complication right now. But hadn't she expected it? She knew the past would come back to throw her universe off course. She had feared this, the very thing her nightmares had been made of since that fateful day long ago.

Leaving Mya and all her friends behind at the restaurant was awkward. She knew she would have hell to pay and did not have the first clue how she would explain things when Mya got in. She had told them she was an only child because it had been easier. She did not want to explain the drama of her early life. Now that the lie had caught up, she knew Mya would not be her normal, understanding self.

Tina shifted in her seat, feeling the uninvited person scrutinizing her. She glanced at the woman, trying to find the adorable child her niece had once been. She could not find a trace of that innocent girl. Not that she thought she would. What had happened to her niece would have killed most grown women, much less a child. But there was no denying that this was her sister Lolita's daughter. She looked just like her mother, a different shade, fuller-figured, but no doubt her child. Tina felt tears well up, guilt and shame threatening to overwhelm her. She should have done more, even if she knew at the time she couldn't.

Tina turned her head and gazed out the window. She didn't dare talk to this woman, not about what had happened and especially not about her twin sister.

"I'm sure you've got something to say after all these years," the woman said angrily.

Tina sat silently, staring into the dark night as warm tears fell.

"But it doesn't make sense," Mya said. She and Tanzi were all who remained at the celebration.

"I know," Tanzi leaned in, moving closer to Mya, taking her hand.

"Why would she lie to me?" Mya asked. "I thought we shared everything!"

Tanzi was just as stunned as Mya. She knew her friend well enough to know if she hadn't told the whole story, she had her reasons.

"Look, we both know Tina very well. She is one of the most honest people in the world," Tanzi said. "We've got to trust her."

"Trust her?" Mya said, snatching her hand away as tears fell uncontrollably. "I want to rip her heart out!"

Tanzi understood exactly how Mya felt, but having a beat-up-on-Tina party was out of the question.

"Look, come over to my house tonight, and tomorrow we'll find out what's going on, okay?" Tanzi said, grabbing her purse as she stood holding a hand out. Mya took her hand, nodding, but the look on her face told Tanzi that Tina would have hell to pay tomorrow.

Tina was perplexed by the young, beautiful woman standing on her balcony far above the streets of Manhattan. When they'd gotten to the apartment, she'd expected a litany of questions that never came. Instead, her niece had gone from room to room as if searching for something. Afterward, she'd gone to the balcony where she'd been for the last hour, silently gazing over the city.

As Tina sat on the sofa, bouncing her knee, her keen eyes examined her niece. She was beyond stunning, almost angelic, unearthly, but with mesmerizing depravity that was so sensually charged, it danced on the eyes. She seemed strong like steel, but a certain fragility was beneath the surface. She looked as though she might sprout wings and soar over the rails.

Tina knew from the second she'd held her in her arms twenty-four years ago that she would be the most amazing child ever. But she'd had a premonition that life would be unkind to her niece. She just didn't know how right she would be.

If a child's eyes could hold a dream and radiate hope, Tina saw her sister Lolita's little girl shining like the morning sun. As she held that little angel, only a few hours old, she stared into the deepest hazel eyes she'd ever seen. The baby frightened and intrigued her. She was riveted, drawn in as if the baby knew the answers to all life's mysteries.

Tina was still jet-lagged from her flight from New York and worn out from non-stop photo shoots, but nothing could have kept her away. She had promised her mother she would be there. They both knew Lolita was in no condition to do this alone. Tina looked over at her fragile older sister tossing in fitful sleep. She had already been through so much, yet she kept placing herself in dangerous situations. She couldn't take care of her one-year-old son, David, who already lived with their mother, and now she had brought twin girls into this world. Their mother, Barbara Ann, had arranged for the girls to stay with her.

Barbara Ann was rocking and talking softly to the other twin when David, asleep in a carrier beside her, let out a loud wail. She reached down and rocked him until he settled down, but not before Lolita woke.

"Please make them quiet!" her sister shouted.

Tina knew it wasn't only the delivery that had her sister exhausted and irritable; it was the drugs she was hooked on. Thankfully the twins had been spared any adverse effects from the cocaine during birth, but the doctors couldn't say if there would be long-term cognitive and emotional development issues. She could have berated her sister and yelled at her to straighten her life out, but it would have done no good. Besides, she knew exactly why her sister needed to anesthetize herself. She walked over to Lolita's hospital bed and gently stroked her arm. Their eyes met, and her sister calmed a little. Lolita's eyes fell on the little one Tina held to her chest.

"Do you want to hold her?" Tina asked. Lolita stared at the child intently, and Tina gently placed the baby in her sister's arms. The baby pursed her lips in hunger.

"I think she's ready to eat," Tina said, smiling as she stroked her sister's hair, wincing at the black and blue marks on Lolita's throat. Her heart hammered, and she wished she could kill her sister's husband, Gary. He'd choked her when she entered labor and ruined his high. A friend rescued Lolita, took her to the hospital, and called her mother.

Suddenly, Lolita was overcome; a pained expression spread across her face as she leaned forward, pushing the child away. Tina quickly grabbed her niece into her arms as she watched the silent river of tears fall down Lolita's haggard face. Tina began to weep as well.

"Take her away," Lolita whispered forlornly, weakly shooing the child away. Her niece arched her back, grimaced, and then wailed as if sensing rejection.

"Baby, don't you want to try to feed them," Barbara said, walking to the other side of the bed.

"Mama, I don't have any energy to feed or care for them," Lolita muttered in pain.

"Alright, baby, I'll get the nurse. We can feed them," Barbara Ann said calmly.

"No!" Lolita yelled. "Take them back to the nursery, Mama. I need to be alone."

Barbara Ann was a struggling woman of forty-three who was about to be a mother to three young children. Tina saw her mother's half-smile and knew the burden she bore. As if that wasn't challenging enough, her greatest pain was watching her daughter live through hell, helpless to rescue her.

"Alright, baby, you get some rest. God and your Mama got your babies, and we'll take good care of them until you can." This time smiling sweetly, she placed the baby in the small rolling bassinet. Tina placed her twin in the other.

Barbara Ann rolled the twins down the hall, and Tina followed with David, glancing back at her sister. Lolita turned away as if to shut the world out. Tina knew it wasn't time for her sister to care for her own kids. She couldn't even care for herself.

As they headed down the hallway towards the nursery, a dutiful nurse appeared and helped her mother push the babies. Barbara Ann smiled at the woman and began to sing soft and low.

"Jesus loves me; this I know. For the Bible tells me so. Little ones to him belong. They are weak, but he is strong. Yes, Jesus loves me..."

Tina remembered how their mother had sung them to sleep many nights to this song. Her love and faith were a constant no matter what they had been through. She shared her mother's love but not her faith. God was on her shit list, and he knew why. But her mother was still the most remarkable woman Tina knew.

When Tina and her mother arrived at Westside Memorial Hospital the next day, they discovered Lolita had walked out against her doctor's advice, leaving her two days old, caramel-colored girls, Savannah and Elisha, behind.

An uncanny feeling of deja vu overtook Savannah as she gripped the rails on Tina's balcony. Jaws shaking and palms sweaty with the awareness that she was here. Finally. *How many nights had she laid on her cot with her hands on her heart, thinking of her sister and transcending the miles from Oakland to New York instantly?* Too many to count. Crying. Wondering. Dreaming of the day they would be reunited. Savannah closed her eyes and drew in a deep breath.

Most people can't understand the bond between twins. She and Elisha were closer than most. They were born eight minutes apart, with Savannah being the oldest. They'd survived in their mother's unwelcoming womb, locked in a protective embrace. No matter the horrors life would inflict on them, at least they had each other. That was until the day their lives were horribly altered, and Savannah was shipped off to Essie's.

As a six-year-old condemned to live in Oakland, California, with the Wallin clan, Essie warned Savannah never to mention Tina's name. Nor could she speak of her parents, her sister, or the events of the terrible night that had changed everything. Essie clarified that if she broke these rules, she would be taken to the Park Street Bridge, hurled over the side, and eaten by hungry sharks. The thought terrified Savannah.

More often than not, Savannah stayed in her small room, which had originally been the back porch. Devoid of furnishings, except for the worn wooden nightstand and a bulbless yellow lamp that sat upon it. Splotchy green walls, a mingle of eruptions of grime and peeled paint. A foul odor and dankness lay thick in the stale air. Pushed into the corner was the rickety cot she sat or laid on. Her only covering was an itchy gray blanket. No visitors or friends ever visited, except for the occasional cockroach that wandered in and an old, dead spider in the half-worn web in the corner over her head.

Despite her austere surroundings, her few meager possessions meant the world to her. A couple of books, her

Cabbage Patch Preemie doll, Celena, and her unfettered imagination. These offered her escape and a ray of hope.

Essie often poked her head into the room, a look of disdain and unkind words on her lips. *Ugly. Stupid. A mistake. Unwanted.* Savannah always had a warning of her approach. The frightening sound of her aunts' heavy feet clumping down the hallway offered one advantage. It gave her time to hide Celena. Essie surely would have taken her away if she knew what the doll meant to Savannah. It had been her sister's doll. The only thing of Elisha's she had left.

One thing was certain. Essie's hatred of her never wavered. Her words attest to it, and her actions convey it. Savannah had to endure painful beatings for minor infractions like leaving the cap off the toothpaste or letting down her long hair from the bun she wore. She dressed in worn clothes from thrift stores while Essie clothed her husband, Pastor George Wallin, and their son, Montez, and herself with the best from Bay Street Emeryville. While Essie's family dined on overflowing plates of mouth-watering food, her meals were sparse, but she dared not ask for more.

She was half-heartedly home-schooled by Essie, who didn't want her in the public school. No reason was ever given, and she learned not to question her. She wasn't allowed to go outside and play with the other children in the neighborhood, but on occasion, she got to go out into the backyard. Those were special days when she looked up into the blue skies and talked with Nana as before her death.

Sunday was the only day she spent outside of the home. Sitting alone off to the side, in church, she would watch the ungodly Wallin crew transform themselves into the most loving Christians. Try as she might, Savannah could never reconcile Nana's loving God with the realities of her life with the Wallins.

Why would a loving God let her Nana, the only person who'd ever loved them, die in a car accident caused by a drunk driver? Why would he give them to a mother and father who never wanted them? Why would he take her sister, the person she needed most, and do so on their sixth birthday? And why would he allow her to be raised by such a vile and hateful person as her aunt? Essie's entire family was on her list, too. In due time, she would exact payment.

She cautiously believed that God had finally answered her prayers for a brief time. Savannah knew Essie was going to kick her out on her eighteenth birthday. In her mind, she dreamed of heading to New York but had no money to get there. So, when she met Michael, she thought things had finally changed for the better. And they had, to a large degree. At first, his family seemed to truly love Christians, the opposite of the Wallins. His parents seemed to care for one another and lavished love and wealth on their son. And Michael, in turn, gave her endless gifts. She could buy anything, eat the best meals, and go out on her own, which she rarely did. She preferred being at home, being a housewife while making plans and daydreaming about being a mother.

On their first wedding anniversary, the church held a celebration for them. An hour into the party, she realized Michael wasn't around and foolishly went looking for him. He was in one of the classrooms, getting "busy" with a church member. She quietly closed the door so as not to disturb them. From that day on, Michael had become a cheater and a liar like every other man.

Contrary to what some might have expected, she didn't really care. Yes, she was disappointed, but all the men she had ever known had been addicted to sex. Why would he be an exception? However, when he beat her and killed her babies, she snapped. Someone else had taken over her body, literally.

Savannah thought about her sister every day. The mirror was a constant reminder. Often, she thought of asking Michael to help locate her, but something always stopped her. Maybe she didn't want to rock the boat and jeopardize her good fortune. All she knew for certain was that her sister wasn't there. The first thing Savannah did when she entered Tina's apartment was to look for signs of Elisha. There were none. Maybe when she turned eighteen, she'd run off, too. Only one person knew the answer.

Savannah turned her thoughts from the past and the bright lights of Manhattan and walked inside. Tina stood up quickly as if she had been lost in thought.

"Where is my sister?" Savannah asked.

Tina seemed confused, but Savannah registered something else in her aunt's expression but wasn't sure what it was. Tina shook uncontrollably. Moments passed, though it seemed like an eternity. The silence made Savannah's head throb. She felt darkness coming on but fought it back.

"Look, Elisha..." Tina spoke softly as if to carefully avoid her question.

Savannah lunged toward Tina. "You know what, I don't want to talk about Elisha yet," she said.

“I want to know why you, of all people, abandoned me when I needed you most,” Savannah fumed. “You left my ass to be devoured by the mother-fuckin’ wolves!” Savannah said, jabbing a finger into Tina’s chest.

“It …was…not…like…that,” Tina stammered as if she were trying to deflect blame.

“Don’t give me any of your fucking bullshit! I know exactly what it was like. I heard you and Essie! I was standing there begging you not to leave me.” Savannah trembled as hot angry tears fell down her face. “But you just turned your back and walked out!”

“I tried to bring you back, but….”

Savannah cut her off quickly. “But what? Tell me!” Savannah glared at her.

Tina said nothing.

“No, let me tell you! Because you didn’t care. Your life here meant more to you than I did,” Savannah yelled as tears ran down her aunt’s face.

“Don’t cry now, bitch. I needed you crying back when I was packed to live with Essie. She tortured me every day.”

“I needed you crying when Montez was using me as his own personal sex slave from when I was seven until I was thirteen years old! And do you know why he finally stopped?”

Tina closed her eyes against Savannah's onslaught.

"Because his daddy, Pastor Wallin, cold busted him. And do you know what happened after that?" Savannah said.

"Montez stopped fucking me, and his dad picked up where he'd left off. That's right, the preacher man liked me to suck his dick and swallow his cum once he got home from preaching his sermon!"

"I didn't know…I would have come and…" Tina pleaded.

"No one…no one was there for me!" Savannah screamed as she sank to the marble floor, sobbing bitterly.

"I'm so sorry," Tina said, embracing her. Savannah pushed Tina away.

"Not as sorry as you're going to be!" Savannah grew eerily calm and offered Tina a smile.

"Please come home," Tina whispered into the phone, looking at the clock on the nightstand. One-thirty a.m. Mya was silent on the other end.

"I want you to know how deeply you hurt me," Mya said quietly. Tina was already filled with overwhelming emotions; she couldn't handle anything else.

"Listen, I know how this looks…but baby, I need you now more than I ever have before," Tina said with desperation.

Mya sighed. "So just push aside what I'm feeling and come and comfort you. Is that what you're saying?"

It had been a long time since Tina and Mya fought like this. But Tina didn't want to fight. She was emotionally spent and gravely concerned about her niece, who seemed mentally unstable and possibly planning to do harm. But in the end, she couldn't turn her away.

"Look, baby, I know you're hurt, but I promise I will tell you everything, then you'll understand."

"I will be there and help you through whatever this is. But when it's over, either tell me the truth, or I'm gone," Mya threatened.

Tina listened to the line go dead and then slowly hung up. How could she ever tell Mya the truth? The truth she wasn't ready to face.

The distant wail of a siren unsettled her even more. As she rose from her bed and walked to the bedroom door, she wondered if she would have to call 911 tonight. She placed her ear to the door and listened. Only the sound of Al Green belting *Tired of Being Alone*. She had reluctantly left her niece drinking Jack Daniel's at the bar off their kitchen.

Her only request had been to put on Al Green. He had been Nana's favorite singer. No doubt the twins had heard him continuously when they'd lived with her. Tina softly banged her head against the door and began sobbing again.

Walking over to the bookshelves, she reached for a book on the top shelf, one she had ignored for years. Alice Walker's *Temple of My Familiar*. She'd picked it up at the airport to celebrate the twin's sixth birthday when she landed at LAX. She had only read the first chapter while waiting to pick up the rental car. But she'd read and reread it when she finally returned to NYC. It changed her life at a time when she needed transformation. She turned to the back of the book and found the small manila envelope hidden between the pages so long ago. It held her family's dreadful secrets. Their unspeakable lies. Things are best forgotten.

Sitting at her desk, she carefully emptied the contents. There were pictures of her mother with a grinning twin on each knee, David sitting at her feet. One of Tina with the twins in front of the Christmas tree as they opened presents. A creased picture of her and Lolita when they were younger. She had torn Essie out of the picture. The faded black and white photo of her stoic grandparents, James and Ernestine Murphy. A picture of her mother beaming with the love of her life, Edward Preston, the man Tina considered her father.

Beneath the photos was a stack of documents. Deeds to property. Life Insurance. Adoption papers. Birth and death certificates. Police report. She unfolded the last record, the one that hurt her the most. Still couldn't comprehend the lunacy. Why? Tina shook her head, still perplexed after all these years. The hardest thing in life to reconcile was always the "why." It was the slow, silent killer, the unrelenting thief.

Even the "why's" she knew, the stories of her family's deep betrayals and painful chapters, couldn't be logically communicated to her niece. The intricacies of the deceit, the labyrinths of unfortunate acts, and the complexity of the coverups they'd all engaged in defied understanding. In the end, the only option Tina had in the face of the unthinkable was to let Essie control the cards that had been dealt. And because of that, they all suffered at the hands of vengeance.

Savannah woke with a start, her body wet with perspiration. She'd had the nightmare again. She looked around the strange bedroom. It took her a minute to recall that she was in Tina's guest bedroom. Her head pounded. She needed something to drink. She walked down the long hallway toward the bar. She knew exactly where it was because she had spent most of the night pouring endless rounds.

She saw pictures hanging on the wall of Mya on the cover of Sports Illustrated, Vogue, Cosmo, and at least thirty other magazines. But it was the Playboy layout that made Savannah stop and pause. She had never thought of sexing a woman until recently, something she would do to get what she wanted. A delicious aroma drew her toward the kitchen. Tina was probably feeling sorry for neglecting her for so many years. But she was sadly mistaken if she thought a place to stay and breakfast would make up for abandoning her all those years ago.

Savannah stood at the kitchen door and saw Mya cooking, wearing a short, peach-colored satin nightgown. A sweet plan began to formulate. Savannah smiled. Fuck the bacon, she thought; she was about to have pussy for breakfast.

Chapter Three

"Perhaps everything terrible is in its deepest being something helpless that wants help from us."

— Rainer Maria Rilke

Savannah was captivated by the image of her naked body in the vast, ornate bathroom mirror. Twenty minutes later, when the clock struck midnight, she would be twenty-seven years old. Damn, she thought, if she wasn't even more beautiful than when she'd first arrived in NYC three years ago. She gazed, hypnotized by her own exotic appearance. She was the epitome of narcissism, captivated by her own allure. She touched her face like a priceless treasure, a chef d' oeuvre. Her fingers slid over her nose, her lips, her chin.

"Who am I?" The thought came as her hands explored. Down the smooth skin of her long neck, over the Harry Winston necklace she wore. Across her strong and feminine shoulders, over the crest of her voluptuous breasts. Her thick nipples stood erect. A tantalizing shiver ran through her. A river of heat worked its way to her center.

Journeying further, her hands glided over her round stomach and ample hips, down her inviting thighs, coming to rest in her garden of delights. She looked up and smiled. Her clean-shaven pussy was her greatest treasure. Her index finger traced her engorged clit, kindling a blaze that increased as she voyaged past her thick lips and probed inside.

Savannah appraised her full-figured body, an enraptured look on her face. She was not ever going to be a size 0, anorexic bitch. She had meat on her bones and was proud of it.

When she first came to New York, Savannah's first mission had been to get revenge on Tina and exact the same devastation she had inflicted upon Michael. But she quickly discovered it wasn't going to be an easy task. Tina existed behind a fortress of loyal friends and had built a strong, thriving business. But Savannah wouldn't be deterred and eventually got what she wanted from Tina. Deep satisfaction spread across her face.

Shortly after she'd arrived, Tina set out to placate her by giving her a place to stay and a career as a model with her agency. Savannah was in great demand not only because of her looks but because she was a natural in front of the camera. It had been a short-lived career, even though initially Savannah had loved it. She could seduce the lens and leave it begging for more. But she eventually became bored with the endless shoots and temperamental photographers. She hated being told what to do and despised the judgmental fuckers who ran the industry.

There was a new definition of beauty emerging, defying stereotypes and embracing a variety of sizes and ethnicity. However, the change came slower than a snail in mud. It was still a world for tall, size two White women who ate nothing but air. The final straw came when she saw the layout she had posed for days prior on Tina's desk. Someone had digitally slenderized her body, and the sight evoked a deep, primal rage.

At first, she went off on Tina but found out it had been the doing of John Blakemore. He was the egotistical head of a prominent magazine, making it his mission to meet Savannah after noticing her across the room at a social event. He'd given Tina's agency multiple assignments just to gain access to Savannah.

He had moved Savannah into her own luxuriously appointed apartment. She had closets full of expensive clothes, shoes, jewels, and cash in her coffers. John couldn't get enough of her, and she willingly serviced his ravenous appetite for a price. She had put up with his old, wrinkled ass until she found out he had ordered the digital improvements.

No matter what John provided, Savannah wouldn't stand for his bullshit. She invited him over under the pretense of exploring more deviant ways of sexing him, and his horny ass arrived within the hour. As he walked through the door, she held up the layout and asked for an explanation. He just smiled and reached for her, saying something about how much he loved her body but that her hips appeared a little large in photographs. Unbeknownst to him, Savannah had set up a hidden camera.

The next day Savannah moved all her possessions out of the apartment, then left a pan of fried chicken on the burner and left. She later found out that most of the apartment had been destroyed when the Fire Department arrived. She mailed his wife a little gift, his cum stains on her sexy Carine Gilson panties, and a USB drive documenting their tryst. She later heard his wife, Gilda, had slenderized his bank account in the divorce settlement. That would teach the bastards to fuck with her.

Savannah hadn't wanted to return to Tina's but did so out of necessity. She had about sixty grand in liquid assets that wouldn't make a dent in getting the place she needed to house her new business venture. She knew she would be a raving success. Men like John would go to any length to be with her, and she intended on milking this realization for all it was worth. She just needed to find a sponsor until she could get it all together.

She formulated a new plan when she returned to Tina's place and saw Tanzi. Savannah would set up her business and get revenge on her aunt. Of all of Tina's friends, Tanzi was closest, maneuvered with great power, and had plenty of money. Tina's dependence on Tanzi only sweetened the pot.

Savannah wasn't attracted to Tanzi in the least. Yes, she was beautiful. She had regal African features, but her midnight skin, perfectly chiseled face, long and stylishly braided black hair, and perfectly proportioned, tall body, did nothing for Savannah. But necessity being the mother of invention and her grandmother being a well-weaved plan, Savannah got busy working on her. Tanzi had a thing for helping the underdog, and once Savannah had garnered her sympathy, she had a place to stay before the week was out.

Tanzi might have been one of the top civil litigators at the prestigious law firm of Friedman, Knight, and Slack, earning millions each year, but she was no match for Savannah's wiles. Within a month, Savannah had worked her mojo so well that Tanzi had purchased an expensive apartment in SoHo for Savannah, where she could work. Then she had perfectly executed the avenging blow to Tina.

Three years later, she and Tanzi were a couple in name only. For Savannah, it was strictly a relationship of convenience. She did what she wanted, and Tanzi stayed out of her way. She didn't know how long they would be together, but Tanzi was a comfortable port in the storm for now.

Tanzi smiled as her limo sped past the restaurant, her face aglow remembering the first time she'd looked at Savannah. Tanzi hadn't seen it coming. She had been focused only on her career, and then Savannah had come like a whirlwind into her life, and everything changed. Before Savannah, Tanzi hadn't been one of those women who fantasized about falling in love. She didn't want a relationship with a man or a woman. She had no aversion to same-sex partnerships. She had friends and business associates who were straight, gay, bi, trans, and pansexual. But she was undeniably asexual. To this day, she still doesn't understand how Savannah had gotten inside her heart. One thing was certain, it had been their destiny to meet.

Being with Savannah was the best part of heaven and the deepest pit in hell. Despite the intricacies, Tanzi wouldn't change a thing. Well, except for one. That persistent feeling held her thoughts captive-aware that their relationship would eventually come to an end. Tanzi always pushed the thought aside, refusing to let fate's approaching hand rob her of the woman who was the love of her life.

Smiling, then laughing aloud, Tanzi shook her head. Yes, it was overly complex dealing with Savannah. She was the epitome of a Leo: egotistical, self-serving, and an expert manipulator. She demanded to be center stage in every area of their lives. That left little room for Tanzi's needs to be voiced, much less met. She learned not to rock the boat because when she did, their lives had teetered on the brink of insanity. She was accustomed to letting Savannah get her way without demanding anything. Especially not love.

It was impossible for Savannah to love anyone. She erected an impenetrable wall around her heart. The events of Savannah's past were to blame for the facade she wore as a second skin. It concealed an inescapable truth entombed in her soul. Savannah wanted love, family, and children. However, she would never allow herself to blindly hope in those ideations again. What little Tanzi garnered about Savannah's upbringing, her marriage and divorce, and the death of her twins made it an impossible task for Savannah. Tanzi understood. A painful past was a scourge on a person's soul. Savannah hadn't been the only one with a difficult childhood. As a little girl growing up in Nairobi, Kenya, Tanzi had been well acquainted with heart afflictions.

From her earliest memories, Tanzia, whose name in Swahili meant "death notice," felt invisible. Maybe it was because her mother, Adehumi, a tall, beautiful Nigerian, had almost died bringing her into the world. Perhaps it was because her father, Mygambi, a handsome, wealthy Kenyan merchant often away from home, had no use for a daughter. Whatever the reason, she felt unseen and unheard. She would often put her ear to the door and listen to the stories her father told her brothers about his travels to other lands or fascinating stories about the old ways. She had to remain quiet and docile when her father was there. But her two brothers, Talib and Temilade, were allowed to run rampant and unrestrained. Their father greeted his sons warmly and allowed them into the inner chambers of his private library, where she spent her days perusing the world's greatest books in his absence. But when her father was there, Tanzia was denied access.

A few times a month, when she saw her father, he would walk by and smile dutifully at her as he watched her perform tasks alongside her mother. He would occasionally commend Tanzia for her skills in learning the ways of women and for being well-behaved. But that was the extent of their interactions. Despite her rigid home and school life, Tanzia never complained. Yes, she longed to be held and cherished, like her mother did her brothers, or to sit on her father's knee, but she didn't ask. For the one time she had, her parents took her on a journey she would never forget.

The sun was high as Tanzi sat in the car's back seat, inwardly smiling as she watched the beautiful Kenyan landscape pass by. Her brothers had been left at home. She thought, finally, they would make me feel special, too. But they had taken her into Kenya's old lands and stopped in one of its worst slums. Her father had stoically pointed out children living in emaciated tents dying of malaria and AIDS. Her father hadn't said a word, but his message was clear: don't ask for anything because this could be your life. So, she learned to settle for what was and not ask for anymore.

Although it had been more than twenty years since Tanzi was brought from Kenya to America, her life there was never far from her thoughts. She had become a civil lawyer to fight for those who couldn't fight for themselves. Her loving adoptive parents, Robert and Jennifer Ridley, taught her how. They were the ones to rescue her after that fateful day when she was twelve. The day that forever changed who she was.

It had been her adoptive parents that had shown her the power of love. They taught her that no matter how the body was violated, how painfully a heart was broken, love could rescue you. Tanzi was determined to let her save Savannah.

A peal of thunder followed by lightning flashed across the night sky. Ominous clouds released a deluge. Tapping on the window like a thousand hummingbirds, the rain infused Tanzi's thoughts with uneasiness. A little anxiety grew quickly into a tsunami, and she dialed Savannah's phone. It went to voicemail.

Tanzi glanced at her watch. She hadn't planned on meeting this late with a client, but they had to prepare for a trial on Monday. She tried to calm herself. Savannah was probably not home from her outing, so there was no reason to hurry. But Tanzi couldn't shake a dark foreboding in her gut. Thoughts of Savannah's last birthday came to mind. A full-blown panic ensued, and she pressed a button and spoke to her driver, Abewoji.

"We need to get home right away," she said urgently.

"Yes, Ma'am," he replied, and they sped off.

On nights like these, Tina was glad that Mya was already asleep. Otherwise, she would've been forced to smile and feign happiness. An insidious depression nagged her, keeping her awake despite the lulling effect of her meds. All these years later, her hurt was still fresh, wounds that refused to heal. Her insane, destructive niece had taken so much from her.

Listening to the rain only made it worse. She wanted to kill her even more because she could no longer enjoy the things she once loved. But she couldn't. She had committed murder out of rage before and knew the cost.

Though she hadn't sought retribution for her niece's damage, exercising restraint had proven immensely challenging. She had lost the business it had taken her twenty years to build. The recognition, respect, and reputation of her boutique firm were gone. Even though she would have never competed with Elite, Ford, or Wilhelmina Model Management, she had built an excellent brand. All her friends and employees suffered, too. They had been blacklisted for their association with her and Preston Enterprises.

The wretched bitch had lied and reported that Preston engaged in fraudulent business practices. They came under state and Federal scrutiny. If it hadn't been for Tanzi's proficiency and how well she had insulated the business, Tina could have been sitting in a federal penitentiary. It had been the death knell for her.

The demise of her business also marked the demise of her friendship with Tanzi. They had been inseparable, the epitome of true friends. Witnessing Tanzi being manipulated and coerced into choosing sides left Tina utterly devasted.

The worst offense, by far, her niece had committed was almost destroying her relationship with Mya. She'd wanted to believe the psycho bitch had forgotten about the past and was building a new life for herself, but she had been calculating all along. She should have seen it coming.

The day started like any other. Tina went into the office early for a host of meetings. Mya, taking the day off, had called to say Savannah was coming by to pick up the last of her things. Of course, Tina knew it was a bad idea for her niece to move in with Tanzi, but she stayed out of it. While meeting with a prospective client, she got a video from

Mya's phone, distracting her from her presentation. Mya was having sex in their bed with her niece.

When Tina pulled up to their apartment, the fury she felt in the taxi had grown into full-blown rage. To fuel the inferno, Mya was asleep and hadn't answered her calls. Tina pulled Mya from the bed, and things went from bad to worse. The police were called. Tina was arrested for battery and spent several days in jail. Mya eventually bailed her out but wanted an explanation. Together, they figured out that Mya had been drugged. They had gone to Tanzi's place but couldn't enter the building. Tina was in the process of having her niece arrested when Tanzi called, stepped in, and squashed it. That was the beginning of the end.

It took over three years of intense counseling and anger management to get Tina and Mya to a better place. Still, the healing was tenuous, especially on nights like these. It was the twins' birthday. A day that had changed so much. But that still didn't change the fact that she only wished for her treacherous niece to die.

Savannah glanced down at the pile of cash lying on the marble bathroom counter, then looked back in the mirror and smiled.

"Bitch, you got it all!" she said approvingly.

It wasn't just the multi-million-dollar Manhattan apartment she shared with Tanzi or her ten-million-dollar apartment in Soho where she worked. It wasn't the limos, the wardrobe closets overflowing with the best and finest. It wasn't her vault in the master closet that held over five million in jewels or a business that brought in almost two million a year plus perks. Nor was it that she could pick up a phone and be on her way to any destination in the world on a luxurious private jet within minutes.

What really mattered was that she was still here; she'd survived and won. Motherfuckers had tried to break her down, to annihilate her, but they couldn't. Especially the Monster. He had said she was nothing. She wished he could see her now.

The richest, most powerful men in the world wanted her. Tonight was proof of that. Although some might call her a prostitute, a call girl, or a professional dom, that wasn't how she defined herself. She used her delectable body and highly skilled mind to service the upper echelon and got paid extremely well.

Her clientele represented the privileged class of Fortune 100 companies, Congress, the Judiciary, and Wall Street. Yet they came to her as supplicants. Her clients rarely wanted vanilla sex; they loved her artful dominatrix service. She loved humiliating them and relished those who wanted her to stick twelve-inch dicks or baseball bats up their asses. They paid her what she wanted because of her superior services and discretion. The belief she would keep their dirty little secrets. They didn't want their wives or the world to know what they really did behind closed doors. She kept secrets, all right. She had plenty of evidence locked in the vault of her Soho penthouse. She had complete dossiers on them, along with video and DNA samples.

But tonight, Savannah had deviated from her usual routine. Normally, she never did groups nor worked anywhere except for her place. But Senator Richard Effingham, a regular of hers for several years, had begged her to entertain his brother Chad's bachelor party. At first, she declined because, for one thing, it was her birthday. Secondly, it was being held at a secure, undisclosed location.

But she acquiesced after a private showing in her penthouse an absent Richard had arranged with a Harry Winston representative. She acquired five items at the cost of just under $350,000. In addition, Richard would pay her $175,000 in cash for just a couple of hours of work. Savannah knew it didn't matter to Richard how much he spent. He really wanted to upstage his brother; their rivalry was legendary. He wanted Chad to see that he had the baddest pussy around. When Savannah arrived at the mansion and noticed the Secret Service, she knew there had to be some powerful dicks inside. Chad's bachelor party had brought together some of the top movers and shakers from Washington, D.C., and Wall Street.

Savannah knew they had come not to celebrate his wedding to Chelsea, the ditzy blonde, size zero daughter of Senator Alexis Colby. They hadn't come for the delicious banquet and top-shelf booze. They came because she was going to be there. No phones, cameras, or recording devices were allowed. Underneath her expensive full-length silver fox, Savannah wore only platinum jeweled pasties, a black satin garter, black silk stockings, black stilettos, Harry Winston jewels, and a clean-shaven pussy.

"Look, no camera," she said, laughing as she pulled the lips of her vagina open for inspection.

When she walked inside, she knew she had reached a new level; everything screamed opulence and big money. Richard greeted her at the door like she was his prized possession. He took her hand, and as she seductively strutted and danced into the room and flung her coat open, a loud echo of claps, whistles, and cheers in praise of her magnificence thundered throughout the palatial room.

To her, the group of around thirty men gathered, who were responsible for making the world spin, appeared nothing more than ordinary. However, her gaze instantly fixated on a distinguished gentleman conversing with Chad. He stood at least 6 feet tall, around 185 lbs, and possessed a fit, muscular physique. His attractiveness exuded a movie star aura. Among all his notable attributes, his eyes were the most striking- penetrating and captivating as they met her gaze.

When he saw her near-naked form, he seemed taken aback. He didn't clap or whistle like the others. His glance unsettled her, turning from surprise to an angry, disdainful glare. However, just before he averted his gaze, she caught sight of something else: was it a hint of rejection?

He quickly turned away, ignoring her presence, as he walked up to Richard and whispered in his ear. He was standing only a few feet away from her, yet it was like she was invisible. He shook Richard's hand and headed for the door without glancing back. Like she wasn't shit. Bastard! It took her a minute to shake the feeling he had left in his wake: an indescribable pain in her stomach, followed by a tenseness she had not experienced in years. But she had put her smile back on and did what she did best.

As she looked in the mirror, Savannah suddenly felt emotionally raw from their encounter. Some of the richest men in the world wanted her, and this man just walked out like she was powerless over him.

“Why does it matter to you?” A dark voice chided from somewhere deep in her mind. It caused her head to hurt, and she grabbed it to stop the pain. But she couldn’t stop the ache nor his eyes from seeing her. It was as if the stranger’s eyes were an evocation of buried torturous ghosts. For years she had kept them securely locked away in steel vaults underground in her mind. Suddenly they unleashed again as if his gaze had created a chink in the protected armor she had placed around her mind.

“Why didn’t he want me?” She asked timidly to the woman staring back at her in the mirror. Instantly, the old feelings of being unloved were back. The hurt and rejection were right behind it. Fervid, unrestrained tears began to fall, a torrent that perplexed her because she couldn't remember the last time she had cried or why she was doing so now.

“What the fuck is your problem?” she screamed at the taunting image staring back at her. “No other bitch gets paid like you!" she shouted as she grabbed the piles of wrapped hundred-dollar bills, holding them up as proof of her worth.

"He didn't want you because you ain't shit! I don't care what you have. Nobody wants you!" a voice said, laughing at her.

Savannah's eyes, enraptured by her naked form, changed as if some ominous veil had passed over them. She saw the dry cum on her stomach and legs. Suddenly there they were, legions upon her, eating away at all her defenses, swarms of poisonous vipers, old voices, chattering demons.

She angrily threw the money at the mirror as fury welled within her, a heated inferno so intense that she felt she would internally combust. She grabbed her head again, placing her hands over her ears as if that would silence them.

"Shut up! Shut the fuck up!" She raged at the wicked laughter and jeering that rose in her head.

"Fuck you, fuck you!" She hissed as spittle flew wildly from her mouth. Something snapped within her, and Savannah began to tremble uncontrollably. He was coming to get her. Her eyes searched for a weapon to protect herself, to defend against his coming. His laughter just got louder.

"Elishaaaaa," she screamed repeatedly. "Help me," she cried as overwhelming hopelessness descended upon her like a shadow: enfolding, wrestling, and conquering. Savannah's anger emerged and took over. She picked up a huge candelabra on the counter and began to bash the mirror wildly until it broke, her reflection distorted.

"Elisha isn't here, she is….." the voice taunted, "Shut the fuck up!" Savannah raged back at the voice as her mind shattered into a thousand jumbled pieces. She took one of the jagged mirror pieces in her hand so tightly blood began to run. She could see him in the mirror, staring back at her.

"Happy Birthday to you," she could hear her sister singing sweetly to her, just as she always did as they blew out their candles. 5

"Elishaaaaa," she screamed again, her hot tears distorting her view.

"Do it! Kill yourself, finally get it over with." She held the shard high, and its sharp blade begged to descend like a guillotine.

"Happy birthday to you!" She sang softly as she plunged the glass.

Tanzi's strong hand locked quickly around Savannah's descending thrust like a hawk's talon grip. Although Savannah's psychotic frenzy energized her, she was no match for Tanzi's brute determination.

"It's okay, baby," Tanzi whispered as she wrapped her other arm around Savannah. They had played out this destructive drama before, and Tanzi had learned the secret to de-escalating her. She finally understood that Savannah's death wish was really a plea for the pain in her life to end.

"I'm here, I'm here, baby," Tanzi said softly. Savannah was wracked by wails emanating deep from within the dark forest of her suffering. Tanzi knew that Savannah's past, locked away in her mind, had escaped again to collect its due.

"I'm here with you, baby; I've got you," Tanzi comforted. Her efforts to ease the tension quickened as she watched the blood dripping from Savannah's hand.

"Nobody loves me; nobody wants me!" Savannah screamed in a fitful rage. As their bodies swayed, Tanzi looked into the fragmented glass.

"I love you, and I want you," Tanzi whispered, her words intended to lead Savannah back to a place of safety.

"No, you don't! You leave me just like everybody else!" Savannah shouted back at her through tearful, childlike eyes.

A tangible pain shot through Tanzi's chest. The innocent little girl Savannah had once been conspicuously challenging her to dispute the reality of her life had been. If little girls were loved and protected, they wouldn't turn into hurting grown women.

"God, where are you when children are hurting, calling out to you for help?" Tanzi thought, perplexed, straining to hear an answer. The familiar silence echoed back.

"When you wake up every morning," Tanzi said, looking into Savannah's eyes, "What is the first thing you see?"

Savannah's body began to relax slightly, her mind searching for the answer.

"You see these eyes looking back at you, revealing how much you are loved." Tanzi paused to let her words sink in. Normally, Savannah wore her self-assurance and conceit like a second skin. At this moment, she was a lost child living in a grown woman's body. Savannah closed her eyes, leaning back on Tanzi.

Tanzi kissed Savannah's cheek repeatedly, eliciting a smile. The jagged shard fell to the floor. They weren't out of the woods yet. Tanzi knew from experience the insecurities could resurface.

"Every morning, I wake up next to you; I am the happiest woman on the earth," Tanzi said, rocking her slowly. "I'm never leaving you!" Savannah stared at her.

"Why?" Savannah asked, doubting it.

If only Tanzi could give Savannah her eyes to see with. Tanzi felt powerless to express the worth of the woman she held, the magnificence, beauty, and power.

"Mirror, mirror on the wall," Tanzi said boldly, "tell my lady it's because she's the finest of them all!"

Savannah smiled widely as Tanzi rocked her slowly to a rhythm only she could hear.

The storm subsided, and Tanzi breathed a sigh of relief. Her sanative ways had won again. She loved this enigma she held. Loved her completely, body and soul.

Wilson Fairmont Dozier, Jr. stood at the door, apprehensive and unworthy to enter. Overwhelming guilt rose in his chest, threatening to choke his life out. Death would be a fitting end for all the pain he had caused her. The lights were low, inviting Will into the room, lulling his resistance, and silencing all complaints. If it had been him lying there, he would have gone willingly. But because

Sophia didn't deserve this, he was determined to fight for her life.

He rubbed his tired face, wiping back the tears. He steeled himself, then walked in, determined to speak the words that would bring her back. Laying his jacket in the chair, he gently climbed into the bed with her. He leaned his face into her and kissed her soft cheek.

"Hello, my love," he whispered as he rested his head on her shoulder. He watched her chest move gently up and down as the machine breathed for her. How could this be happening to his wife? All she had ever done was love him, which cost her everything.

"I've missed you," he said, knowing how she had always loved hearing it when he returned home. It had been years since he had said it to her. He had let so many things get in the way. He had done so many things that had wounded her heart, yet even till the end, she had forgiven him.

"Baby, I was thinking today that when you get better, we should look into purchasing that vacation house in South Carolina you've always loved," he said, trying to sound hopeful.

"I talked to Richard about it earlier when I flew in some of his friends for his brother's bachelor party," he said as his thoughts circled back to the woman he had been fighting not to see ever since. Will knew from the second he entered the mansion that he should have turned down Richard's invitation to join the party. He should have been at the hospital with Sophia, but he had wanted to put off meeting with Dr. Bentley again. His wife had been on life support for five days and was declared brain dead.

He was glad when Senator Richard Effingham called and asked Will to fly friends into New York for his brother Chad's bachelor party. He should have refused and told him what had happened, but he didn't. The flight had been a relief for him.

When Will pulled into Teterboro and shut the jet down, he should have let his passengers depart and head back to the hospital, but he couldn't. He willingly accepted Richard's invitation to what he knew would be a distinguished gathering. After all, Effingham only moved in the most powerful circles in the world. He hoped it would rest his mind from the decisions he was being asked to make. How wrong he was.

When the half-naked woman walked in, everything dead within him had come alive, electricity surging through him, causing tremendous pain. She was undoubtedly the most stunning woman he had ever laid eyes on. And he had lain eyes, as well as other body parts, on women worldwide. The vision of her standing there bejeweled in that fur had made his groin stiffen, and on its heels of lust, he had been filled with the most intense rage. She represented what he hated most, the thing that stirred his dick and cost him literally everything.

Will looked up and saw Dr. Bentley's searching eyes, and he did the only thing he could. He took her carefully in his arms and wept.

Savannah looked down at the warm water beading on Tanzi's black satin skin and felt utter and complete sadness. She didn't love Tanzi; in fact, she despised her most days, and yet here she was again, holding onto her like a life ring so she wouldn't drown in this sea of craziness. The insanity seemed worse with each passing birthday. Today, she and Elisha were twenty-seven years old. She wondered where her sister was, how she was doing, and if she was thinking about her, too. She would continue to search for Elisha. They shared something that no one else could understand.

The thought made Savannah's tears well. She laid her head back against the marble wall of the shower, closing her eyes. She fought against the pain still snaking through every inch of her body.

She knew one day Tanzi would get tired of this and leave her.

"I'm never leaving you, baby," Tanzi said as if reading her mind.

Savannah knew she meant well, but a long list of people had broken that promise. She didn't dare trust, ever again. At times like these, it amazed Savannah that even though Tanzi made millions, had degrees from both Harvard and Yale Law Schools, and could have anyone she wanted, she stayed with her and put up with all her madness.

"It's okay, baby," Tanzi said softly. Savannah was too emotionally drained to protest but knew it wasn't.

The sultry voice of Anita Baker singing "*Lead Me Into Love*" was like an elixir to Savannah's wounded soul and pulled her away from her sad thoughts.

When Tanzi drew close, the pleasure of it chased away the residue of pain. They touched breasts, nipple to nipple. Electricity surged through her as Tanzi took her full caramel breasts into her hands, expertly in an erotic circular motion as her nimble fingers touched and pulled.

Still cupping her breast, Tanzi kissed her lips gently at first, and then her tongue, hot and sweet, explored Savannah's mouth, licking, probing, and sucking. Tanzi gently pushed Savannah's hands over her head, licking down her neck as the warm water cascaded over their bodies.

When Tanzi's mouth found her thick nipple, she took it in, sucking wildly; it made her body tremble. When she released the swollen mound, she kissed it, then moved to her other breast and gave it the same treatment.

Stepping back, Tanzi took Juicy Couture Shower Gel and squeezed it over Savannah's breast, rubbing it with her hands, lathering, and cleaning. Savannah knew why Tanzi had to cleanse her first. She had to wipe every trace of the men. Although they had fought about Savannah's chosen profession for two years, Tanzi acquiesced for two reasons. One, she hated fighting, and two, she knew she would never win.

As Tanzi's strong hands moved over every inch of her stomach and legs, Savannah let the water run over her face, washing all the bad thoughts away. When Tanzi's hands, soapy and wet, slid over Savannah's pussy into her honey pot, the thrill made her shiver and moan. Anita sang so sultrily, creating the perfect mood.

Savannah's hips gyrated slowly into Tanzi's hand as she probed, fingers dipping into the darkness, wet and inviting. A fire was raging between her thighs, uncontainable and spreading. Tanzi stood, turned her around, and washed her back, massaging and caressing as she went.

Tanzi turned Savannah's body, rinsing her front and back. She pressed Savannah into the cold marble, getting on her knees, pushing her ass cheeks apart, and letting her tongue work its lustful magic.

When she licked her pussy, it looked like the opening of a dark, blooming rose drew her in. With a seductive rhythm, Tanzi fingered her ass and her pussy while sucking her clit. Savannah gasped from the pleasure of it.

"Damn," Savannah said, her breath catching.

Tanzi spread her legs open. Her tongue probed her mouth, and their eyes fastened on each other. Savannah's hand reached for Tanzi's ass and held her tightly as they moved into each other. Their engorged clits stroked, and the pleasure made them move feverishly against each other.

Tanzi's hands moved up the slopes of Savannah's firm breasts as she descended, running her tongue seducing her clit, as Savannah opened fully for her.

"Oh, baby!" Savannah yelled out in pleasure. She was on the verge and ready to go over.

Savannah closed her eyes and moaned; the sound reverberated off the walls. Her back arched as aftershocks of pleasure ripped violently through her body, bringing billows of ecstasy. As her body shook and rocked, a shocking vision assailed her, ending the throes of enraptured bliss. The pain had returned; she was back at the bachelor party, and he was watching her.

Chapter Four

"I'd like to die like this...with the dark fingers of the water closing and unclosing over these sleepy lights and a sad bell somewhere murmuring good night."

—Kenneth Patchen

Will sat across from Dr. Bentley, dreading this conversation.

"Will, I know this is a burdensome time for you." Dr. Bentley folded his hands on his large mahogany desk. Will stared at the framed degrees slightly above the doctor's head. "I need to discuss your wife's condition." Will remained silent. "Sophia is brain dead; this means…."

The doctor's voice faded away as Will recalled that fateful night. A week ago, he landed in Teterboro. Several U.S. House leaders de-boarded his plane as he received a frantic call from Sophia. He slumped back in his seat and rubbed his eyes. At first, her voice was very faint. There was crying and gasping for air.

Sophia wasn't the kind of woman to get emotional. She was eight months along. His first thought was for the baby. Maybe his countless prayers that she would lose the child had finally happened.

Will had never wanted a child, but a child had been all Sophia wanted. She had pleaded with him to change his mind for eight years, but he'd adamantly refused. She had been a good wife to him, but the baby thing had come between them. Her constant pleading and nagging made her presence unbearable for Will, which was one of the reasons he loved being away.

Finding out about the baby had been one of the most dreadful days of his life. He'd come home after being gone for several weeks and saw Sophia in the dining room, aglow in the candlelight. Soft music played, and the table was spread with all his favorite foods. She kissed him so passionately that he got an instant erection. She moved him to his seat, where a gold gift box awaited.

When Will opened the box and saw a positive pregnancy test, he hurled it across the room. He paced, pounding his fist into his other hand. He stopped in front of her. She looked away.

"How the fuck did this happen?" The ferocity of Will's words seemed to strike her, making her body tremble.

"Will, I...I...." Sophia put her hand over her mouth as tears flowed.

She had betrayed him in the worst way, went off birth control without his consent. Instead of using his hands to hurt her, he stormed out and remained away for a month. Although Sophia had called and left numerous apology messages, he remained cold and distant. He hadn't touched her or the baby growing in her belly. If she lost the baby, Will thought, it was just punishment for her betrayal.

"Will, why? Why did you do it?" Sophia cried on the phone. The question surprised him. It wasn't the baby; it was him. Then it dawned on him; she must have learned about one of his numerous affairs. He had always been careful, but maybe he had left a clue. Deep down, a part of him wanted her to know. It would make it easier when she finally left him.

"What are you talking about?" Will asked.

She said the name Rosaria, and Will came undone.

Will had always valued his anonymity and left no trails to his identity. Rosaria, a sexy Latina with a huge set of tits and a dynamite ass, had been a one-night stand on a layover in Miami. Then, three months later, to his surprise, she called. When asked how she got his cell number, she ignored him and simply told him she was pregnant. Will laughed loudly and hung up on her.

Will knew it was nonsense. He abided by a set of strict principles. He consistently wore protection and removed it himself. In the woman's presence, he took it to the sink and ran water into it. He would then hold it up, demonstrating there were no leaks.

"So, don't call me with any bullshit," he'd say before flushing them. He had said this to Rosaria, so he was straight as far as he was concerned.

The second time she called, she'd said, "Sophia Dozier, 129 Benedict Road, Staten Island," and had his undivided attention.

She explained that her father was the head of the FBI in Dade County, Florida, and that she had used his connections to track him down. She also told him how much trouble she would make for him if he did not do right by her.

He denied that she could be pregnant by him, reminding her that he had flushed the condom. She then reminded him of what had happened afterward. After he'd gotten rid of the condom, she smiled deviously and knelt before him.

"Oh, I love a brilliant man. I will make you mine!" she'd said. She took his dick in her mouth and eagerly forced him to cum. It had been some of the best head he'd ever had. Afterward, she'd revealed that she'd been going to a fertility clinic and hadn't become pregnant. When she saw him, she knew he was the one. She'd gone into the bathroom and inseminated herself. Will was chagrined, knowing he'd been tricked into baby drama a second time. Rosaria was due September twelfth; Sophia was due the following day.

This news sent Will's world spinning out of control. He hadn't feared so much what Rosaria could do; it was what her father could do to his future. For the last fifteen years, he had worked methodically to realize his dream of owning a luxury charter jet company. The last thing he needed was a bogus investigation by the FBI. His clientele valued loyalty and trust, even above his superior flying skills. With one hint of an investigation, everything would topple.

Rosaria assured him that she didn't want to make trouble for him. All she wanted was just a little attention until she had the baby. Will initially went along with her game until he could figure something out. Over the last five months, he had obliged her with occasional phone calls and a few visits. Lately, she'd been more demanding of his time. He hadn't returned her calls for several weeks to teach her a lesson. She must have called Sophia to pay him back.

"Sophia, where are you?" he said calmly, trying to distract her from questioning him further.

"I'm almost to ..." He'd heard her terrifying scream, then a loud explosion.

"So, Will, what would you like to do?" Dr. Bentley asked.

Dr. Bentley's voice jarred him back to reality. Will was trained to deal with catastrophic events but wasn't prepared. He got up to leave and stopped dead in his tracks. His best friend Ricky Huntington stood, holding a small baby girl in a pink blanket. Her eyes, so much like her mother's, pierced him through the heart.

Bennie asked a ton of questions as Angelica got dressed. "Where are you going? Where's breakfast? Who's gonna iron my shirt?"

She kissed him sweetly, replied, "You will," and walked out.

The day was going to be about her. She was looking forward to indulging in the two things she loved most, after her family, food, and shopping. She spent most of that crisp autumn day motoring from one Staten Island store to another. She finished her day with a stop at Da Noi Restaurant in Staten Island, her favorite Italian eatery. Angelica started with Mussels in white sauce, then dined on Rottollo Montanara pasta, and finished with Marsala veal. She'd ordered their delectable tiramisu to go, even getting some for Bennie.

Hopping into her Volvo, she pulled out onto Victory Boulevard. She saw a black sports car bearing down upon her in the rearview mirror.

"What the hell?" she said as she swerved hard, grabbing the bag with her tiramisu as it slid to the floor. She was glad no oncoming traffic had been headed her way. The car sped by with a group of rowdy teenagers inside. One of them flipped her the bird while laughing, mocking her panic. "Faccia di Merda! " she yelled. Sons of bitches could have killed her.

Anger erupted as she watched them speed away, weaving in and out of traffic. Someone could get hurt. She reached for her cell phone and dialed 911. She watched the car approaching a busy intersection, wondering if they would stop. A light-colored Mercedes entered the intersection just as the 911 operator answered.

"911, what's your emergency?"

The scene unfolding before her terrified Angelica, and she was momentarily speechless. She saw the black sports car smash into the tail end of the Mercedes, spinning it like a child's top.

"911, what's your emergency?" the operator repeated.

"Oh my God," Angelica said, approaching the intersection as cars began to stop. The black sports car sped away. Angelica informed the operator of what had happened, and the operator riddled her with questions.

“Is anyone injured?”

Angelica hurried out of her car, trembling violently as she walked towards the twisted wreck. She didn’t want to approach the car, but that was somebody’s daughter, wife, or mother. She could make out a woman in the driver's seat. A crowd was gathering, but no one moved to help.

Angelica pushed past her fear, reached the driver's door, and pulled it open. The woman looked like she was in shock; her beautiful face was wet with tears.

“Are you alright?” Angelica asked the woman. “I called 911, and help is on the way.”

The woman didn’t appear injured, but what she saw next panicked her. The airbag had deployed against the woman’s huge belly.

“They need to get here quickly because she is very pregnant,” Angelica told the operator.

“Ma'am, can you tell how badly she is injured?” the operator asked calmly.

“I don’t see any blood. I don’t know if she’s injured or not.”

The woman moaned as if she experienced only slight discomfort and leaned back against the headrest. The sirens in the distance calmed her.

"They're almost here," Angelica said, reaching to hold the woman's hand. She looked at Angelica with kind eyes and took her hand.

As they touched, Angelica felt an electrical charge. It reminded her of what she often felt as a young girl in church. Her mother had called those holy moments the touch of God.

Angelica made the cross sign and uttered softly, "Lord, have mercy."

Angelica's mother often told her she chose her name because she was an angel sent by God. She wasn't super religious or anything, but she knew her purpose today was to be here.

"My name is Angelica; what's yours?" she asked.

"Sophia," she said weakly. "Can you find my cell phone?"

Angelica looked around and saw the phone on the passenger side floor. She couldn't reach it because the car had come to rest against a utility pole.

"My husband is on the phone," Sophia whispered, "I've got to let him know."

"I'll get your phone in just a minute as soon as they get you out," Angelica said. Sophia closed her eyes again, and Angelica feared she would pass out.

"Stay with me, Sophia," she said, rubbing the woman's hand. "What are you having?"

The woman opened her eyes, and tears fell. "A girl," she said, smiling through the tears.

"What are you going to name her?" Angelica asked, relieved that the sirens were getting closer.

"Chloe," the woman whispered, offering the name like a prayer.

The fire truck was the first to arrive at the scene, then the ambulance and police. There was a whirl of activity as first responders barked orders and took command of the scene. Angelica tried to retreat, but Sophia held on tightly.

"Stay with me," Sophia pleaded. Emergency workers separated them and moved Angelica back.

"I'm going to be right here," Angelica reassured.

"Please, get my phone…Will," Sophia said.

"Just as soon as they get you out," Angelica said, maintaining eye contact.

The paramedics began treating Sophia. She looked okay, but she had been hit hard. Angelica was comforted that help had arrived, but she couldn't shake the feeling that Sophia was in danger. She began to pray.

"Ave, o Maria, piena di grazia." "We have a thirty-year-old female, approximately thirty-eight weeks pregnant," a young paramedic said on his radio. The words flowed from Angelica in Italian. She heard someone behind her praying along in English. She made the sign of the cross, praying it would be enough.

This was Sophia's first pregnancy. She wasn't due for three more weeks. When the paramedic put the oxygen mask on, she cried out like she had been stabbed. "Oh God, help me!

"She is experiencing severe cramping. Her heart rate has increased, and her pulsing oxygen value has dropped into the low 80s," he shouted as they began to rush her toward the ambulance. Angelica was running with them until she suddenly remembered the phone. "Wait…wait!" Angelica yelled at them. "I'm going with her, but I've got to get her phone."

She knew that Sophia's husband must be frantic. She quickly made her way to the car and retrieved the phone. "Hello?" Angelica said, not knowing what to say as she ran towards the ambulance.

"Hello? Who is this?" a man asked.

“This is Angelica Lamberti. I’m here with your wife,” she said as she climbed into the ambulance.

“Tell me what’s going on?” he asked.

Angelica watched the medics start an IV. Sophia looked relieved to see her on the phone.

“She was involved in a hit and run,” Angelica said. She asked the paramedics what hospital they were going to.

“We’re heading to Staten Island University Hospital. Hurry!” Angelica said and ended the call.

She saw red spreading over the white sheet and didn’t want to betray her fear to Sophia’s husband. Angelica took Sophia’s hand.

“Your husband is on the way,” she said, smiling.

Sophia and Angelica shared a look that said everything; this wouldn't end well.

“If anything happens to me….” Sophia said, “Tell my husband….” She stopped, straining for breath. “Tell Will I love him, that he has always been the love of my life.” Sophia’s eyes closed.

“Sophia…Sophia!” Angelica screamed. “Stay with me!” Sophia fought to open her eyes.

“Tell him to take care of our baby and let her know how much I love her.” Angelica heard a paramedic talking into the radio as she held onto Sophia’s lifeless hand.

Angelica looked around the hospital waiting room area and marveled at the love of Sophia's family and friends. They had been there for the last seven days, comforting each other and sharing their stories about this remarkable woman. Angelica had been there every day, too, sharing how Sophia Dozier had come into her life and changed her forever.

As she listened to others talk about how Sophia had cared for them, she understood why, on that fateful day, she'd driven down Victory at that moment. Sophia had held the hands of many, so it was only fitting that in the hour she needed it most, God, through Angelica, was holding her hand too.

Will walked into the waiting room, and everyone looked up. He didn't make eye contact with anyone. He sat at a table in the corner, head in his hands.

"Mr. Dozier, I'm Angelica."

Will looked up at the stranger. Couldn't she see he didn't want to be bothered, he wondered?

"I was with Sophia on the way to the hospital."

Will remembered.

"Thank you for being with her," Will said.

A hush fell over the room, betraying the presence of Dr. Bentley. He was a close friend of the family. He and Sophia's father, a neurologist, shared a practice before he died of prostate cancer at forty-two. Sophia's Uncle George, who had just gotten into town, was the first to speak, "Doc, what happened to her?"

Dr. Bentley responded, "Well, let me say that seven days ago, when Sophia was brought in, everything humanly possible was done to save her and Chloe."

Uncle George interrupted, "I don't care about all your excuses! I want to know why my niece is on that machine."

Dr. Bentley continued, "At first, she was placed on life support because she had lost too much blood and was not responsive. Once we surgically delivered the baby, we left Sophia on life support to give her husband time to make certain decisions."

"But why didn't you give her blood and save her?" Uncle George asked.

"Sophia lost a lot of blood from a severe uterine tear before she arrived here. No amount of blood would have saved her," Dr. Bentley said.

Uncle George looked at Dr. Bentley, "But she's on life support. Can't you bring her back?"

"Sophia is brain dead. That means an irreversible end of all brain activity. Machines are supporting her body to breathe until her husband decides to…".

Before Dr. Bentley could complete his sentence, Uncle George interrupted, "But I've heard of people coming out of a coma. How do we know she won't wake up?"

"Brain death and persistent vegetative state are two different things. Some comatose patients can recover, but their brain still has some activity level. But that's different from someone with no brain activity," Dr. Bentley responded.

Virginia, Sophia's mother, took her brother George's hand, patting it gently as he hung his head.

"I want to assure you that every lifesaving procedure was done for Sophia." Dr. Bentley answered a few more questions and then asked for privacy to speak with Will and Virginia.

"The reason I asked for this meeting is to discuss Sophia's wishes and to determine our next step. Virginia, while these decisions are Will's alone, I've asked you to be here for support." Dr. Bentley paused, taking a document out of his pocket.

"May I?" Virginia asked for the paperwork.

“Will,” Virginia said as she reached for his hand. Will’s jaw clenched. “Sophia drafted a living will when she found out she was pregnant. If something happened to her, Sophia didn’t want to be kept alive by artificial means.”

Will put his head down, resting it in his hands. Dr. Bentley approached the bereaved husband, “Will, I know this is a devastating situation. In addition to the termination of life support, your wife also wanted to be an organ donor. It’s listed on her driver’s license.” When Dr. Bentley held the license out, Will smacked it from his hand.

“We never talked about this!” Will screamed. “Not about any living will or organ donation. You just want to cut her up?”

Dr. Bentley said, “Will, a transplant team will respectfully harvest her organs, and her sacrifice will benefit many people.”

“What the hell is wrong with you, people? Don’t you fucking touch my wife!” Will shouted as he stormed out.

“He needs a little more time,” Virginia said, rising as Dr. Bentley embraced her. “Let me talk to him, and I’ll get him to honor my baby’s wishes.”

Will walked over to the bed where his wife lay. She was as beautiful and alive as ever.

"Dr. Bentley has lost his damn mind!" he said, taking great care to rub hand lotion into her dry skin.

The machines' rhythmic whooshing noise and beeping were the only sounds in the room. He yearned for her to wake up, look into his eyes and forgive him.

"Please wake up!"

Virginia peered into her daughter's room window and saw Will lying in bed next to Sophia. Now he was sorry, crying, and bereaved. Where was this concern the last eight months of her daughter's life? She wondered. She knew about the night her daughter told him she was pregnant, about how he'd left and cut her off during what should have been the best time of her life. Virginia was completely heartbroken. A mother should never have to bury her child. *Never.*

Virginia entered the room, wiping away tears, and stood at the bedside. She knew her daughter would want her to provide comfort instead of beratement.

Virginia lifted Sophia's hand to her lips and kissed it gently. Then swept the hand against her cheek as her tears covered it. Kissing it a final time, she placed her daughter's hand back on the bed.

"Will, the Sophia that we knew is gone. This is just her body," Virginia said softly.

"You don't understand. I can't let her go," Will said. He buried his face deeper into Sophia's shoulder.

"Will, Sophia was a gift to all of us, and her memory will live on with us always."

"How can you give up so easily?" Will said, looking up through his tears.

"We aren't giving up, Will; we're letting go," Virginia said. She bent down and hugged him as they wept together.

Will and Virginia stood in Dr. Bentley's office.

"Is she going to be in pain when you turn off life support?" asked Will.

Dr. Bentley got up from his desk, walked over to Will, and put his hand on his shoulder.

"Will, your wife is far beyond pain's reach."

"Do the donor thing and end Sophia's life support," Will said, then turned and walked away.

Ricky held his goddaughter, Chloe. When he discovered that Sophia was pregnant, he hoped he would be important to the child's life. But he didn't expect to be the one bringing her home from the hospital or being her temporary father. Will fled the hospital after life support was turned off. Virginia was overwhelmed with preparations for Sophia's funeral, so he and his wife, Regina, volunteered to take care of Chloe.

Ricky knew his best friend was hurting in unimaginable ways. Removing your wife from life support had to be the hardest thing a husband could do. Will hadn't been the best husband and hadn't wanted this child. But he knew his best friend's heart, knew he would come back and be a good father. Chloe opened her eyes, stared intently at him, and began to wail.

"It's all right, precious," Ricky said, lifting her to his shoulder and gently rubbing her back. He knew a little something about being a daddy. He and Regina had three kids, the center of his world.

"She's probably hungry," Regina said, entering the room with a bottle. She sat beside him as he stuck a warm bottle in the newborn's mouth. Chloe immediately began to suck, still staring at him. Ricky looked over at his wife with gratitude. Ever since they had heard about Sophia, he had been offering thanks to God that he still had his childhood sweetheart.

“I got the kids bathed and put them into bed. They have many questions,” she said as she leaned against her husband.

“I do, too,” Ricky said as he rocked Chloe. He wished he could take Will’s pain away. He couldn’t, but he knew someone who could. God was the source of strength and comfort for him and Regina, especially in times of trouble. Ricky lifted his voice in prayer.

Sarah Dozier looked at her unkempt son and intuitively knew that life as he’d known it was over. Will collapsed into his mother's arms, and they fell to the floor. A mother didn’t have to be told that her child was broken and needed refuge. She’d brought him into this world, wiped his tears, kissed his scrapes, calmed his fears, and listened to his dreams.

“Mom, I killed her,” Will said. He was incoherent with grief. Sarah rubbed her son's head and let him get it all out. Her questions could wait. Life-defining moments require a mother to love unconditionally. She was determined to let her embrace rescue her son.

Will had always possessed an uncanny knack for thriving amid chaos. His composure remained unwavering;

he had an innate ability to filter out the cacophony and zero in on solutions. His late father, the illustrious attorney, Wilson Fairmont Dozier, Sr, instilled such invaluable skills in him.

As fate would have it, Will's education and training advanced through various stages. He embarked on a transformative journey at the prestigious U.S. Naval Academy in Annapolis, honing his abilities. Subsequently, he ventured to the renowned Naval Air Station in Pensacola, where he delved into advanced flight training at NAS Whiting Field. His dedication and skill earned him acceptance into Aviation Officer Candidate School, culminating in his commissioning as a naval officer.

With the highest academic achievement within his class, Will proudly donned the Navy's coveted Wings of Gold. Not only that, he was handpicked as the epitome of potential among his peers, hailed as the "most promising naval officer." These accolades served as a testament to his unwavering commitment and unwavering excellence.

Each progressive step in Will's journey seemed like a stepping stone toward a life of triumph and accomplishment. But now, he couldn't help but see it as an elaborate deception, a cruel hoax that had left him feeling utterly inadequate.

All his training, meticulously designed to prepare him for any situation, had failed to equip him for this particular ordeal. Will had honed the art of emotional detachment to a fair degree, yet this time, his feelings refused to be ignored. His existence, once familiar and secure, had been irrevocably shattered. And the weight of responsibility pressed upon him, for hadn't he brought this calamity upon himself? He carried the burden of an indelible curse, a haunting reminder of the pain he inflicted upon his father and Sophia.

There was only one path to redemption, a singular remedy for the transgressions he believed he had committed. He knew what he must do: he had to pay the price for his actions, to atone for the damage he had caused to those he held dear. The road to salvation lay before him, fraught with uncertainty and self-inflicted wounds, but Will was resolved to tread it with unwavering determination.

If Will had never come into existence, his father, a revered figure, a hero whose impact resonated with people across the nation, would still be breathing, tirelessly making a difference in countless lives. And if Will hadn't endured the aftermath of his father's demise, a remarkable, loyal, exquisitely beautiful woman wouldn't now lie lifeless in a desolate morgue on Staten Island.

The weight of his presumed curse burdened him, an insidious belief that led him to avoid the prospect of fatherhood altogether. His motive was noble, an attempt to shield others from the agony he felt destined to inflict. He believed he didn't deserve the roles of a husband or a father; the gift of love seemed unattainable, an honor forever beyond his reach. To him, love was an elusive privilege he could never earn, an accolade he felt perpetually unworthy of.

Days had blurred into an agonizing continuum as Will pondered these thoughts, his mind consumed by contemplation. His father's passing haunted him from the tender age of eight. And after that heart-wrenching loss, he contemplated ending his own life, succumbing to despair.

Those around him assumed that his desperate act, ingesting his mother's pain pills, stemmed solely from the profound grief that accompanied the absence of his beloved father. But the truth was far more complex, a hidden layer known only to him. In her own anguish, his mother had convinced him that she couldn't bear the thought of losing him. She had implored him to honor his father's memory by forging ahead and living a life of extraordinary significance.

Now, with his mind ensnared by these haunting memories and conflicting emotions, Will grappled with his existence, purpose, and the price he believed he must pay to honor the ones he had lost. His mother had believed the best about him, but she'd been wrong.

"I've reached the end of the line, Mom," he whispered, his voice barely audible, as he reached deep into his father's gun safe, retrieving the cherished Glock. It had been his father's favored weapon, the very one he had clutched tightly on that ill-fated night of his passing.

Clad only in his boxer shorts, Will stumbled out into the balmy night, his movements unsteady, seeking support from a nearby pillar. Memories flooded his consciousness when he gazed out across the expansive twenty-acres of the family estate. His father had acquired this property in the late seventies, a notable victory against the tobacco industry resulting in the largest jury award in the state. But it was more than just a grandiose mansion his father had constructed; it was a haven, a sanctuary intended for Will, his sole progeny, to raise his own family in Raleigh, North Carolina.

"I'm sorry, Dad, but that dream won't come to pass," Will murmured, his words etching through the heavy night air as he slowly descended the stairs into the encompassing darkness. Clutching a whiskey bottle and his father's treasured firearm, he traversed the path toward the private shooting range, a sacred ground that his father had meticulously crafted for their shared moments. Countless hours had been spent there, where they sought solace and contemplation, exchanging stories and aspirations. Within those hallowed confines, his father had instilled in him the values of honor and integrity, revealing the true essence of an upright man. Now, Will recognized the abysmal depths of his failure to uphold his father's teachings.

"Dad, I'm so sorry," Will choked, his tear-filled eyes betraying his agony. Collapsing onto the ground, his dwindling strength giving way, he wept for the loss that consumed him. His father had always stood as his hero, guardian, and unwavering champion. The ache of his absence now intensified, exacerbating the already suffocating pain and grief. Just as surely as he had caused Sophia's untimely demise, he bore the heavy burden of his father's passing. The media had spun tales of Wilson Fairmont Dozier, Sr., careening out of control, his vehicle propelled at reckless speeds around a treacherous curve. But Will knew the truth, the haunting reality that lay concealed behind the distorted narratives.

A soft breeze caressed the swaying trees, momentarily tricking Will's senses into believing he heard his father's voice beckoning him. He strained his ears, desperate for any sign of his father's presence, but only silence enveloped him. Taking one final, protracted gulp, the gun rested upon his lap, its weight a grim reminder. The amber elixir cascaded down his chin, a bitter testament to his conviction. There seemed no other escape from the relentless anguish but to extinguish his own existence. In doing so, the torment would finally be laid to rest, burying the secret that had robbed him of everything he held dear.

Tears streamed down Will's face as he pressed the gun against his temple, his trembling hand poised to pull the trigger. From the depths of his being, a familiar voice urged him forward, compelling him toward the irreversible act.

Tonight, he believed, there should be more than one death. Will had contemplated flying to Miami, crashing his jet into Rosaria's condominium, eradicating her existence and all its trifling consequences. The thought of inflicting pain upon the 17-year-old pot smoker arrested for causing Sophia's death also danced within his mind. But no one deserved the embrace of death more than the person who had precipitated his father's demise on that fateful night.

That individual bore responsibility for the loss that had consumed every fragment of his life.

Amidst his tumultuous thoughts, the sound of approaching footsteps punctuated the air. Will's gaze shifted, his eyes meeting his mother's somber presence. Instantly, sobriety washed over him. How could he consider ending his life in this place, he wondered. His mother had endured an insurmountable share of suffering already. He couldn't subject her to another loss that would undoubtedly shatter her beyond repair. He needed to find another location, away from her heart-wrenching gaze.

"Son, I know you're in pain, but taking your own life is not the answer," she said gently, settling beside him. He couldn't bear to meet her gaze, burdened by guilt and anguish. In a gesture of compassion, she carefully retrieved the bottle and the gun, placing them out of reach.

"I've spoken with Ricky and Virginia," she continued, holding his trembling hand. "I know what transpired."

"You still don't understand... not everything," he replied, his voice strained.

She gently lifted his chin, compelling him to face her. "Then explain it to me because I can't bear to lose you either."

Will couldn't muster the strength to meet her eyes, his tears flowing ceaselessly, fearing the devastating consequences that his words would unleash. She had been an extraordinary mother and wife, weathering the storm of his father's passing with resilience. He couldn't subject her to further pain, for revealing the truth would surely fracture her spirit as irreparably as his own death. The knowledge would only lead to her resentment, blame, and the permanent severing of their bond.

"Whatever it is, my son, you can confide in me," she whispered, her touch tender against his face.

Will's gaze shifted beyond her, staring into the inky darkness as memories of the day when his world crumbled flashed before his eyes, forever etching its harrowing imprint upon his soul.

How many wake-up calls does one life warrant? Will pondered the question as he walked arm in arm with his mother, their steps leading them toward the gathering of mourners, family, and friends who had assembled to bid farewell to his departed wife.

All eyes turned to them as they entered the room. Will discerned a mixture of understanding and judgment etched upon the faces before him. Judgment, he comprehended, for he had forsaken his wife and daughter, leaving the burden of funeral arrangements upon her grieving mother. Despite his reluctance to be present, he acknowledged that this was precisely where he needed to be.

Will and his mother had engaged in numerous heartfelt conversations since that fateful night when she interrupted him at the shooting range. He had bared his soul, revealing the true circumstances surrounding Sophia's untimely demise. He mustered the strength to confess the events of his youth and the reasons behind his father's ill-fated journey that fateful night. He knew his revelations had devastated his mother, but she concealed her pain. Instead of casting blame or condemnation, she offered solace that transformed his perspective.

Ricky and Regina stood at the forefront of the room, Chloe safely cradled in Ricky's arms. Will cautiously reached out, drawing his daughter close to his wounded heart. Together in their bond of friendship and godparent duty, Ricky and Regina enveloped them with unwavering support. Though shattered, he drew fortitude from their unyielding outpouring of love. While forgiveness remained elusive, he discovered a reservoir of courage, enough to forge ahead with life. It was what his father and Sophia, who had loved him unconditionally, would have wished for him.

Finally, Will's gaze rested upon the casket that held his wife, the weight of grief threatening to consume him entirely. He steeled himself, finding solace in the love and support that encircled him. When he looked down at his daughter, an overwhelming sense of gratitude washed over him.

Chloe's radiant smile reflected a boundless trust, an innocence untarnished. It seemed to whisper, "I always knew you would return, Daddy." He vowed to never disappoint her. This marked the final awakening, the ultimate revelation he would ever need.

Chapter Five

"Never are we nearer the light than when darkness is deepest."

—Swami Vivekananda

Savannah sat by the oversized clock under a bevy of multicolored Tiffany-style lamps in the whimsical restaurant Serendipity 3 on East 60th Street in New York. She was sipping a Frozen Mochaccino wishing; instead, it was a quart of Jack Daniel's. Usually, this playful place brightened her mood. Today, it had an insignificant effect. She was frustrated and unhappy. A dangerous combination. Even though she wore Gucci: a plain short-sleeve polo shirt, jeans, sunglasses, and a New York Yankees hat with her hair pulled back, people were staring at her. She was used to it, but today it was a pain in the ass. She wasn't in the mood for attention.

The private investigator she had enlisted to locate her sister finally called, arranging to meet her at that very place. Savannah had been trying to recover from a drinking binge and was in a funky mood. There was no palpable excitement in his voice. He claimed to have a mere update for her, but she wasn't interested in goddamn updates. What she desperately needed was for him to find her sister.

This marked the fifth investigator she had hired in three years. None of them had succeeded in tracking down Elisha. If Peter didn't have concrete news this time, Savannah was prepared to unleash her wrath upon him with the white parlor chair she was sitting on. Glancing at her watch, she let out a deep sigh. He was already ten minutes late, and she had reached her limit. She grabbed her phone, ready to dial, but froze when she heard an infant's cry. Following the sound, she spotted an attractive couple across the room. The man gently lifted the child, soothing it against his shoulder, and the baby's cries subsided. Savannah's heart ached. The scene radiated genuine love as the couple conversed effortlessly while indulging in a spoonful of The Golden Opulence Sundae. Savannah had savored that pricey, decadent treat with Tanzi. Yes, it was undeniably delicious, but that wasn't the reason this couple was smiling.

The affection shared by the family was palpable, enveloping them in a visible glow. Savannah tried to turn away but couldn't tear her gaze from them. It was the very dream she had longed for but had been cruelly denied. Why not me, she wondered. The answer, an all-too-familiar one, resurfaced: She was never deemed worthy of love.

"So what!" she screamed inwardly. Love was the last thing she wanted anything to do with. It was a deceptive fantasy. She had traded in that illusion for something real that wouldn't let her down—money and power.

Ignorant, deceived bitches. Go ahead and live in your fantasy world. "You think you have it all now, but that will soon change. Love always eventually fucks you over," she rued.

"Good day, Ms. St. Clair," a husky baritone voice resonated. Savannah scowled. She had crossed paths with the investigator once before, but today he seemed even more unnerving. She raised her gaze as the detective settled himself across from her. He was a short, stout man with a glistening shaved head and a full beard. His complexion bore a pasty pallor, and his eyes loomed large, piercingly inquisitive. His bulbous nose was a testament to his former days as an NYPD detective, marked by heavy drinking.

"You're late," Savannah spat. "My apologies; I was awaiting a fax from Los Angeles," he replied, placing a substantial manila envelope on the table. Savannah's heart drummed in sync with her pounding head. A flush of heat suffused her face. A young, excessively thin waitress with a lazy eye appeared. Savannah couldn't help but think the girl needed to step behind the counter and enjoy a few bowls of ice cream to put some meat on her bones.

"Nothing for me," the detective declined. His unwavering gaze remained fixated on Savannah, unsettling her considerably. "Did you find her?" Savannah blurted out. "Not precisely," he began, but before he could continue, Savannah seized the envelope. She tossed twenty dollars on the table and leaned in, mere inches from his face. "You're fired, dickhead!" she spat and strode away. She would have to embark on the search for her sister alone.

Even amidst the suffocating darkness, she is intimate with every inch of the decaying gray cinder block wall, its surface marred by peeling, white paint. Years have been consumed in a clandestine dance of meticulous study, weaving intricate plans for escape.

She harbors a deep-seated hatred for those responsible for her confinement. She spews venom their way with each visit they make, bearing food and a peculiar red drink. They snatched away everything from her on that fateful day. They persist in holding her captive, denying her family any knowledge of her whereabouts. The question of why continues to elude her grasp, leaving her mind entangled in perplexity.

These walls surrounding her, silent sentinels to her nightmares, have absorbed her anguished screams, delirious rants, and the ceaseless cascade of tears that have etched paths down her haggard face. Yet, they remain unmoved, their indifferent gaze reflecting no semblance of mercy or empathy. In this sinister realm, where time coils like a serpent, she is consigned to dwell—an eternal specter caught between the yearning for freedom's sweet embrace and the malevolence of a wretched existence that denies her constant pleading for death.

If one dares to believe she is feeble, lacking fortitude or perseverance, let them fathom the battles she valiantly fought. Let them tread the treacherous path she traversed, stepping into her weathered shoes, immersing themselves in the depths of her tormented existence. Only then would they comprehend that long before their own resolve crumbled, she persisted. Thus, should they dare to pass judgment, let it be an accurate reckoning. Let them not cast their eyes upon this hollow husk of a woman and recoil in repulsion. For within this vessel once dwelled a vibrant child, a resplendent butterfly, until life dipped her delicate wings into the viscous tar of its cruelty.

The course she found herself on was never of her own volition. Once, she had a sister who cherished her with a love surpassing all else. Together, they wove dreams of a glorious future. But then, like an unyielding force, Mother Destiny intervened, dictating a path she had no say in. Her dreams were not merely deferred; they were violently uprooted by hands imbued with rage, ensuring no blossoms would grace the garden of her life.

Her gaze is inexorably drawn to the narrow window, where moonlight cascades, igniting a dormant spark buried deep within her being. She senses the specter of life stirring, clawing its way from the depths of its grave, filling her with dreadful anticipation. Yet, her mind remains ensnared in a haze, a relentless guardian stationed at the door of her fragmented memories.

"Savannahhhhh!" she screams, her voice a parched, cracked whisper. But it is merely a taunting apparition birthed by her own tortured imagination. The relentless passage of time, marked by the countless years of her captivity, has assuredly erased her from the collective memory of everyone that knew her. Her eyes, weary and forlorn, retreat from the moon's ethereal glow, returning once more to the worn surface of the gray cinder block concealed beneath its patchy coat of flaking white paint.

Tanzi sat on the edge of the bed, putting on a pair of Chanel alligator and lambskin pumps, preparing to head to work. Her worry was palpable. Savannah hadn't come home the last night nor returned any of her calls. Even though her absences had become a recurring theme in their lives, Tanzi wasn't comfortable with it. Tanzi was jolted by her ringing phone.

"Finally!" she screamed, relieved until she saw it was her mother. Tanzi had been avoiding her mom, the woman who had rescued her and sacrificed so much. She couldn't answer the call because she didn't want her mother to worry. The second she heard her voice, she would know something was wrong. Such was life, having a mother who prayed devoutly. Instead of taking the call, she stared out the window. The early morning looked perfect. A vivid blue sky, the sun illuminating powder puff white clouds. Early March, so she knew the air would be chilly. She was far from Nairobi, yet her mind instantly spanned the distance.

After touring the slums of Nairobi, Tanzi had become even more invisible at home. So, it was no surprise that months after her eleventh birthday, when the "ubakaji" vicious rape happened, her birth parents abandoned her.

She had been an innocent victim, a dutiful girl walking home from school when six men had abducted her. Lying in a hospital bed after the savage attack, she received word that she couldn't return home. She was sent to live in an orphanage.

Days after her twelfth birthday, as she lay delivering a child, she prayed for that death notice to finally catch up with her and end this painful life. Her prayer for death had not been answered, but her plea for the end of her painful life was granted. Her adoptive parents were the reason. After they got her, everything changed, including her name. She was no longer Tanzia, a notice of death. She was Tanzi, the persistent spirit.

It had been almost twenty years since Tanzi left Kenya for America. She still felt the pain of betrayal but knew love could rescue her. Her adoptive parents taught her that lesson. She would have to figure out how to prove to Savannah that she was worthy of love. She stood, straightened her clothes, and headed for the door.

After leaving Serendipity 3, Savannah's emotional state deteriorated. She'd gone back to her SoHo apartment and continued her tirade. She had spread carnage everywhere, but she wasn't done. She slashed her expensive bespoke

Charlotte Thomas bed linen with a long butcher knife in her hot hands. Then she turned on her European down Batiste pillows. Strips of cotton and satin and feathers flew everywhere. She sat on her bed amidst the wreckage, breathing heavily.

"Why are you so enraged?" A calm query came from the familiar voice, the tormenter that resided inside her head.

"Why? Why?" she hissed. "I want my sister!"

Peter Farmington had made bold claims of his expertise, but he had failed to deliver like those before him. Despite the fleeting glimpses of progress by a few investigators, Elisha remained a ghostly figure, vanishing into the depths like a covert operation orchestrated by the CIA. Even Tina, with her supposed insights, provided no solace. The question burned within her, a relentless torment: Why would someone snatch her away? The manila envelope lay before her, tempting yet terrifying, holding secrets she was too fearful of confronting. Shifting on the bed, huffing, she dropped the knife on the floor and sobbed bitterly, rolling her naked body into a ball. A piece of her was missing as long as her sister was missing, too. She knew everything would change if she could just find her sister. Without Elisha, there was a hollow emptiness that couldn't be assuaged. She reached for the nearly empty bottle of Jack

Daniel's and took a long pull. The fiery liquid ran through her, quieting all the questions. Finally, she succumbed to the whiskey and slid down the rabbit hole of dark memory.

The rain fell hard against the dirty windowsill as Savannah and Elisha held each other. They were cold and trembling. They'd never suffered nights like this when their Nana was alive. She'd often said that God was on his throne and all was right in the world. Now both girls wondered if that was true. Elisha leaned into her sister while she sucked her thumb, as both stared out into the dark night.

After Nana's death, it took the authorities three days to contact their aunt Tina, and she'd quickly flown in from New York and whisked them out of the foster home. Reluctantly, Tina called her oldest sister, Essie Wallin, to help with the funeral arrangements and to try to find the twins' mother. Eight days after they buried Nana and David, they found Lolita in a rundown crack house in South Central Los Angeles. The twins waited anxiously in the car with Essie while Tina went inside.

When Tina came out dragging Lolita, the girls were overcome with panic. Elisha began to cry, and Savannah patted her sister, trying to calm her. The stranger in the back seat beside them was cursing Essie and Tina. It was as if she didn't even see the girls. A war of angry words erupted inside the car. Essie said that Lolita was responsible for Nana and David's death. Suddenly, the car had become silent; the raging words stopped, and then a piercing scream so loud that it threatened to rip the car to shreds. The woman wailing, Tina said, was their mother.

Essie and Tina took Lolita to Nana's grave. She broke down again and cried uncontrollably, begging her mother's forgiveness. Lolita collapsed at David's grave, and her sisters had to carry her away. When Lolita emerged from her drug-induced haze three days later, she vowed to get clean and sober and raise her girls. Tina had to return to New York. Essie, who felt Lolita shouldn't stay alone in Los Angeles, forced her and the twins to move into her home in Oakland, California.

Several months later, the twin's father, Gary, came to Oakland to get Lolita and the girls. They moved back to Los Angeles with him, living in a two-bedroom apartment, unable to move into Nana's house because Essie forbade it. The house was up for sale, and until it was sold, this rundown apartment was home. The filthy walls were caked with dirt and graffiti. Lolita had scrubbed, trying to make it more presentable, but it hadn't helped. The girls slept on the floor, covered in old, tattered blankets, while their mother slept on a bare mattress. They ate once a day, sometimes two, if Gary hadn't taken the food stamps to buy liquor or drugs.

Their mother fought desperately to uphold her promise of staying clean from drugs, but when things turned grim, and Gary didn't return home, she sought solace in alcohol. In her intoxicated haze, she would keep the girls awake throughout the night, reminiscing about the "good old days" and painting a glorified picture of their father. Savannah saw through the façade and held contempt for her feeble mother. Elisha, however, clung to every word, longing for a connection to their absent father. With Gary gone for months, Lolita resorted to "dating" men who would visit their cramped apartment. Savannah overheard her mother boasting to one of the men about her irresistible allure, claiming it was the secret to keeping them enthralled and ensuring their return. It was through these arrangements that the bills were paid. *One night, the twins had been awakened by music and laughter. Savannah got up to see what was happening, but Elisha pleaded with her to return and lie down. However, some force she couldn't explain drew Savannah, and she bent down and peered through the dusty heat register. Soon, Elisha was beside her, and they both watched. The sight sickened and excited*

Savannah, and she couldn't tear herself away. Her mother was pressing into the naked body of a stranger, his pants down around his feet. His long "pee-pee" was sticking out. Her mother, in black high heels, was rubbing it. The man pulled up her skirt, revealing her mother's "secret." Elisha begged them to return to bed, but Savannah wouldn't move. She wanted to see what was going to happen next.

They watched as their mother dropped to her knees, saying something they couldn't hear, and took him into her mouth as the man held her by the hair. He yelled as he shot milky-looking stuff all over their mother.

Days later, when their father came home, the twins watched through the vent as their father did the same thing to their mother. He didn't give her any money but violently beat her for "messing around." Savannah ran to her mother's defense, picked up a chair, and threw it at her father. It hit him in the back, drawing his attention away from beating their mother. He staggered to Savannah and slapped her hard. Elisha stood screaming and crying at her sister's side.

"Both of you little bitches get back in your room," he said angrily, slurring his words as he grabbed Lolita's hair and pulled her towards him, readying to slap her again. Savannah ran towards him, kicking and screaming.

"Leave her alone!" she yelled as she received another blow. Dazed, she stumbled backward.

"Stay out of grown folks' business," he fumed and slapped Lolita again, so hard blood ran out of her mouth.

"Go back to bed, girls," their mother pleaded. Trembling through tears, Savannah and Elisha reluctantly obeyed. When she and Elisha got back under their blanket, she felt insurmountable hate as she rubbed her hot, swollen face.

"One day, I'm going to kill him!" She swore in the darkness.

Their father had left the night he slapped Savannah well over a week prior. She'd hoped he would stay gone. But their mother had been gone for days, and they had eaten the meager rations of crackers, peanut butter, and a box of Fruit Loops. Elisha began to whimper, and Savannah held her tight as her stomach growled. Although she was only minutes older, she felt like Elisha's mother.

"Don't cry, baby girl; I'll get you something to eat, okay?" Savannah said comfortingly.

"Is Mama coming back?" her sister asked, tears streaming down her fragile face as if Savannah was the wisest of sages.

"She'll be back," Savannah said confidently.

"What about Nana, David, and God? Will they be back?" Elisha said, her hazel eyes searching Savannah's for an answer. Pain and anger played across Savannah's face as she stared out the dirty window into the dark, thunderous night.

"No!" Savannah said through clenched teeth to her sister. "Don't worry, I'll take care of you." She vowed as she tenderly lifted Elisha's chin until their eyes met.

"All we have in this world is each other! Don't ever forget that baby girl!"

Savannah awoke, momentarily unsure of where she was until she saw her clock on the nightstand. It said 4:15 a.m. Wiping her eyes, she looked around at the mess she'd made. Pain coursed through her naked body. A familiar stench lingered, an unpleasant reminder that she'd probably been dead to the world for several days.

The best thing she could do was to go to sleep permanently. *Why was she fighting to live?* So much would be settled if she stopped living, especially the pain. Nothing was ever going to change. The indisputable truth was that everything had gone to shit in her short life. *What is the point of living when you know every time you love, inevitably, you will lose?*

Tanzi couldn't believe it had been five days. Savannah still hadn't answered any of her calls or texts. She turned the television off and headed towards the bedroom, where she would spend another night alone. She wanted to go to the SoHo apartment but knew it wouldn't end well.

As she slipped off her satin robe and slid into bed, another part wanted to wring Savannah's neck. *Did she not understand that when someone cares about you, the last thing you should do is ignore them?* As if on cue, her phone rang.

"About damn time!" she screamed, reaching for the phone. It was her mother again. She knew her mother was already overwhelmed by her father's recent heart attack, and she refused to put any more on her. But it wasn't fair to have them worry if something happened to her.

"Hey, Mom," Tanzi said, feigning happiness.

"Hey baby, I just wanted to hear your voice. You've been so heavy in my heart."

Tanzi heard the lilt in her voice and knew her mother was trying to mask her pain. Tanzi knew why, too. She had gone to her for advice after Savannah's birthday suicide attempt almost six months ago now. In the following days, her mother had been a source of strength and encouragement, but it had taken a toll on her father.

Tanzi thought her mother would keep her issues with Savannah a secret from her dad, but she'd been crazy to think so. Her parents shared everything. When her mother told her father what she was going through, he became so fearful for his daughter that he suffered a heart attack. Tanzi wouldn't make that mistake again; she would keep the latest drama to herself.

"Everything is fine, Mom. I've just been really busy at work. How's dad doing?" Tanzi said to change the subject.

"He's being stubborn about his diet. Maybe you can talk some sense into him," her mom laughed.

Tanzi answered, "I sure will; put him on."

"How's the most beloved daughter in the world?" her dad said with such enthusiasm Tanzi could see his ocean-blue eyes dancing.

"I'm good, Dad," she said.

"Are you just saying that to keep me from worrying about you?" Her dad asked.

"Now, would I do something like that?" Tanzi answered.

"Yes, you would," he responded, chuckling.

"Really, Dad, I'm just overwhelmed at work," pausing to debate whether to tell him that Matthew Friedman had offered her a partnership in the law firm.

"And life is just very complicated right now," Tanzi said.

"With Savannah?"

Tanzi knew exactly how her father felt about her relationship with Savannah. He was a Christian who didn't support gay relationships. But he loved his daughter unconditionally, so he'd gotten past it. What Robert couldn't get past was Savannah attempting to keep Tanzi from spending time with her family. Occasionally, they would come to her office to visit. They usually avoided conversations about Savannah, but she was always the elephant in the room.

"Dad, you know how I feel about Savannah," she said, hoping to avoid a discussion.

"Well, you know how I feel about her too, but it's your life, so I won't subject you to another one of my sermons."

"Now there's an answer to prayer," Tanzi laughed.

Robert laughed heartily and replied, "You're beautiful and brilliant, but now you're a smart aleck too!"

She smiled, happy to hear him laugh. Sitting in the hospital with her mother after his near-fatal heart attack and bypass surgery three months ago was traumatic. During that time, she sat by his bedside, reflecting on the great sacrifices he had made for her.

Tanzi had been rejected and abandoned by her biological father, Mygambi, but her adoptive father rescued her. Mygambi only briefly acknowledged her presence, but her dad went out of his way to show and tell her how much he cared. He did many things that demonstrated his love for Tanzi, but one of the most endearing was how he cared for her hair when she was younger.

Tanzi's hair was long and coarse, and it would have been easier for him to send her out to get her hair relaxed or braided, but he didn't. Her dad had spent many hours with natural hair care specialists learning how to attend to his daughter's mane. He always stressed the importance of maintaining her heritage. Though his skin was white and hers was black, he was her father in every way. While brushing, combing, and plaiting, he would share with her what was happening worldwide, especially in Africa. He always made her feel proud that she was both African and American.

"I just want you to know that we love you and want you to be happy," he said with great emotion.

"I know, Dad," her eyes welling with tears.

"Your mom and I are here for you," he said.

Tears streamed down her face. "I won't forget. Dad and we all need you, so promise me, you will behave," Tanzi chided.

"I will, just for you," he vowed.

"We love you, Tanzi," her mother said in the background.

"I love you too, bye." Tanzi hung up and let the tears fall as she buried her face in her hands. She had so much to be grateful for, wonderful parents and an illustrious career, yet she was completely unhappy. She wanted most to have a good relationship with Savannah, but that was slipping away. *Why did life have to be so complicated?* She didn't want to feel this pain. It weakened her and made her question everything about herself. Her childhood fears of not being good enough or worthy of love resurfaced. Although she had law degrees from Harvard and Yale and was one of the best negotiators in the city, she couldn't fix the mess that was her life.

Matthew Friedman removed his reading glasses and rubbed his eyes to alleviate his fatigue. It seemed that he hadn't slept for days, tormented over Tanzi. He sensed she was drowning, yet he felt powerless to save her. Her performance at work hadn't faltered one bit, but he'd seen it in her eyes: a distant look of pain, a resignation of some kind. He'd offered her the partnership because she deserved it and because he thought it would make her happy, but her sadness remained.

He put aside the latest reports from the World Health Organization and his foundation, the Nwanji AIDS Project, that he was perusing to distract himself. It didn't work. In fact, the latest statistics of millions of children dying from AIDS or being orphaned in Africa only made him feel more tormented. Most of those who knew of his benevolence to Africa thought it was just a good cause he supported. It wasn't. It was deeply personal.

Matthew fell in love with Africa the first time he set foot on its soil as a ten-year-old, visiting his humanitarian father, Dr. Simon Friedman. His father's skill as a doctor helped to save many Kenyan children. Even though he was a young white boy from a faraway land, the children of Kenya accepted him. By his third trip at fifteen, he knew he would live in the Motherland someday. During his fourth trip at age sixteen, he'd promised Neema, the Kenyan girl who'd stolen his heart, he would.

He reflected on the last time he saw Neema. Her beautiful midnight skin was dusty and broken. Her divine, sparkling eyes fought to see him one last time as her gentle hands reached out. She didn't deserve to die. Even now, thirty-six years later, it is still very painful. Neema was violently taken from life by the hands of her father, who'd discovered the two were lovers. The buzzing of his phone pulled him back from memories of Africa.

"Yes, Annie," he said.

"Sir, I just wanted to let you know that everything is ready for tomorrow's press conference," she said quietly.

"Thanks; I'll see you tomorrow," he responded.

The press conference would shut the mouths of the naysayers at the firm who balked at Tanzi becoming a partner. While acknowledging Tanzi's value to the company, the senior partners fought him about moving her up. At the root of their objections were the two things that kept most women in the U.S. from their rightful place: white male privilege and jealousy. He was determined to prevent either from standing in Tanzi's way. So, when he'd learned of their latest client, he'd arranged for Tanzi to take the lead.

This client's case had been front-page news for weeks, sparking protests against torturous police brutality. In his estimation, Tanzi was the best lawyer in the firm. She would set the stage for the national spotlight to shine on their firm. Not that he cared, but he knew the senior partners did.

Matthew wanted Tanzi to win. She had worked diligently for this, and he had guided her in some small way with partly selfish motives. She had always reminded him of Neema. He couldn't save her, but his dedication to Tanzi helped to right the wrongs Neema had endured.

It had been fourteen years since Matthew first laid eyes on Tanzi. She had saved him, brought him back from death’s door. The truth was, he loved her.

Chapter Six

"Beware that, when fighting monsters, you yourself do not become a monster."

— Friedrich Nietzsche

Tanzi couldn't believe what had just happened. "Ms. Ridley," Tanzi's secretary said, tapping lightly on the door as she entered.

"Yes?" Tanzi answered.

"Mr. Friedman asked if you would come to his office." Tanzi was silent. *How could she get out of the meeting with him?* She thought.

"Ma'am?" Her secretary intoned.

"Tell Mr. Friedman I'll be there," Tanzi answered.

As her secretary closed the door, Tanzi leaned into her massive ornate mahogany desk, burying her face in her hands and sighing. "Get a grip on yourself," she said aloud.

How would she face Matthew? Her hasty departure from the boardroom meant the end of the partnership offer she'd worked so hard for.

"This isn't fair," tears capsized over her eyes. Tanzi was excited when Matthew told her she would be the lead attorney on a high-profile case. After reading over the file handed to her minutes before the press conference on their newest client, a 16-year-old female, she felt sick in her stomach. Detaching from the emotional aspects of the case had been Tanzi's specialty. But not this time. As she listened to their client, giving details of being taken from the stroll at 47th Street to an abandoned building, it was too much for Tanzi. She trembled as the girl told how she was forcibly raped, sodomized, made to perform oral sex, viciously beaten with clubs and fists, had gasoline poured on her, and then set afire.

Tanzi's firm filed a $100 million civil suit on behalf of the teenager. The suit was against N.Y.P.D., the City of New York, and the three officers who'd violated her.

The perplexed look on Matthew's face, as she ran past him at the press conference left their client, six other attorneys, assistants, including Matthew, and about forty of New York's top journalists and photographers stunned in her wake.

She was a 22-year-old aspiring legal eagle studying at Harvard when she first met Matthew and realized they shared a destiny. Tanzi had been deeply affected by his tenacious defense of victims and his compassion for the world's needy. He had been a guest lecturer who had so moved the crowd with his passion and intellect that they gave him a five-minute standing ovation. He earned greater respect in Tanzi's eyes when he spoke of his work with the World Health Organization and how he gave fifty percent of his income to rid AIDS and poverty in Africa.

After his lecture, Tanzi introduced herself, and as they spoke, she could tell he was equally moved by her. Matthew offered her an internship during her summers. Upon graduation, she was offered a top position with his firm. The jealous jackals at the firm, who felt he favored her, had been tearing at her flesh since her arrival. Never mind that in her eight years with the firm, she brought in three times what the others did. But her cowardice today had ruined everything.

Leaving her desk, she walked to the window of her twenty-fifth-floor office. *How would she ever be able to explain to Matthew the nightmare that had destroyed her soul many years ago?* She thought. It all returned and haunted her as she listened to their client. Tanzi was just as scared and disfigured inside as the teenager was outside. Both Tanzi and her client had been sentenced to life as victims of men who disregarded their humanity and counted them worthlessly. She owed it to Matthew to tell him what she'd kept secret and hoped he would understand.

Tanzi looked at the clock again, inwardly shook her head, and took another sip of wine. How predictable it was that Savannah wasn't home yet. She always found a way to be MIA when something really mattered to Tanzi. Her promotion from senior associate to equity partner had been something she had worked so hard for and finally achieved.

As she headed into Matthew's office earlier, she asked him not to take her off the case. Tanzi explained to Matthew the reason. He stood from his desk and gently escorted her to the Louis XV sofa in his spacious office. There was something so consolatory and kind about his demeanor that Tanzi instantly felt at ease.

"I have often wondered what gave you the passion and keen insight to fight for the victims we represent. Now I completely understand," he took her hand.

"Tanzi, you're the bravest woman I have ever known."

As they talked, Tanzi realized that what had been a great mentoring relationship had become so much more. Matthew stood, motioned her over to his desk, and handed her a bottle of champagne with a gold bow. She instantly recognized the bottle from his limited edition 12-bottle box set by Perrier-Jouet.

"Could it be?" she wondered.

Matthew took her hand, his eyes beaming as he saw her surprise. "I have more confidence in you now than ever, and the partnership is yours."

Tanzi hugged him so tightly he gasped for air. She thanked him profusely and ran from his office with one thing on her mind: she couldn't wait to celebrate with Savannah. Once she arrived home, she put the bottle of Perrier-Jouet on ice, slipped into a luxurious bath, then dressed in her favorite satin gown. Luther Vandross's Greatest Hits played as she waited for Savannah. And waited and waited. Finally, hours later, Tanzi heard Savannah at the door, and although she was extremely pissed, she decided to let it go so they could get on with celebrating.

The first sign of trouble was when she heard Savannah struggling to get her key in the door. After several moments, Tanzi opened the door, and Savannah staggered in. Tanzi helped her to the table where the now cold dinner awaited. There was silence between them for a moment as Tanzi began serving food.

"What's all this?" Savannah questioned, slurring her words.

Tanzi glared at Savannah. Acting as if she hadn't personally spoken with her earlier in the day, telling her she had great news. Tanzi got over her angst and shared the news about the partnership. She expected Savannah to be happy for her. But no sooner had the words left her mouth that Savannah stood up, feral, and threw her plate, full of food, at Tanzi. The plate barely missed her and landed against the wall.

"Bitch, you already spend too much time in that office now! You think you're gonna be there around the clock?" Savannah stood and staggered over to Tanzi, who remained seated and silent.

"Do you hear me?" Savannah roughly pulled on Tanzi's braids until her head was back, and she was staring up at her. She was struggling to breathe but still didn't say a word.

"So, you think making a partner means something to me?" Flinging her head loose, Tanzi's face almost hit the plate of food on the table before her.

"You must think I'm a goddamn fool," Savannah fumed, walking around the room.

"You think I don't know you're fucking him?"

Tanzi rose, heading for the bedroom. Savannah walked angrily over and blocked her way. "Answer me!"

"What are you talking about, Savannah?" Tanzi glared.

“You’re fucking Matthew!” Savannah pushed a hard finger into her chest.

“I never let anyone touch me,” Tanzi snapped. Savannah grabbed her neck roughly.

“So, you’re going to play me? One of the partners there told me what you two do behind closed doors!” Savannah’s red, angry eyes bore through her. “Maybe I’ll let you go on and get me a sweet thing to take care of me.”

“How can you say that when all I’ve done, from day one, is taken care of you,” Tanzi panted, her voice barely audible as Savannah’s grip tightened on her neck.

“Taken care of me? Bitch, I’m the one who takes care of you,” Savannah yelled into her face and pushed her away. Tanzi stumbled and grabbed the chair to keep from hitting the floor. She ran quickly into the bedroom and tried to lock the door, but Savannah burst in.

“Deny, you’re fuckin’ him; go ahead!” Tanzi just looked at her, her defiance making Savannah’s face turn dark with fury. She punched Tanzi hard in the stomach and threw her to the ground. Savannah roughly straddled her.

“Get off me,” Tanzi struggled to free herself.

“Who the fuck are you ordering around? I’m not that weak bastard you're fucking!”

"It's not like that!" Tanzi yelled back at her. Savannah slapped her face hard, and blood gathered at the corner of her mouth.

"You lying bitch, I know you're fucking him!" Savannah said.

"Why do you have to ruin everything," Tanzi spat at her.

"If you were home doing your job, I wouldn't have to be out there getting sex from someone else!" Savannah yelled in her face.

Tanzi rapidly beat Savannah's chest. "Fuck you, Savannah! How could you?"

"You're just like all the other disloyal motherfuckers in my life!" Savannah screamed as she viciously beat Tanzi like a prized pugilist.

Tanzi was too deadened to fight back, and when Savannah finished with her fist, she stood and began to kick her as Tanzi balled up and took the blows.

The phone rang loudly, startling Tanzi from her sleep, and she grimaced as she reached for it. It had been three days since Savannah's beating, and her body was still badly bruised and battered. Her stomach quivered anxiously as she looked at the caller ID, hoping it was Savannah finally calling. She was disappointed when she saw it was at the front desk of her apartment. At first, she thought to ignore it, but a horrible thought instantly occurred. What if it was the police coming to inform her that Savannah had been found dead?

"Yes," Tanzi paused, not wanting to hear the news.

"Good morning Ms. Ridley; Ms. Tamara Haley is here to see you."

Hearing these words caused a jarring shame to rise in Tanzi. She could not let her personal assistant see her like this. "Tell Ms. Haley I'm not available."

"Yes, ma'am, as you requested, but Ms. Haley told me to let you know if you said you weren't in, she was going to camp out in the lobby until you let her up," he replied, waiting.

Tanzi knew she would do it too. She had to cover up evidence of the beating from Tamara's scrutinizing eyes.

"Give me about ten minutes and then let her up," Tanzi said, disconnecting the line. Tanzi's movements caused extreme pain, and she wondered if one of her ribs had been broken. Initially, she had thought about going to the hospital but didn't because it would trigger contact with the authorities, and the press would get wind of it. She struggled out of bed as the pain mingled with her great humiliation.

Tanzi finished applying the MAC foundation to cover her black eye when the door chimed. She did her best, but if Tamara looked closely, she would see it. As soon as she opened the door and saw the look on Tamara's face, she knew she had failed.

"Jesus, you look like shit!" Tamara said as she walked briskly carrying bags from Starbucks and H & H Bagels.

"Hello to you too!" Tanzi chimed and guided her assistant into the sitting room.

"And why are we going in here?" Tamara feigned a whisper. "Is Ms. Thang here getting her rest from her hellcat excursions?"

"No, Savannah's not here, and neither is my staff. That's why the house is a mess!" Tanzi sat down in a beige Queen Anne chair.

"*My house* is a mess with three badass heathens running everywhere! Your house has never been a mess." Tamara put down the bags on the table.

"I came to check on you because Matthew said you were taking a few days off," Tamara loaded a sun-dried tomato bagel with cream cheese. She placed the bagel on a paper plate and handed it to Tanzi.

"So, what's going on…and don't lie to me," Tamara ordered angrily.

“I’m fine,” Tanzi said, taking a sip.

“Girl, you’re gonna make me baptize your ass, lying like that.” Tanzi remained silent.

“Did you think I wouldn’t notice that skank bitch hit you?” Tamara lifted Tanzi’s face and touched it under her eye. Tanzi winced and pulled back.

“It’s nothing, really,” Tanzi waved her into a chair.

“I know you’re not gonna say some lame shit like that.” Tamara sat across from her, shaking her head.

“Please calm down.”

“H- E- L- L- O? You do remember how many times you came to the hospital to visit me after my husband bashed my skull in?”

“I know, but….”

“And who was it that finally got my kids and me to safety?” Tamara stood, walked to Tanzi, and took her hand. “Because of you, I was one of the fortunate ones who lived to talk about it.”

“But, it’s different with us,” Tanzi started, but Tamara interrupted.

“Yeah, okay. Eat,” Tamara ordered, pointing to the plate.

“You're such a bully to be so little.” Tanzi said, taking a small bite of the bagel as she eyed the feisty 110 lb, 5’2” paralegal powerhouse, who had been the first to welcome her to the law firm so many years ago. It took Tanzi a minute to warm to Tamara, not just because of her razor-sharp tongue but also because of Tanzi's colorism at the hands of others who were a lighter hue of black, as was Tamara.

As much as progressive African Americans wanted to believe that all black skin tones were created equal, that hadn't been Tanzi's experience. Her darkness walked into every room ahead of her intellect, wealth, and even womanhood. She had been made keenly aware of it upon arriving in America. Yes, colorism existed in Africa when she was a young girl. However, most youths in her school were her complexion. In America, she was not only "Black," she was "African." The combination often slung in double disdain.

Although her parents tried to shield Tanzi from the realities of white privilege and colorism, both were inescapable. In the elite community in which they lived and the schools she attended, she was always conscious of the preferential treatment given first to those born white and then to lighter-skinned blacks. By the time she had entered the distinguished halls of Harvard, she'd built up a firm shield to protect herself.

Tanzi did not seek to retaliate for the slights, slurs, and outright racist comments thrown at her by both her white and black counterparts. Instead, her retribution was in scholarly ascendance. All the comments had ceased when she strolled across the stage summa cum laude. Later, when she arrived at the Friedman law firm and was greeted by Tamara, who was fair-skinned, she quickly sized her up as just another detractor, smiled faintly, and ignored her. Days after her arrival, Tamara cornered her in the bathroom, hands on her petite hips and a fire in her eyes.

"Look, Ms. Thang," Tamara said, glaring at Tanzi. "Whatever your problem is with me, you better resolve it quickly." Tanzi gazed coolly at her, and this seemed to irritate her more.

"You may be Ms. Summa Cum of Harvard, but your black ass has just been placed in a tank full of piranhas," Tamara said, pointing at Tanzi. "And if you plan on surviving, you need me to help you navigate these waters. Like it or not, Mr. Friedman appointed me to help you because I'm exceptionally good at what I do," she backed Tanzi against the wall.

"Now, you can keep treating me the way you are, or you can get with the program because only two people here give a damn if you make it. Mr. Friedman, who believes you can walk on water, and me, whose job it is to ensure you do," Tamara smiled faintly. "So don't fuck with me because I'd hate to beat the ass of such a beautiful and brilliant woman!" Their partnership and friendship were born that day.

"You know what amazes me about you?" Tamara said, rising and grabbing a bagel and taking a huge bite. "You ruthlessly fight injustice in the world but do nothing about the injustices perpetrated on you."

"Savannah and I just have a few problems to work through, that's all."

"You are brilliant and stupid," Tamara murmured. Tanzi rose and moved toward the window, looking out.

"I just need to take better care of her," Tanzi whispered. Tamara walked toward her friend.

"There's a fine line between codependency and being a caregiver. One is about control and obsession, and the other is about love and mutual respect. They may look the same, but they aren't," Tamara paused as the silence enfolded them.

"Thank you," Tanzi said, rubbing her friend's hand.

"You once told me to fight to get my life back, and I asked you 'why,' and you said, 'Because you're worth it,'" Tamara walked over to the chair and picked up her purse.

"Well, I've got to get back to the office; somebody's got to keep things going while you run after the Harpy."

"God don't like ugly, Tamara!"

"And he ain't too fond of an asshole either, so don't be one!" Tamara shot back as she walked out and slammed the door behind her.

Savannah picked up her cell phone, looked at the text message, and smiled. Tanzi called her over fifty times in the last ten hours. "That will teach your dumb ass to fuck with me." She purposefully ignored her and partied from Upper Manhattan to SoHo with a vengeance. When she saw the wife of one of the managing partners in Tanzi's firm at a restaurant in SoHo, a perfect plan came together.

Now that woman was sleeping next to Savannah. She would be the knife she used to cut Tanzi's heart out. When her phone rang again, she picked it up and remained silent. Tanzi repeatedly called out to her, the panic in her voice rising. Savannah hung up, knowing things would turn out just as planned.

Robert looked deeply into Jennifer's rueful, Irish green eyes, his wife of thirty-five years, and knew she was worried. He looked out the kitchen window over the lush gardens of their manicured estate in upstate New York. It usually gave him a great sense of peace. Not today. Outside, the bitter cold mingled with harsh, falling snow. His hopes for their daughter had disappeared just as quickly as their Kentucky Bluegrass under the velvety whiteness.

"Honey, all we can do is keep loving her and pray that she will be alright," Robert embraced his wife.

"I know, but I want to speak with her; maybe she'll listen to me this time," Jennifer said, reaching for her cup of tea.

"You know, if we do anything else, she'll only pull further away. She can be stubborn when she wants to," he chuckled.

"I wonder where she gets that from," Jennifer said, playfully jabbing her elbow into his hearty girt. They sat in silence for minutes.

"Well, I'm going to go take my meds," Robert stood slowly, holding onto the table. "Are you coming?"

"I'll be along shortly," Jennifer said, patting his hand. He squeezed her hand and headed towards the door. He turned and looked back at her. He knew his wife well. She wasn't coming along any time soon. She was going to be up, praying.

Chapter Seven

"If you prick us, do we not bleed?"

—William Shakespeare

Tanzi knew she was too weak to leave but ignored the pain, stepped into the elevator, and pushed the lobby button. She could not stand by and watch Savannah's life end this way. None of this would have happened if she'd cared for Savannah better and worked less. For months, their relationship had sped like a fast-moving train toward a cliff, and she had done nothing to improve things.

As Tanzi headed towards the lobby, the doorman nodded and greeted her respectfully.

"Good evening, Ms. Ridley; your car is waiting," he said, holding the door.

"Thank you."

A biting chill gripped her face in icy talons as she stepped outside. Her chauffeur was standing beneath the elegant canopy and took her arm to guide her safely over the snow-covered sidewalk. She knew he was wondering why she was going out at this time of night, but he was discreet and would never ask. Suddenly, they were hit by a strong gust of wind. She stumbled, but both men were there to catch her before she hit the ground.

"Are you alright, Ms. Ridley?" they asked in unison.

"Yes. I'm fine," she said as they steadied her, helping her to her feet.

Tanzi stood there for a moment, chilled by the frigid night air. She sensed something else. It was as if the wind were howling a warning, telling her to turn back. Like the image in a fortune teller's crystal ball, a voice within her, an omen, told her this night would end badly.

"It's quite treacherous tonight, ma'am," the doorman said. "I'd be more than happy to get one of our staff to run an errand for you."

She knew it was foolish to be out here, but she needed to get to Savannah. "No, I've got to handle this myself, but thank you."

The wind suddenly dropped as she headed towards the car, and an eerie stillness took hold. The void of words didn't stop the quiet from urging her. *Go back!* But she couldn't. Savannah needed her. *Please, God, don't take her from me*, she whispered as she got into the car.

Sadie Jones peeked into the large oven and smiled as she saw that her Pecan Sweet Potato pies were baked to golden brown perfection. She took pride in everyone, saying she made the best pies and cakes anywhere in Hattiesburg, Mississippi. She took the pies out and carefully placed them on the counter. Although her seventy-five-year-old body was still in good working order, she didn't want to take any chances of dropping these special gifts for her pastor. She adjusted the oven's temperature and put in the Lemon Pound and Coconut Dream cakes. She would have her son, Nelson, mail them all by special delivery tomorrow.

Even though she was living in New York now, she couldn't forget about Pastor Haskins. As she closed the oven door, she chuckled at the thought of him in the pulpit, sweating, wiping his brow, and talking about 'Big Mama's Coconut Dream Cake.' That's what everyone called her: Big Mama. Not because of her size; she was only five feet tall and weighed barely a hundred pounds. It was because of what others called her "powerful" presence and booming voice. She glanced at the time; *eleven-fifty-six p.m.* It was definitely past her normal bedtime hour, but she could not sleep.

Being in her son's penthouse apartment had taken some time to get used to. The place was so big you could fit three Hattiesburg houses in it. It shared the twentieth floor with one other apartment. She hadn't met their neighbor yet, but she knew she would. A delicious sweet potato pie was a great way to make an introduction.

In her neighborhood in Hattiesburg, she was always there to welcome new people moving in. This generation didn't seem to have the manners and thoughtfulness her Momma raised her with. Everyone was so busy rushing around that they barely spoke. It shocked her soul when she exited the plane in New York City. Too many people!

Moving to New York had been a concerted effort by her six sons, who felt she was no longer safe in her neighborhood. Without her input, it was decided that she would move in with her second youngest son, Nelson, and his wife. When they greeted her in the lobby upon her arrival, her first thought was that they were living too high on the hog. When her son showed her around the penthouse, she knew it was too big for one family to live in.

As hard as it was, she kept her opinions to herself, mainly because she was so very proud of the man her son had become. Secondly, she refused to be like many of the older women in her neighborhood who sat on their porches gossiping. She wanted to be there with an encouraging word, giving people hope. So, she told Nelson how proud she was of him.

Sadie turned her head as something outside the kitchen window caught her attention. As she ambled towards it, she saw the darkness of night dancing with light snow flurries. But it was something else that drew her closer. *Was that angel's wings in the distance?*

Suddenly, Sadie felt a chill, goosebumps climbing down her arms. She moved away from the window as she felt the spiritual presence outside enters the room. There were two things Sadie was very acquainted with; the power of God and the power of darkness.

Some might have considered her delusional in communicating with God, but Sadie knew better. She was a Christian believer in a supernatural God who spoke directly to his children.

"Yes, Lord?" she said aloud.

Sadie's heartbeat picked up its pace. She sensed that someone was in trouble, which meant she was being called to intercede. *But where and who?*

"Okay, Lord, what's going on?" She asked, holding her hands up.

She stood still, listening to his instructions, and walked to the door. Sadie looked out the peephole; only two penthouses were on this floor. She had never seen the neighbors, but the hallway had no activity. Even though she couldn't see anyone, she knew with certainty that she had been called to the door. She began to pray aloud.

"Lord, I thank you for peace and protection. I bind up the demonic forces that are busy in this place. Satan, the Lord rebukes you! You're a lie, and the truth ain't in you!"

Sadie looked at the peephole again and saw a beautiful woman with long neat braids pulled back in a ponytail. There was a powerful presence, a golden light all around her, meaning someone was praying for her. Angels were on duty, covering her.

The woman hesitated as if in fear. She stood outside the door, a key poised in her hand. Sadie opened the door.

"Hello, Baby, are you alright?" she asked.

The woman jumped as if she'd been stunned by an electric current.

"Yes, ma'am," the woman said, her expression a mix of dread and uncertainty.

Sadie knew it wasn't the truth; she definitely wasn't alright.

"It's a cold night to be out and about. I just made the best pie you've ever tasted, and I have some hot cocoa if you would like to join me," she smiled.

"No. But thank you, that's very kind," the young woman answered.

"I'm Big Mama."

"I'm Tanzi."

"You sure you don't want to join me?" Sadie said, wiping her flour-covered hands on her apron. She shook her head no. She could see the woman's mind processing.

Sadie stood there as the woman turned toward the door, ready to put the key in. "Tanzi, do you believe in God?"

Tanzi silently regarded Sadie.

Sadie didn't wait long for an answer.

"Well, believing is good, but listening and obeying is better. Go home, chile'. You can't fix this the way you're going about it. God has already told you that tonight."

"Besides, your momma is prayin' up the throne room for you. Go home, call her, and let her know you're okay."

Sadie could feel a stillness of icy cold creep into the hallway. Sadie thought people often thought they were victims of fate or some other controlling force, but she knew differently. Whether we recognized it or not, the power to choose was always ours.

"You can either walk through that door, or you can go home. Either choice comes with a price. You must decide which one you want to pay for."

Sadie stepped back inside the apartment, smiled, and regarded Tanzi. She felt a release in her spirit.

"Always remember who you are, baby."

Sadie closed the door. A sense of peace flooded her, and she headed back into the kitchen and peered in the oven at her cakes; they were baking perfectly. Sometimes, people were just like cakes; baking them perfectly took life's fiery trials. No doubt, the young woman will have some regrets tomorrow. But it would all eventually work together to make her who she was.

"Cover her, Lord," Sadie said as she went and boxed up her pies.

Tanzi's hands shook violently as she entered the massive foyer, her eyes adjusting to the darkness as she listened for signs of life. She had been afraid to use the key because she was terrified of what she might find. Her encounter with the little woman who called herself "Big Mama" hadn't improved. *"Go home, chile; you can't fix this the way you're going about it!"* The woman's admonishment made intellectual sense to Tanzi, but her heart wasn't buying it. She needed to be here for Savannah.

Tanzi's eyes focused on a delicate silver stiletto lying on the floor and a trail of garments too small to belong to Savannah. Rage welled within her. While she had been suffering, Savannah had been out like a goddamn

Christopher Columbus discovering all the ass she could. *How could she do this?* Tanzi thought, feeling like the biggest fool in the world. She had endured days of panic, and here was Savannah, alive and well and fucking someone else.

Tanzi heard the rustle of sheets coming from the bedroom, and paralyzing anxiety gripped her so tightly she felt nailed to the floor. She heard a muffled moan, deep and wanting. Before she knew it, she was moving forward, unbridled anger driving her on. She crossed the living room in long strides, the Maasai warrior in her surfacing, ready for a fight.

She stood in the bedroom doorway, clawed by the sight before her, raking her heart and drawing blood. Savannah was on top of Debbie Knight, the woman's tongue dancing around Savannah's dark nipple. Her slim legs were wrapped around Savannah as if she owned her. It was bad enough that she was fucking someone else, but Debbie Knight, of all people! Suddenly, all Tanzi saw was red.

"What the fuck is this?" Tanzi screamed, rushing angrily towards them.

A look of fear registered on Debbie's face. She muttered something unintelligible as she quickly untangled herself from Savannah and moved to the farthest side of the bed.

Tanzi covered the distance in a flash, throwing Debbie's naked body to the floor. Tanzi landed on top of the screaming woman and locked her legs around her small body, immobilizing her.

"I'll kill you, bitch!" Tanzi screamed as years of a rage held prisoner in her soul exploded. Her blows rained so hard that all Debbie could do was cower while she screamed for Savannah to help her.

Blood was streaming down Debbie's face, but Tanzi didn't care. She grabbed her long, strawberry-blonde hair and started beating her head against the marble floor, intent on releasing every bit of her hurt. She could hear Savannah's voice in the distance, but she wouldn't stop.

"Let her go," Savannah yelled as she landed a kick to Tanzi's side. She grabbed Tanzi by the throat, pulling her backward. The pain was so great Tanzi released her grip on Debbie. Tanzi struggled for breath, unable to understand how Savannah defended someone else over her.

Debbie scrambled away, grabbing her clothes as she ran through the door and out of the room, yelping like a wounded animal.

"I don't know who the fuck you think you are coming into my house, bitch! You don't run shit!" Savannah glared at Tanzi.

Tanzi was hurting in every way a person could possibly hurt, but what tore her heart the most was how Savannah had stepped in to defend Debbie. She had never been there for her like she had. Had never made sacrifices, dried the tears, or taken years off her shit. At that moment, Tanzi hated Savannah more than she had ever hated anyone. She struggled against Savannah's grip and finally rolled free, gasping for air.

"I hate you!" Tanzi yelled. Her tears ran freely, hitting the floor like angry raindrops.

"Then get the fuck out!" Savannah yelled, kicking her again. Tanzi writhed, the pain so excruciating she thought she would black out.

"Get out of my house and get the fuck out of my life! I don't need you." Savannah loomed like some kind of grotesque monster seen through Tanzi's tears.

"How could you?" Tanzi said, the weight of betrayal and the pain pinning her down.

"Can't you see? I don't want your dumb ass anymore!" Savannah said. She pulled on her robe as if she could care less.

Tanzi struggled to her feet, body wracked with pain, and stood there dazed. *Was it really over after all she had given? Was this how it ended, her broken and empty?*

Savannah sauntered to the bathroom. Tanzi's voice, dripping with venom, echoed in the room.

"I will make your life hell, Savannah; watch what I tell you!"

Savannah stopped and turned to face her.

"What did you say?" Savannah said, her face contorted with rage. "Are you threatening me?"

Savannah walked to her nightstand and produced a handgun. Tanzi didn't flinch when Savannah approached.

"I don't give a fuck! We can both die tonight," Savannah said, pressing the muzzle against Tanzi's head.

Tanzi closed her eyes as her life flashed before her. This was it. She knew it but was surprised to discover she didn't care. She was tired, tired of fighting, and tired of hurting. Tanzi opened her eyes and stared Savannah down. Tense seconds passed between them.

"All I ever did was love you. What happened to us?" Tanzi asked tenderly.

"You stopped loving me," Savannah mumbled, then turned away.

"No, I didn't," Tanzi said quietly, placing her hand on Savannah's shoulder. Turning to face her.

"Yes, you did," Savannah said.

"I've always been here for you," Tanzi tried to reason.

Savannah tossed the gun on the bed. Tanzi took her into her arms and held her tightly.

"What do you want, Savannah? Just tell me what you want, and I'll do it."

"I need you to be only with me. Quit your job."

Tanzi knew Savannah was asking her to give up the partnership and everything else. But how could she ever walk away from Matthew? He'd put everything on the line for her. Tanzi could see the hurt in Savannah's eyes. She worked insane hours, seventy to eighty a week, to further her career. She'd been blind to what it was doing to Savannah. Maybe she could take an extended leave.

"I will always choose you, Savannah." Tanzi held her tighter. She wouldn't let Savannah down.

Chapter Eight

"The most terrible and violent of our own afflictions is to despise our own beings."

—Michel De Montaigne

Have you ever had one of those days when you couldn't take one more thing? When Tanzi heard the tremor in her mother's voice, she knew this would be one for her. It had been eight long months since Tanzi caught Savannah and Debbie together. Initially, Tanzi was hopeful because, at first, Savannah had acted like an angel, bearing gifts, romantic wining, and dining, but it was just that—an act. Savannah quickly returned to verbal and physical abuse, and the drinking worsened. Somewhere along the way, Tanzi stopped caring. She had let Savannah do whatever she wanted.

For the last several months, Tanzi fell deeper into funereal depression. She had cut off communication with everyone, choosing the company of her thick comforter and the blackout drapes she had installed. She didn't remember when she'd last eaten or bathed. Last night against her unspoken wishes, Savannah, inebriated, entered the bedroom, turned on the lights, and ordered Tanzi to get up.

After ranting about the condition of the bedroom and Tanzi's unkempt appearance, the night ended with a one-sided fight. Savannah fought while Tanzi retreated into the sanctuary of wanted numbness.

Afterward, Tanzi lay awake into the early morning, contemplating why she'd stayed entangled in the spiral silk of Savannah's poisonous web. Her vibrating phone jarred her out of her thoughts.

Seeing her mom's number, she looked at the screen and answered the phone. "It's Dad Tanzi…" her mother, Jennifer, said slowly, "…and it doesn't look good."

"Where are you?" Tanzi asked as she arose out of bed.

"I'll be there soon, Mom," Tanzi said as she quickly ended the call, pushed back the covers, and headed toward the bathroom. She could hear Savannah stirring in the bed behind her.

"Where do you think you're going?" She spat.

Tanzi ignored her inquest as she entered the bathroom and splashed cold water on her face. She wouldn't look in the mirror because she knew the horror she would see. It was too late to be concerned with that now. Ignoring the putrid smell of her body, Tanzi grabbed a pair of jeans and a sweater. Just as she slipped into her slides, she saw

Savannah staring at her. She tried to walk past her, but Savannah blocked her way.

"Savannah, move out of my way," Tanzi said, pushing her back. When Savannah roughly grabbed her arm, she quickly broke free. She'd allowed Savannah to cut her off from everyone she loved. Not today.

"Keep your fucking hands off me," Tanzi fumed, meeting Savannah's gaze with a deep penetrating glare.

"I asked you a question," Savannah moved menacingly closer. Tanzi didn't flinch or move. A tense silence filled the narrow gulf between them.

"I'm going to see my father," Tanzi said with finality, walking toward the bedroom door and grabbing her purse and phone.

"Who…that white man?" Savannah railed. "He ain't your fucking daddy."

As she walked out of the bedroom, the decision that Tanzi had been making for months was concrete. All that she tried to be for Savannah, in the end, none of it mattered. She was done with the tyrannical rule of Savannah.

"So what are you gonna do…leave me?" Savannah yelled after her. "Bitch, you'll be back, and when you do, I'll make you pay!"

When Tanzi entered the hospital room, the sight of her father's pale, lifeless body, covered with tubes, hit her hard. She'd prayed that he would be okay, but her hopes for that miracle faded fast. Guilt, like a heavy blanket, wrapped painfully around her. She couldn't remember the last time she saw him or communicated what he meant to her. Her tears spoke of sorrow her lips couldn't utter as she stood paralyzed by grief.

Tanzi felt a hand gently resting on her shoulders. "I'm here, Tanzi." It was Matthew. He had been a faithful friend to her parents even though she'd abandoned all of them. He'd sent cards and flowers inviting Tanzi back to the law firm whenever she was ready. She was glad he was here. As Tanzi looked into her mother's eyes, she shook her head, letting the river of tears become an unquenchable ocean. Her mother, crying an ocean of her own, embraced her.

"Matt and I are going to step outside and give you some time alone with your Dad," her mother whispered as she kissed Tanzi's cheek and gently patted her back. Tanzi slowly walked to the bed as they left the room, sat on it gently, and took her Dad's hand.

“Dad, I’m here,” Tanzi said quietly, wiping her tears. Robert fought to open his eyes, and when he did, Tanzi smiled at the man who had traveled around the world to get her. And how had she repaid him? By abandoning him when he needed her most. A weak smile formed across his weary face. He tried to reach a hand up to touch her but couldn’t. She took his hand and lifted it to her face.

“My beautiful girl,” the whispered words flowed like a forgiving spring over the pain lodged in her heart. Even as her Dad waited at death’s door, he reached back across the dimension once more to let her know how completely he loved her.

“I love you so much, Dad. Please forgive me for…” her words were cut short as he moved his hand to her lips to block her words.

“One of the greatest days of my life was when we got you. I only want one thing for you…live your life to the fullest and find the love that you deserve,” her Dad said as he smiled again and gently closed his eyes.

Savannah slammed the phone down so hard the table shook. *Where the fuck was Tanzi, and why wasn’t she answering her phone?* Tanzi had been gone for four days, and Savannah, who had returned to her SoHo apartment to service a client, had constantly been checking with the doorman at their home, but there had been no signs of Tanzi. As a desperate last measure, Savannah had called Tanzi's mother but had reached her voice mail. On the evening news days ago, she had heard that Robert Ridley had passed away. But not even that should have kept Tanzi from returning her calls or coming back to make things right.

Anger had been Savannah's constant companion over the past few days; she had killed Tanzi in her mind in thousands of different ways. But now, a troubling fear gripped her. *What if this time Tanzi was really gone?*

"Fuck that bitch!" Savannah shouted.

A sound from the front room silenced Savannah, and she stood still, momentarily listening. She thought she heard Tanzi put her key in the door and rushed to meet her. She opened the door expecting Tanzi there, but the hallway was empty. She slammed the door hard and walked back to the bar. Savannah picked up the half-empty quart of Jack Daniel's Black Label, held it to her mouth, and let the warm liquid run down, a fire burning through her. "*Thank God for ole Nearis Green.*"

Savannah fumbled with the remote for the CD and finally found Al Green's Greatest Hits. She knew all the songs by heart; her Nana had played them from when she and her sister were born. The tears flowed uninhibited; she was again alone in this fucked up world.

How Can You Mend A Broken Heart came on, and Savannah sang along with Al as a deep pang gripped her and mingled with a bitter tear that flowed over her quivering lips. As memories flooded her hazy mind, Savannah wished she had selective amnesia. She wouldn't have to remember *everything*. But she had always had perfect recollection. Her Nana said that was because she was an "old soul." Her memory was both a blessing and a curse.

A blessing because there were many things from the first five years of her life that she wanted to remember. Like the joy she had known being with her Nana, climbing up in her warm lap and listening to her melodious voice. Savannah would be on one side and her twin sister on the other while her big brother David played with his cars at their feet. Like watching her Nana cook in the kitchen, baking pies and cakes and letting them lick the bowl, laughing while David threw flour at them. Like the comfort of Nana's body as she laid across her lap while she wrote in her journals, like falling asleep, holding her sister's hand, and sucking her thumb.

Like bedtime prayers, when Nana would make them feel safe and tell them that God was on the throne, watching over them and all was right in the world. Like knowing deep within that, she was completely loved.

But her perfect memory was also a curse because she remembered every detail of how their lives had suddenly changed just after their fifth birthday, and her world had fallen apart. She remembered Nana calling God's name and the dreadful sound of twisting, crashing metal.

She remembered the terrifying fear that gripped her heart, the cold, eerie silence, and then her piercing scream from the backseat of the Taurus. Nana died at the scene, and David died two days later. The drunk driver had lived, walking away without a scratch. A part of Savannah died that night too.

"How could you do this to me…how could you leave me like this?" She screamed.

Matthew sat on his veranda, listening as midnight crept in. With it also came thoughts of the beautiful woman sleeping in his guest bedroom. He and Tanzi had been inseparable since they had reunited at the hospital. She needed him, and he had been there. It was very difficult for Tanzi to bury her father, and he could tell how tenuous her emotions were. He knew it wasn't only because she had lost her father but also because she had finally decided to leave Savannah. He didn't want to pressure her in any way, but time was winding down for his return to Africa; Nwanji Orphans Center was scheduled to open in less than a month, and he needed to be there for his daughter Mwende; he and Neema's love child.

Matthew's memories journeyed back to the land that had always felt like home. The place that he had visited with his father, Dr. Simon Friedman. From Matthew's first visit to Kenya, his heart had found its destiny there. He had run the land and experienced it fully. Year after year, upon his return, he had acquainted himself with all of the kids in the village. But when he was sixteen, something he wasn't expecting happened; he fell in love. It happened as soon as he laid eyes on Neema. She had always been a good friend to him, but she had grown up in ways that had taken his breath away. She was sixteen now and womanly; her beauty riveted him. They had spent every moment together that summer.

They would sneak out and lie, talking under the midnight sky until the sun came up, sharing their thoughts and dreams. The closer it got to his departure, the sadder they both became. Being separated would be unbearable, and the pain drove them so close that they exchanged comforting words and their bodies in each other's arms until they blissfully fell asleep. They had been found by Neema‘s father, who had beaten her unmercifully. Matthew tried to intervene, but he was restrained by other Kenyans who had taken him to his father. It had caused such an uproar in the village that even though they needed Dr. Friedman, he was banned from their village. Matthew’s father lectured him incessantly about his foolishness, but Matthew was inconsolable. He’d watched Neema’s father beat her until life left her eyes. She had been killed for loving him.

When Matthew turned eighteen, the summer before attending Harvard, he returned to Africa to walk the land he and Neema shared. He wasn’t ready for what greeted him; he learned from some of those who appreciated his father's help that Neema hadn’t died that day. She survived and was sent to live with her mother’s family. His heart rejoiced to know that she was still alive and that he could find her again. The next news left him stunned and silent. Neema was pregnant with his child, but both she and the baby had died during childbirth. That moment had changed him forever.

For many years, his anger made him one of the most ruthless attorneys in New York. It wasn't until many years later that Matthew received a letter from a friend in Kenya, letting him know that Neema had died, but their daughter, Mwende, had lived. As an infant, she had been sent to live in a neighboring village where she'd had a rough life and had contracted HIV. Matthew had dropped everything and went to Africa to find Mwende. When he first laid eyes on her, he saw the magical blending of his and Neema's love. But their reunion wasn't what he expected; she hated him and wanted nothing to do with him. He pleaded with her to let him explain, but she spat in his face and walked away.

It was like losing Neema all over again, and he was in such pain that he was sure that dying was the only solution. A week later, when he had spoken at Harvard, he met Tanzi, and everything changed. She had resurrected him from the dead and given him a reason to live. Years later, Matthew and his daughter were reunited. He had gotten the chance to explain everything, and she had forgiven him. He wanted to bring her back to the States, but she refused. Her mission was in Africa, making a difference in the lives of children living and dying from AIDS. He vowed to do everything in his power to help her.

He was supposed to be leaving for Africa several days before Robert had a heart attack, and he had chosen to postpone his trip. He didn't want to leave Tanzi, but he had promised Mwende he would be there in the next few days. He couldn't disappoint his daughter. Matthew felt torn; he knew he and Tanzi were destined to be together, but his daughter needed him too. He stared out into the night sky as the stars twinkled brightly. Just maybe things would finally go the way he hoped.

Big Mama felt that familiar tug on her heart, calling her to pray. She and Jesus had walked together long enough that she knew not to question. She struggled a little but finally got down on her knees. Instantly, she felt the brush of the angel's wings and smiled. *Thank you, Jesus.* Her thoughts drifted towards the apartment down the hall; she knew for a certainty that was the main reason she had been brought to New York. It had been eight or nine months since she had seen Tanzi standing at the door, but the one that lived there always entertained "guests" at all hours of the day and night. Yes, Big Mama knew what she did for a livin', but it didn't bother her.

Big Mama thought about the brief encounter they had several days ago. She finally got the okay from God to introduce herself and headed to the door with one of her freshly baked apple pies. As she opened the door, she saw a man coming out of the woman's apartment who looked like a Senator always on TV. Several men were waiting there and walked with him to the elevator. The woman, who barely had any clothes, stood at the door looking strangely at Big Mama. She could have gone back inside the apartment, but Big Mama walked down the long hallway and stopped in front of her door.

"I just finished baking the best apple pie you ever had, except maybe for your Nana's," Big Mama said.

The woman trembled as if she had seen a ghost as Big Mama held the pie. An awkward silence went between them, and she took the pie a moment later. "My Mama used to say a good pie could solve whatever was wrong in life," Big Mama said, holding her hand. "I'm Big Mama, by the way, and you are?"

The woman seemed to have lost her voice. "I'm Savannah," she said slowly.

"Is that the name your Grandmother gave you?" Big Mama said, gazing intently at the woman. She could tell her question made the woman uncomfortable.

"How did you know my Grandmother named me, and how did you know I called her Nana?" She said, somewhat irritated. Big Mama smiled at her. That was the only answer she could give. Her gifts were still a wonder to her as well.

"Some things in life just come to you when you've lived as long as I have," she said, chuckling. "I'll be seventy-six on March 28th."

The young woman looked like an unseen hand had slapped her. She slammed the door in Big Mama's face as hard as possible. Their encounter had been strange, but she could see through to the woman's heart. Outside, she seemed cold and uppity, but that was just an act. No matter what, Big Mama was intent on keeping this assignment.

Sometimes you know that a major change is coming, which will lay waste to all you trusted, leaving your dreams desolate. Like when the rumbling of an earthquake begins, terror grips you, not because you fear the unknown. But because you turned a deaf ear to the divining seismologist that lives within. You knew the magnitude would be devastating when it came, but you foolishly believed you could outrun the earth when it opened to swallow you in.

Standing in the epicenter of her life, Tanzi surveyed the widespread damage and knew she had no one to blame but herself. From the second she had laid eyes on Savannah, she knew it would be the kiss of death, but she had licked the poison off her lips anyway. Others had seen it clearly and tried to warn her, yet she wouldn't listen. *Why?* She'd been asking herself that question for days and still had no answer. She had rehashed all the painful details of their relationship; so much of it had been ugly for sure. But there had been many good times too. *How could she just throw away all of her time in their relationship?* More importantly, *if she went back, could they make it work?*

It was sad; she had built her life around a future with Savannah, and now... *Who am I if I'm not with her?* The question had riddled her mind. She hadn't planned on being single again, but who was she kidding? She had been solo in this relationship, living the worst loneliness. *Being there with someone who isn't there with you.* The truth was, whether she moved on or went back, her heart was irreparably broken. She had lost so much; her friends, family, career, and herself. Now there was much regret, a river of haunting pain. There would be no quick fix, no easy antidote; Tanzi knew this for sure.

Yes, it was painful leaving Savannah. Yes, she had always promised to be there for her, but she couldn't return. It would be the complete end of her. Sitting on the veranda of Matthew's home, Tanzi closed her eyes and took a deep breath. She didn't know where to begin rebuilding her life. She remembered her father's last words as tears ran gently down her face.

"I only want one thing for you...live your life to the fullest and find the love that you deserve." Her dad's last words echoed in her mind.

Tanzi felt a gentle breeze whisking across her face and knew her Dad was there to help her. He had always been. He and Matthew. *Matthew.* She smiled at the thought of him. He had always been her strength, her champion, her protector. His support had meant the world to her. Last night had been an amazing reprieve from her pain as she listened to him passionately talk about moving to Africa. "I've always heard you talk about Africa, but you're going to *live* there?" she asked. "What is it with you and Africa?"

Matthew took his time and told her every detail about Neema and Mwende. He seemed to be contemplating how much to tell her. Then he stood, took her hand, and she followed him to his master suite. The most beautiful painting she had ever seen was over his specially crafted Jab Anstoez's Majesty Vi bed. The woman in the work bore an uncanny resemblance to her, and Tanzi looked at Matthew for an answer.

Matthew had also told her the details of what he and Mwende had planned to do to make a difference in Kenya with women and children, especially regarding AIDS. He paused and asked her a very difficult question; had she ever wondered about her daughter's fate? She had been a child of twelve, giving birth to a daughter conceived from the most brutal act she had ever endured. She had lost everything as a result of the rape. Although she'd never held the child, she explained to Matthew, she had felt connected to her in some indescribable way. They stayed up all night talking about Africa, loss, and love. As the sun rose, he asked her if she had ever considered returning to Africa. "No!" She said, laughing.

"You know there's an old African tradition that says when your umbilical cord is buried in the ground of Africa, you will come back home." Matthew chided her.

The birds sang sweetly as Tanzi sipped green tea and looked out over Matthew's beautiful grounds. All seemed peaceful, and for a moment, she felt hopeful. She thought about her mother and sent a prayer of comfort to her. Life without her Dad was going to be hard.

Tanzi's phone startled her as it began vibrating. She picked it up; Savannah. She could only imagine what way she would plan to hurt herself this time. Tanzi had always been there to rescue Savannah, or so she thought. The truth is that only Savannah could do it for herself. Tanzi sent a silent prayer to Savannah. *Be well.*

The doorbell chimes pulled Tanzi away from her thoughts about Savannah. Several moments later, Matthew walked up to her. "Tanzi," he said softly. "The car is here to take me to the airport." Tanzi felt the tears flowing again. *How could she lose Matthew too?*

"You can stay as long as you like," he said, handing her keys. "Loretta will take care of everything you need." She stood and held onto him tight. His embrace strengthened her. He had always been her best friend.

"I will call you as soon as I arrive." He said, kissing her forehead and turning and leaving.

She heard Matthew's steps moving away from her and felt overwhelming sadness. She didn't want to be without him. But she didn't know if she was ready for Kenya; it was a place that had caused her so much grief. Besides, she needed time to figure out so much. Or did she? Maybe this time, she needed to trust the African Proverb her father, Robert, had told her long ago; *"To get lost is to learn the way."*

"Matthew, wait!" She yelled as she headed for the door.

"I love you too, Baby; take care of yourself," Big Mama said, smiling brightly as she hung up the phone.

"Did you get a good report?" Her son Nelson asked.

"Yes, praise the Lord," she replied as tears of joy rolled down her cheek. She was always so glad to hear from all her sons; she had six of them, especially Eric. He was her youngest and had, in many ways, a more difficult road than the others. He was only six when his Daddy died, and he'd taken it the hardest. He had hated God and her for many years and had turned to drugs and crime in his early teens.

"He'll be released in two weeks," Big Mama said.

"I know; I've already spoken with the Probation Office and made arrangements to get an Interstate Compact Agreement so he can live with us instead of in Mississippi," Nelson said. "It's going to be a transition for him, but we've got him."

"Amen, son! Thank you so much," Big Mama said, grateful for Nelson opening his home to his baby brother. It had taken Eric almost twenty-five years to find his way. He was incarcerated for killing a man and would finally be released. He still didn't like God too much, but he loved her. *Hallelujah!* Her hand went up, waving gently.

When a mother called out her child's name, all heaven stood still before God. Yes, a woman could reshape destiny. Change all that was, no matter how impossible it seemed. Big Mama had been on her knees for many years; finally, the harvest had come. Witnessing the miracle that Eric's life had become made her tenacious for the next one. Someone was ready for a miracle, and Big Mama knew just who it was.

Savannah woke up lying naked on the floor, an almost empty bottle of Jack Daniel's resting like a lifeline beside her. She reached for the bottle holding onto it as she tried to get up, her legs moved unsteadily beneath her, and she hit the floor hard. "Shit!" She cursed, slurring the word as she struggled to rise again, grabbing onto the table and wavering as she pulled herself up and fell back onto the sofa. She reached for her phone several times before getting a grip on it and clumsily dialed Tanzi's number. The voicemail instantly came on, and as Tanzi's greeting ended, she railed.

"I can't believe you..... was just.....like everybody else.....you fucker...fucking.....cunt," Savannah fumed as she belched loudly. "Well hoe.....you don't have to.....worry about me anymore.....and don't come to try to rescue.....me either," Savannah said as she lifted the bottle and drank the last drops.

“I hate your.....fuckin ass.....you black bitch.” “I see you..... for who you really are, you fucking.....bitch.” The message beeped, and the phone disconnected. "Oh, you gonna....hang....up....on.....me?" Savannah said, trying to redial but dropping the phone on the floor.

Savannah threw Jack Daniel’s bottle hard against the wall, knocking a vase to the floor. It broke into many pieces, and Savannah did the sign of the cross with a heavy hand that fell upon her stomach. “Bless me, Father, for I have sinned,” she laughed. Savannah struggled to reach for the phone, but each attempt moved it further from her grasp, and eventually, she tumbled onto the floor. Lying there, she sadly looked around her massive penthouse. Even though it was filled with everything she once thought made her a success, it meant nothing now.

She couldn’t understand why her life always came to this moment; her heart was broken, engulfed with immeasurable pain and aloneness. But here she was again. A river of tears rolled down her face. Savannah grabbed the phone and hit Tanzi’s number; again, it went straight to voicemail. “I’m leaving...this life because I’m tired. You can have all...this shit."

"This is my fucking...last will and test...test…a...ment!” Savannah screamed, bawling into the phone. “I ripped up all your…shit too! How are you gonna...be a lawyer now? Huh? You will have to go back...to running naked…in the bush, you nappy-head African bitch."

The line disconnected again, and Savannah laid still momentarily and then rolled onto her stomach, beating the floor as sobs wracked her body. *God, what did I do to deserve this?*

Savannah stopped crying as she heard movement in the hallway outside her entry door. It had to be Tanzi. She smiled as she pushed up on the sofa and staggered to the door, holding on to the walls. She was going to beat the fuck out of Tanzi right after she hugged her. Savannah swung the door open wide. Her smile faded as she looked down the hall. It was empty. She slammed the door hard at first and then decided to leave it open just in case Tanzi didn't have her key.

As Savannah saw her naked reflection in the gilded mirror in the entryway, she stared back. Her wild mane looked matted, and her body looked broken. "What the fuck are you looking at?" Savannah raged. The image stared back and sadly shook its head.

"Mirror, mirror on the wall, I'm looking at the most fucked up bitch of all!" The image said, smiling. Savannah looked around, picked up a large candlestick, and swung at the mirror repeatedly, shattering it into hundreds of pieces. She dropped the candlestick and grabbed wildly at the taunting image. "I will kill you!!" Savannah blared as the pieces of glass spooned jagged chunks of redness out of the depths of her flesh.

Big Mama headed out the door with a purpose. Strawberry Whipped Pie in hand and a spring in her step. She knew the young woman's heart would be ready this time. As she approached the apartment, Big Mama noticed the door was ajar and felt an urgency pulling her. She knocked.

"Hello?" "Hello, It's Big Mama from down the hall," she said, pushing the door open. There was only a stark silence. She saw the naked woman lying on the floor. Crimson pooled beside her; it was blood.

"Oh, my dear Lord Jesus," Big Mama screamed.

Chapter Nine

"Who were you before the taking? Before the indelible pain and crushing suffering burrowed so deeply into the dark of your glorious soul?"

—L.D. Jackson

The twins tilted their heads back, gazing lovingly at the bright sun. Their red plastic sunglasses made the sunbeams dance as they soaked up the August rays. The girls dressed alike from head to toe, except that Savannah wore bright red, her favorite color, and Elisha wore pink. Their long brown wavy mane was plaited in two braids and tied with beautiful satin ribbons. The excitement was so full it was bursting through their pores, and they couldn't contain the jubilant peals of laughter coming from deep within them.

They were princesses in frilly dresses with laced socks and shiny patent leather shoes. Their mother, Lolita, had given them each three small gift boxes as they had eaten their favorite breakfast of thick, syrupy golden pancakes with whipped cream faces and strawberry eyes. They had squealed with delight as they had unwrapped their boxes and discovered identical 14kt gold heart earrings with matching necklaces and bracelets. They were wearing their treasures as they held hands.

"Everything's gonna be alright now, baby girl," Savannah said, breathing in the hot, beautiful day. The grass beneath them felt like cotton candy clouds, and Savannah bounced as she squeezed her sister's hand. Elisha bounced with her, giggling joyfully.

Savannah and her sister were finally together, and the past's horrors were over. Warm tears ran down her face as she remembered the heartbreak she had felt without the other side of her heart; Elisha. No one understood what it was like to have everything you needed and then have it snatched away with such finality. When each loss only added weight to the boulder lying thickly in your heart. How could you come back from that?

What could you exchange for guilt and loneliness? What would you pay just to have it all back for one suspended moment? What could ease the pain when you deserved the heartbreak? How grateful would you be for one chance to make it like it was? Nothing, nothing except...the return to the world before the taking.

Savannah had been given a gift, mercy undeserved yet granted anyway. She took her sister in her arms and repeatedly kissed her hot cheek as their tears and hearts mingled. She let the grief wash away; it was over. No more losing.

Elisha stood and began dancing; gleeful pirouettes mingled with soulful struts. Savannah laughed so hard that her sides hurt. The pink princess felt the return, joy, and love as she moved with pure abandonment. "Elisha, stop it!" Savannah shrieked, trying to catch her breath. It seemed her sister had moved some way from her. "Elisha, you are going too far; I can't see you!" Savannah yelled as she suddenly became frantic.

In one instance, the sun was gone, and night had crept in. Savannah could barely make out the silhouette of her sister. She could still hear Elisha's giggles, but within seconds not even a hopeful apparition of her sister was there. Savannah stood, unable to speak or move as gentle hands pulled her out of the maddening darkness, and she fell back, spinning into an infuriating, ivory light.

The intense joy, then pure terror that Savannah felt, swirled around in clouds of fogginess. It dwindled and became a dull achiness as she stirred. Closer to wakefulness, it became pure, agonizing pain, and it took her several tries before she managed to open her eyes. The most hurtful thing was realizing she hadn't been with Elisha.

As the stark understanding came of where she was, the sterile whiteness of the hospital room was a blaring, arrant reminder that, once again, she couldn't shake the cruel adder of life. She wanted to cry but couldn't; rage held her tears at bay.

Out of the corner of her eye, Savannah could see a hazy figure in the chair beside her. It was her nosy-assed neighbor. As she focused, anger swirled, and with it came an excruciating headache. She couldn't believe Tanzi hadn't come back for her, the bitch.

Savannah tried to move her hand but was too weak to lift it. It felt as if she was locked in some type of vise. Her eyes fell upon her bandaged wrists and arms, strapped to the bed rails as if she was being held prisoner. "What the fuck?" She tried to say aloud, but her dry, cracked lips held her words in. A few muffled whispers were all that escaped.

The old woman stirred, noticed that Savannah was awake, and sat up smiling. "I'm so glad you are awake, Precious," the woman spoke, holding onto a small black Bible.

"It was touch and go throughout the night, but we knew you would make it."

"What are you doing here, and why do you even care?" Savannah replied with angst in her voice. She wanted this old woman to leave her alone.

"Oh, I care, alright," Sadie said, grinning brightly. She stood and poured a little water into a cup, placed a straw in it, and placed it on Savannah's parched lips. She sipped, rolling her eyes at the little do-gooder.

"Well, don't," Savannah said, leaning back into the pillow. Her body hurt all over. "I'm not going to be one of the stars in your raggedy ass crown."

The woman chuckled so loud that the room seemed to gravitate. "Baby, at my age, the last thing I'm worried about is my crowns!"

Sadie put the cup down and adjusted Savannah's pillow. She sat back down, smiling as if she knew the answer to the $25,000 question.

"Don't you have a church meeting to go to or something, old woman?" Savannah asked, trying to move off of her painful hip.

"I have nowhere I'd rather be than right here. Besides, your Nana has me here for a reason," Sadie said, holding up her Bible and waving it.

Savannah wanted to throw something at the old bitty. She had some nerve acting like she knew her Nana; she didn't. If her Nana had been here, she would have walked Savannah out of this life so she wouldn't feel any more pain.

Dr. Stephen Wouk sat his pale, tired, hefty frame in the small waiting room chair, wishing it had no arms. It was a tight fit; he was not obese yet, but a few more pounds and his BMI would definitely be 30. Even though it was uncomfortable, he was glad to have a few minutes off his feet.

Dr. Wouk listened intently to Mrs. Sadie, a slender, kindhearted woman whose conservative navy suit and milk chocolate flawless skin concealed her age well. She described the previous day's events and her relationship with his patient, Savannah St. Clair, with impeccable detail. Her savvy son, Nelson, a Tyson Beckford look-alike, also spoke of his attempts to locate her family and/or friends.

"I appreciate that information; it helps us to understand what the patient is experiencing. Even though Ms. St. Clair is awake now, we still have an extremely serious situation." Dr. Wouk said, pausing to remove his glasses and rubbing his eyes.

"I don't think she was trying to kill herself, Dr. Wouk. I think she left her door open so someone could find her," Mrs. Sadie said as concern spread across her face.

"That may be the case, but we don't know for sure." Dr. Wouk said, looking at her and then at her son. "The statistics show that nearly one million people in the world die by suicide yearly, and there are another 10 to 20 million non-fatal attempted suicides yearly."

“From what I understand, she had a recent break up of a long-term relationship,” Nelson said, looking carefully at his mother and then back to Dr. Wouk. “Maybe she is just depressed or trying to get attention.”

“A suicide attempt and a suicidal gesture are difficult to distinguish because intent and motivation are not always discernible. Many people in a suicidal state are genuinely conflicted over whether they want to end their lives.”

“But she is such a young, beautiful woman with so much to live for; why would she want to kill herself?” Mrs. Sadie asked.

“Some who try suicide attempts are crying for help, or it can be an attempt to communicate their despair and hopelessness. But it is difficult to know if someone genuinely intends to kill themselves."

“Dr. Wouk, what if I agree to assist with outpatient care for her just so my Mother won’t worry?” Nelson said, rubbing his mother's hand. “I mean, with us looking in on her, she should be okay, right?”

"Nelson, most people who try suicide don’t complete it on a first attempt. But those with a history of repeated attempts are significantly more at risk of eventually succeeding. And we don't know how many attempts she has made, but from my estimation, this is not her first time."

"So outpatient care wouldn't be feasible?" Nelson asked.

"My colleagues and I concur that immediate commitment to a psychiatric facility is warranted. It is not just a suicide attempt. Ms. St. Clair has numerous psychotic disorders that need immediate attention." Dr. Wouk said, rising to leave.

"But what if she doesn't want to go to a psychiatric hospital?" Mrs. Sadie asked as her son stood and helped his mother with care.

"We are preparing a petition for involuntary commitment."

"So that is why she has restraints?" Nelson asked, shaking the doctor's outstretched hand.

"Yes. Currently, she is at risk of harm to herself or others."

"When will she be moved?" The generous older woman inquired as she clutched her worn bible.

"It may be four or five days; we must ensure she is physically stable first. We had several complications and had to give her a blood transfusion. So that is our main focus right now."

"Thank you so much for speaking with us," Nelson said with an enchanting smile.

Dr. Wouk looked for a moment at the woman who obviously cared deeply for the young woman she had only known a short time. "Ms. Sadie, I also believe in the power of prayer. We lost Ms. St. Clair during surgery, and I believe she came back for a reason."

Mrs. Sadie cradled his hand and pat it with a wide grin. "I'm going to help her find that reason!" She stated with surety.

Sari sighed loudly as she swept her waist-length black hair back over her delicate, olive-complexioned shoulder. She had dressed comfortably in wide-legged merlot-hued trousers and a soft palm cream, v-neck tank top, anticipating spending most of the day with Michelle, who had again been admitted to the hospital after a severe beating by a john.

Sari knew she shouldn't be surprised that Michelle had left the hospital in the middle of the night. She still craved the danger of the streets, and running away was all she knew. Even though she wished it was different, Sari understood; Michelle didn't want to be let down again. The young teen had sixteen years of disappointments.

Working in the teen center saddened and inspired Sari at times like these. She had been a homeless runaway teen over a decade ago and knew firsthand the risky, desperate street life. But despite the many times she thought she would die in the streets, she had made it out. After she had been rescued miraculously, she knew it was her dharma to help young women like Michelle. She would be there for Michelle when she was finally ready.

Sari looked down at the two books she had brought for Michelle. Oh well, I'll donate them to the library, she thought as she left the empty hospital room.

As she walked down the hospital corridor, Sari wondered what she would do with the rest of her day and stopped when she saw an older woman walking out of a room. The woman smiled brightly at her as she approached, and Sari smiled back. The woman's presence invoked reverence and had an internal glow that Sari could see all the way down the hall.

“Good morning, baby,” the woman spoke softly and winked. “She’s waiting on you,” she said as she kept walking, turned the corner, and disappeared.

Sari smiled at the universe as she looked down at the books she carried. They hadn’t been for Michelle after all. She knew this meeting had been specially arranged by the Divine. She assuredly walked down the hall and stopped at the room where the kind woman had left.

“Hello,” Sari said, her round eyes smiling at the stunning woman lying in bed. Even in her current state, she was enchantingly beautiful. Dead silence filled the room as the woman disturbingly stared at her. Sari walked in confidently and approached the bed.

“Do I know you?” the woman said, her tone acidic.

There was an exchange that Sari allowed to happen; a holy moment.

“Yes, you know me,” Sari said quietly.

“From where?” the woman asked, frowning.

“We come from the same source,” Sari said, looking at the women deeper. The woman seemed agitated but remained silent.

“I had come by to see one of the young girls that come to the center where I volunteer and to bring her these books," Sari said. "But she left the hospital some time last night." Still, the woman remained quiet.

"I'd like to leave these books with you," Sari said, noticing the woman's hands were restrained.

"Do I look like a public library to you?" she said, her anger palpable.

"No. You are a beautiful woman who has suffered much of your life."

Sari put the books down on the table by the woman's side.

"My name is Sari; what's yours?"

"I really don't give a damn who you are!" The woman yelled. "Get the fuck out!"

"I understand," Sari said gently. "I'm going to leave these books for you, and there is information about our center. When you are ready, come and see us."

The woman tried to kick the hospital table over but couldn't reach it. "Get the fuck out bitch!"

"I'll be expecting you," Sari said as she looked at the board in the room. "Ms. Savannah."

Savannah had wanted to murder many people, but at this moment, the one who topped her list was that fucking flea-bag excuse of a doctor. He didn't know who the fuck he was dealing with, talking to her like she was some three-year-old.

"Try...it..mo..ther..fucka," Savannah tried to scream, but her words were barely a whisper. Her head hurt, her mouth was dry, and her drowsiness, like a curtain, was pulling down.

"Baby, that's the Thorazine shot Dr. Wouk gave you," she heard her nosy neighbor say.

"Go...go…" Savannah tried to tell the woman, but her words were stuck in her head; all she could see and feel was blackness.

Savannah didn't know how long she had been in the hospital, but it was dark outside, and several dim lights in the room cast haunting shadows of yellow that danced on the walls. The hum and quiet beepings of the machines were annoying, and her ass was still sore from the hard bed.

Savannah wanted to get up but still felt too light-headed to move. She rested her head back on the pillow to let her head stop spinning. She noticed that the ugly hospital gown was gone, and she had on one of her red satin gowns. She also noticed that one of her arms had been removed from the restraint; the other was still tethered as if they were trying to test the level of her insanity. She defiantly pulled against the cuff, and it wouldn't budge. She wasn't crazy; it was all of these motherfuckers that needed straight jackets!

Her vivid vision of what she had done in her apartment returned. When the doctor had told her she had expired on the operating table, she despised more that they had fought to bring her back to this place.

With slow scooting movements and much effort, Savannah turned on her side and accidentally pulled one of the monitors loose. The loud beep and flashing were deafening, and the little old lady asleep in the recliner beside her bed jumped up, startled. Savannah was surprised to see her still there.

"It's alright, baby, Big Mama's got it," the woman said as she pushed the button for the nurse.

The auburn-haired nurse greeted them with a smile and stopped the monitor from buzzing.

"In another hour, it will be time for your meds. Can I get you anything else?"

Savannah's cell phone ringing startled everyone. The nurse handed it to her and walked out. She thought it had to be Tanzi but didn't recognize the number.

"Hello?" Savannah said annoyingly into the phone. There was silence for a moment.

"Hello," Savannah knew Tina's voice instantly, even though it had been years since they had spoken.

"I just wanted to call and let you know that Essie died several days ago. I flew out to see her before she passed. She had some things for you that were Nana's. I just thought you'd like to know,"

Suddenly, Savannah's hands began to tremble, and she couldn't breathe. Then everything went black.

Chapter Ten

"Your pain is the breaking of the shell that encloses your understanding."

—Kahlil Gibran

As Will taxied his Gulfstream 650, aka *Mistress of the Skies*, down runway 6-24 at Teterboro Airport in New Jersey to the entrance of Signature Flight Support, he could only think about his princess Chloe. He glanced at his watch; 0900. She had probably been up for under an hour, settling to eat her favorite peach oatmeal with wheat toast triangles. She would try to get her Grandmother to share her messy meal, holding out her spoon while smiling brightly. She was such a beautiful, happy baby, undeniably the joy of his heart.

Who would have thought that Will, who unapologetically declared he *never* wanted to be a father, could be this much in love with a little munchkin who couldn't even spell Daddy yet? He had realized after much soul searching while gazing into the hazel eyes of his little wonder that it wasn't that he didn't want to be a father. The fear of loving someone so deeply and then losing them had been at the root of his wanting to remain childless.

Not that the fear had lessened any; it hadn't. In fact, it was much more profound and debilitating now that Will had Chloe. But how he dealt with it was a remedy that had worked for him since his father's death when he was young. He engaged in good, old-fashioned fear avoidance. He locked the beast up in the deepest reaches of himself in a dark, teeming dungeon where he contained that which was uncontainable.

Will no longer warred with the beast either because he knew it was useless. Fear and losing had proven themselves worthy opponents. The argument that fear was *"false evidence appearing real"* had proved itself a lie. The truth was fear, and its evidence was very real. It was real that he had lost both his father and Sophia. No matter what a person did, it was never a matter of *if*; it was only a matter of *when.*

One day, Will would lose Chloe, and it would kill him. That was inevitable. He could only act like he didn't know this truth and enjoy each second with her.

However, the risk of loving and losing ended with Chloe. Will had decided to never marry again or have a serious relationship. The psychologist he had visited in the months following Sophia's death called this *"loss aversion; a person's tendency to strongly prefer avoiding losses to acquiring gains."* Damn right, he was into loss aversion, no matter what points Dr. Robin Carter had made.

"We normally make poor decisions when we try to avoid loss." Dr. Carter had said to him, looking over her expensive horn rim glasses.

"Turning down opportunities for love and happiness in your future could harm you and Chloe." Dr. Carter had gently warned as he had stood up. That was some trite bullshit someone said who didn't know the first thing about the heartbreak of losing.

Will was going to avoid loving at all costs. Faulty logic or not, he had narrowed his field of loving to Chloe, his mom, and a few friends. That was it.

"I've got it from here, Captain." Will's Second-in-Command, Theo Alexander, said his perfect set of pearly whites gleaming as brightly as his golden blonde hair. Theo was savvy, confident, and hand-picked by Will. He was an ideal combination of leader and schmoozer.

"Captain, do you have enough time to run home and kiss the little angel?" Theo asked as he began the post-flight check.

Will had been seriously entertaining it since they'd left San Francisco. It was about 25 miles from his home, but the traffic would be murderous. They were scheduled to pull out in a couple of hours, but that still wouldn't be enough time. Besides, it would probably be extremely difficult for him to leave her again, so he decided against it. But he could get in a quick video chat.

"Love you, baby girl," Will said as he blew kisses ending his 30-minute call to Chloe. It was always so bittersweet seeing her while he was flying. She looked adorable in her favorite cotton candy pink leotard and tulle tutu, her hair beautifully coiffed in two pigtails with satin bows. As he spoke to her, her hazel eyes sparkled. He chuckled; she was so much like her mother.

Will stood and stretched, looking over the interior of his craft to make sure it was pure perfection. The beige and coffee interior had clean lines, metallic accents, high-tech galleys, 27-inch-wide executive club seats, and a comfortable and private sleeping area. Yes, it was the very definition of both luxury and elegance.

Beverly, his curvy brunette flight attendant, handed him a cup of his favorite coffee, Fazenda Santa Ines, a rich flavor of berries and caramel that always had a stimulating effect on him.

"Just what you need, right?" Beverly said, smiling as she lightly patted his chest.

"You know it," Will said, smiling back. Beverly had been a perfect addition to his crew for over eight years. They had always been very casual and friendly but never sexual. He had learned long ago not to have *relations* with his staff or clients.

"Do you need to stretch out for a while?" Beverly asked, concerned. "I could wake you before the client boards."

Will understood why she asked; the next three days were supposed to be his days off, of which he only got five per month. But when Senator Effingham called and said he needed Will to fly him to San Francisco on unexpected business, he had obliged. The senator was an important part of the rollout of Will's jet venture, SuperLux Air Group, and he was always on-call for him.

Originally, Will was supposed to fly the senator to San Francisco and stay for at least three days. He saw it as a perfect opportunity to head to his estate in Napa and get some much-needed work. But just as they had arrived in the bay area, the senator had asked for a tremendous favorite; a friend in New York needed to be picked up and flown out to the bay area.

It had been a long leg for Will and Theo, but once they landed again in San Francisco, he could still be poolside in his home in Napa before sunset.

"Yes, Bev, I'm going to stretch out here for a while," Will said, yawning. "Don't forget to wake me." he smiled.

"I've got you, Captain," Beverly said, winking as she took the remote and lowered the lights.

Yes, Will was a little tired, but he loved nothing in the world more than flying, except being with Chloe.

After all of the thousands of hours Will had logged, the feeling was even more reverent; a marriage made in the very best part of heaven. He smiled widely, thinking of how wonderful his life was, and drifted gratefully to sleep.

"Look, old woman, I don't need a babysitter," Savannah said to her neighbor, who was standing at the door of the senator's limo.

Sadie looked back at the hospital and then looked at Savannah questioningly.

"Are you sure about that?" she asked as concern spread across her face. "You've been through quite an ordeal besides your Nana…."

Savannah interrupted her. "Look, I know you think you want to care about me but don't. I don't need you or anybody else."

Savannah nodded to the waiting bodyguard to close the door, but the woman placed her tiny frame in the way.

"Look, chile, there is *nothing* you can do about me caring for you," she said, patting Savannah's arm. "Besides, I see past all that stuff you're talking about."

Savannah rolled her eyes at her and waved her hand, dismissing her. "Whatever, old woman."

Sadie was silent as she pensively looked at Savannah, then reached into the car and hugged the brazen young woman. "You know your Nana, and I shared more than birthdays," Big Mama whispered. She could feel Savannah's body tense.

"We are both here to help you see who you really are, Beloved." Big Mama said as she released her and stood back from the door.

Savannah stared indignantly at her. "I know who I am!" she snapped. "Why don't you go find somebody that gives a damn about that bullshit you're talking about."

"I'll be waiting for you when you return," Sadie said, smiling widely.

As the car pulled off, Savannah was glad to finally be rid of her nosy, do-gooder neighbor. The old lady wouldn't leave her side, as if she had gotten a personal summons from Jesus to watch over her. And she didn't care if the little pie lady did share the same birthdate as her Nana; that didn't mean she knew a *goddamn thing*.

Savannah was also glad to be out of the fucking hospital. Despite Dr. Asswipe Wouk's "findings," she wasn't crazy and wasn't some bum squatting in Penn Station guzzling Boone's Farm. She had shown their asses, talking about no matter who she was, she wasn't being released. After the Senator had made some calls, they quickly let her go. Albeit was a conditional release, and she had to agree to start Assisted Outpatient Treatment once she got back from Oakland, she had no plans of ever doing so.

"Senator Effingham?" Sally, the red-haired secretary, said quietly as she leaned into the boardroom. He hated the intrusion of his thoughts about Savannah but knew the Senior Partners were probably ready to resume business.

"Yes," Richard said, sipping his lukewarm black coffee.

"Mr. Bradley said they would be ready for you in 15 minutes," his secretary informed.

"Thanks, I'll be there."

Richard was more than just a little concerned about this thing with Savannah. His greatest worry wasn't the chink in her psychological armor. He was sure she would get back to her usual confident and controlling self. What he needed to assess was the fallout for him if she died. He knew she was shrewd and calculating and had something on him in case things went bad. He needed to secure whatever it was so his political and personal life wouldn't suffer.

That's why when Savannah called him, he had pulled some powerful strings to get her out of the hospital before they transferred her for psychiatric committal. He called in a favor from the Chief Medical Administrator at the hospital. He had filled him in on her diagnosis; "*severe psychotic illnesses and a major depressive disorder, and was a danger to herself and others*" and that in addition to her mental health issues, she had a *"grave substance abuse problem."*

To ensure that Savannah didn't disappear, Richard had sent two of his best men to extract her. After his business was precluded, he would ascertain exactly what she had on him and make sure that it disappeared. If he encountered any opposition, as much as he liked their sexual escapades, he would make her disappear also.

The thump of Will's heart quickened as the woman walked out of the private jet terminal, and the closer she got to the aircraft, the faster his heart raced. She was flanked by two of the senator's Secret Service-style agents, members of an elite private security contractor who had been in bed with the senator for over a decade. These men weren't about protecting but calculating risks and disappearing problems.

Will knew these "risk management" specialists had racked up hundreds of kills in the Iraq-Afghan wars and would relish the opportunity to add more bodies to their list. They were usually only on assignment for Senator Effingham if he needed to get rid of somebody that wouldn't cooperate with his committee plans or if he expected serious trouble. So the fact that it was *her* that these cold-blooded killers were escorting made Will extremely uneasy.

Damn! Will said out loud. If he had known she was the one he had returned to get, he would have declined the senator's request or sent one of his other pilots. This smelled to high heaven, a shit-storm of behemothic proportion, and Will wanted nothing to do with it or her.

As the thoughts swept across his mind, Will knew that it wasn't just what he didn't know about this trip that concerned him; it was also what he did know that disturbed him. *Why the hell do you care?* Will thought, scolding himself. He knew he shouldn't give a damn that she was flying out to meet Senator Effingham or that she was his private paramour. She was nothing to Will. Then why the hell was he so upset that she was about to board his aircraft?

Her black trench coat caught a breeze and flew open, revealing a smart yet classy tan pantsuit that she wore with expensive black high heels. She wore dark sunglasses, and her long locks were pulled back in a ponytail. Her movements across the tarmac were fluid; sensuous without needing to be sexual. She wore no makeup except a faint gold lipstick and didn't look anything like she had the first time he had seen her. Yet her beauty was undeniable. Behind her, she pulled a rolling suitcase.

Will took a deep, frustrated breath, feeling like he was seriously being pulled off his game. Normally, he loved being an exceptional pilot and a masterful planner with good judgment. Right now, the only good judgment Will wanted to display was running her over with his jet.

"Sir...Sir...Captain Dozier?" Will could hear Theo somewhere off in the distance. It shifted his mind from his murderous thoughts back to the cockpit.

"Yes?" Will said, still distracted. Theo was standing with a questioning look on his face.

"Senator Effingham's guest, Savannah St. Clair is ready to board," Theo said, waiting.

Will knew exactly why he was standing and why he had that stupid look. He had methodically trained his staff to meet and exceed his high-end clienteles discriminating needs and high expectations.

Will's cardinal rule was that he and his staff *always* personally greeted and welcomed each passenger aboard his jet. It was just one of the many things that had earned him a stellar reputation in the luxury aircraft industry. But he had no intention of doing so with her. He would leave her to the capable hands of his flight crew.

"Go greet her." Will snapped at Theo as he put on his headset and looked over the flight plan. He could feel his pilot's confusion, but he didn't care. For her, he would make an exception to his cardinal rule; he wanted nothing to do with her.

Savannah had declined food and drink service, dismissed the crew, and settled back in the comfortable, beige leather cabin recliner. It was much better than that hard-ass hospital bed she had been sleeping in. She was glad to be out of those shackles too. *Motherfuckers treated her like she was some runaway slave.*

Savannah's head pounded as a swirl of emotions assuaged her, leaving her completely exhausted and broken inside. Over the last six days, Savannah had been repeatedly asked by a team of doctors, *"Why do you want to die?"* These were supposed to be the most knowledgeable psychiatric minds in New York City, yet they were clueless. It wasn't death that Savannah had been after. Death was the only way she could get what she really wanted; an end to this enduring pain.

Savannah's only viable hope was that there would finally be a cessation of the torment once and for all in the vortex of death. Not just an end to the torment of pain but more so to the torment of hope. The cruelest thing in life was hope; it made murderers and liars out of the best of men and convinced the worst of men that they could be better men.

Yes, Savannah finally understood that hope was an equal opportunity deceiver. She had been born and raised in the hood of South Central Los Angeles and lived in New York's luxurious spaces. She had lived with the crack-addicted and spent time with the movers and shakers of the world. She had given sex for free to poor men and sold herself for hundreds of thousands to rich men, both of which talked about how awful their lives were.

It didn't matter if one was sitting on a worn-out crate in front of the corner liquor store drinking Pabst Blue Ribbon or sailing in the South of France on a 550-foot yacht drinking a Dalmore 62 Single Highland Malt Scotch. The rich were just as miserable and panged as the poor; the rich just had greater ways to deceive themselves it was not so.

Misery and pain weren't only a matter of economics; the masses were all a bunch of self-deceived assholes. No matter what their race or ethnicity, their gender; gay, bi-sexual or transgender, their age, married, single, divorced, or widower, their religion, atheist, or unbeliever, the world was filled with unhappy people who were pathological liars and no matter what they did, they couldn't outrun their pain.

Others could do what the fuck they wanted, but this time Savannah was planning a fool-proof exit strategy. She just needed to see what Nana had left her first.

Savannah used the cabin management system, lowered the shades, and turned down the lights. She needed to forget the last six days and where she was headed. She kicked off her heels, put her feet in the seat, and covered herself with a coffee-colored Cashmere throw.

Savannah heard the landing gear go down and knew they were close to San Francisco. Although the flight had been super smooth, she couldn't rest, much less sleep.

Instead, ghosts danced, taunting her mind; no matter what she did, she couldn't shut them out. What the hell was she thinking about making this trip back to California? Back to the scene of the crimes perpetrated against her life. The place where the innocent girl she once was, had died. Where her twin's bleached-out bones lay in a trashy landfill.

Savannah glanced at her watch; it was almost noon. That meant that by the time she got to the gravesite, they would probably just be getting ready to put the Wicked Witch of the West in the ground. Savannah was glad her mean aunt Essie finally got what she deserved, the nasty cunt. She wanted to see her fat, ugly ass go into the ground. It meant all the others on her revenge list would soon follow Essie to hell.

The landing of the plane jarred Savannah back from her thoughts. Normally, she hated everything about flying, but this flight had literally been like floating on air. Whoever was piloting this plane was the best, no doubt.

Soon after taxing to the gate, the brunette, a svelte flight attendant, approached carrying Savannah's trench coat and rolling her bag. "On behalf of Captain Dozier and the staff, we hope you enjoyed your flight."

Savannah nodded without saying a word as she looked out the window. A light rain was beginning to fall.

"May I help you with anything else, Ms. St. Clair?" the attendant asked politely.

"That will be all," Savannah said, dismissing her and turning her gaze back outside. The sky darkened, and the rain began to pour. It was as if the sky was crying for her realizing she was utterly and absolutely alone.

As Will taxied the G6 to the entrance of the charter hangar at Oakland International Airport, he powered down the luxury jet and had to power down his emotions. He couldn't believe that once again, in the last 24 hours, the senator had changed his plans. Will was furious that he had to fly back to pick up Effingham's play toy. Shortly before taking off from Teterboro, the senator had called requesting that Will *"take good care of her because she's having a rough time."* The senator had the nerve to ask him to babysit his bitch!

Will didn't care that the senator had "i*mportant business matters to attend to*." He did not want to accompany her to some funeral in Oakland nor take her to his estate for several days until the senator could join them. Fuck all of that! She had bodyguards; let them babysit her.

Will's phone rang as he powered off the engines; the senator promised the sun, the moon, and the stars.

"Will, it would mean the world to me," the senator begged. "I'll wrap up here in several days and meet you in Napa to finalize plans on SuperLux."

Will finally acquiesced, against his better judgment. He would have dumped her off the Golden Gate Bridge if he didn't need Senator Effingham's support. She was the last woman on earth he wanted to be near.

As Will left the cockpit, he immediately noticed the bandages on her arms and wrist and the tears running freely down her face. Both unarmed and unnerved him. It would have been easy to ignore her before, but to see her in this emotionally weakened state made him feel sympathy for her. But it was short-lived. As soon as she saw him, shock and loathing registered on her face. He sent the look right back to her.

She quickly put on her sunglasses as if to hide the aching feline she had been moments before. She covered her bandages with her coat and stared at him, surveying his uniform and face.

The intense silence was broken when Theo walked out of the cockpit and asked, "Sir, should I secure the jet here, or will we be flying into Napa?"

"Secure the jet here, Theo. Ms. St. Clair and I will be driving to Napa," Will said arrogantly, knowing this would irk her. It worked, and he smiled as he saw her come undone. The senator hadn't notified her he would be chaperoning her in Oakland and then to the estate.

Her fucking boyfriend had left that detail out. Good, the less she knew, the better.

Savannah remembered distinctly the first night she had laid eyes on him. Her birthday was almost a year ago. The night she had felt such rejection and humiliation at his scrutiny. She never let him know how small and inadequate he'd made her feel. Why was he here, and why were they going to Napa? She was supposed to handle her business in Oakland, meet the Senator briefly in San Francisco, and then return to New York.

The look of superiority on his face made her angry. How dare Richard make alternate arrangements without letting her know. She didn't plan on going anywhere with his ass! She looked past him to the tall Blonde man with him.

"Captain, could you tell me why I would go to Napa?" Savannah asked, quite annoyed with the whole thing.

"Actually, Ma'am, that's Captain Dozier," he said, smiling brightly, nodding towards the arrogant son of a bitch.

"I'm just his admiring flunky." He said quickly and then stepped back into the cockpit. Savannah was furious. There was no way this Motherfucker would be taking her anywhere!

Her move irritated the hell out of Will. Although his navy blue, bespoke double-breasted uniform clearly denoted his captain's insignia, decorated with four gold stripes on his shoulder epaulets and four gold stripes around his lower blazer arms, a gold winged badge and embroidered gold patch with a gold star enclosed in a gold laurel wreath, most people in the beginning days of his career had been just like her.

In Will's early years, it had bothered him to no end when the passengers treated him like he was the hired help. They had often looked past him while his European staff was spoken to as if they outranked him. Most hadn't known that Will's net worth was just as much, if not more, than theirs. But now, Will's reputation was so pristine; it hadn't happened in a long time. It had taken him time to understand his father's lessons: navigating the sea of bullshit and being an intelligent Black man in the matrix of white elitism. But it especially galled him when Black people did it.

Will saw her scanning his uniform as if wondering how he could be the captain. It was a long, amazing story, but one she would never hear. He intentionally let his gaze cut her like a skilled surgeon's knife. He wanted her to know she hadn't gotten to him. The moment was tense and hostile between them.

Despite Will's attempt to appear aloof, he felt his jaws tightening and sweat running down his back. The harder he tried to deny her electric allure, the more her sensuality; the curve of her womanness got to him.

It looked like she would apologize for her slight, but it had gone just as quickly as it appeared.

"Don't worry about apologizing," Will said with a smirk forming on his face. "It's alright that you would mistake me for a co-pilot. I might have done the same thing, thinking you were a lady instead of a slut."

In an instant, she was on her feet, inches from his face, anger pouring from her.

"What the fuck did you just say to me?" she spat.

"The truth!" Will said, smiling as he turned and departed his plane.

Chapter Eleven

"If God were suddenly condemned to live the life which He has inflicted upon men, He would kill Himself."

—Alexandre Dumas

Will was standing by the senator's limo, silently cursing himself for being such a fool. He was supposed to be lounging by the pool at his estate in Napa, working on his business plan. Instead, he was at a cemetery in Oakland, standing next to the harpy *Tisiphone*, whose murderous surveying was palpable evil.

A large crowd of mourners gathered under draped maple trees was a short distance away. They were listening to a minister, adorned in a black robe, who stood before a bronze coffin resting on an aluminum bier. The mood was dark and staid.

Will glanced at Savannah's angry face and wondered who the person in the coffin was to her and why she stood, intensely scrutinizing the gathering but didn't join them. She had rushed out of New York to be here, yet she didn't move forward. Instead, she stood beside him while the senator's henchmen, who had driven a black Escalade behind the limo, flanked his left.

Will didn't need this complication today, especially since it was tied to her. He might have had more sympathy for someone else, but not her. She only earned his loathing.

"Is this where you wanted to be?" Will asked, clearly annoyed.

Her pursed lips silenced any words she might have spoken, but her dark lantern eyes spoke volumes. Will followed her glare and saw a well-dressed African American woman walking toward them. She carried a small suitcase as if it were a valuable treasure she had been asked to guard. The energy volleying between them was nuclear reactive, and Will wanted nothing to do with the impending blast, but he could tell it was too late; he would be a casualty of this radioactive fallout.

Tina knew when her niece pulled into the cemetery the long black limo, followed by a top-of-the-line Escalade, was her style. She was still deceived by riches as if they could hide the despicable person she had become. They couldn't; she was still a demon, just well-dressed.

Tina still felt intense anger toward her niece for the hell she had put her and Mya through, but there was pity for her too. Tina still remembered the sweet joy of a girl she had been.

The twin whose eyes had always danced with hope. How long ago that was...

Tina pulled up to the cute little three-bedroom, Spanish-style home in South Central Los Angeles that she had helped her sister Lolita find. Yes, it was sparsely landscaped and needed some work, but it was a good starting place with a big backyard for the girls.

As Tina exited the rental car and straightened her clothes, she was stunningly dressed in a summer white linen short set with white high-heeled sandals and tasteful gold jewelry. Others always said she looked like she had just stepped out of Vogue magazine and always loved the compliments.

Grabbing the bags of clothes, toys, and goodies she had brought from New York, Tina was happy even though it had been a long flight. It had been a rough year since her mother and David had passed away, but things seemed to be coming together for her sister, Lolita. She never missed her beautiful niece's birthdays.

Tina headed up the driveway towards the backyard like her sister had told her since they would have the girls' party out back. As she got closer to the backyard, she could see the girls lying in the grass happily, which made her smile. The twins were dressed in the sundresses she bought at Bergdorf Goodman. They were the prettiest girls in the world.

Tina also saw her judgmental sister, Essie, with a big floppy straw hat, a long blue jean skirt, and an old, white t-shirt. She was pushing a lawnmower and sweating profusely. Essie stopped mowing momentarily, wiping her forehead and breathing deeply.

"Girls, git yo' self out the way if you ain't helpin'! We got work to do around here, and I ain't got all day to do it!" Essie screamed at the twins.

"The good Lawd done gave you this house and 'expects you to keep it nice," she said while swatting at a mosquito.

"Yes, Ma'am," Elisha said shyly as she nudged Savannah to do the same. Savannah rolled her eyes at her aunt, and both of them burst out with peals of laughter.

"Leave my girls alone!" Tina protested loudly, placing the bags on the ground as the two screaming and giggling ran into her arms. She squeezed them both tightly, planting big kisses on them.

"Auntie Tina, you made it!" Elisha said happily.

"I wouldn't miss being with my favorite girls on their 6th birthday," she said, planting more kisses on their cheeks.

"Well, well, Jezebel made it in with her high-flaunting self!" Essie hissed, rolling her eyes with disdain.

"Just look at you! Your butt hangin' all out. Mama would turn over in her grave if she seen you looking like a whore!" Essie shouted.

Tina ignored her remarks, reached inside the bag, pulled out a large white box, and opened it. The girls' eyes spread wide as they reached inside, pulling out a huge chocolate chip cookie. As they bit into the cookie, they smiled with delight.

"Come on, my special ones, let's escape the wicked witch!" Tina smiled at her sister as she picked up the gifts and herded the girls toward the house.

"You got some nerve!" Essie shouted with her hands on her large hips. "God's gonna send you straight to hell."

"Good! That means I won't have to see your ugly, holier-than-thou black ass!" Tina shot back. She felt Elisha's grip on her hand tightens. She looked down and saw the pretty-in-pink, pig-tailed hair princess with tears about to fall from her eyes.

Elisha had always secretly been Tina's favorite of the two girls. Not just because she was the first person to hold her but because, like Tina, she was highly sensitive and had an innocence that would leave her vulnerable in this life. She needed to protect her at all costs.

"Tina!" Lolita exclaimed joyfully, coming out of the back door. Tina knew her sister was hoping to diffuse her enraged sisters. Old wounds were never far away when they got together.

Tina was determined not to ruin the twins' birthday; they had been through enough. She would save that fight for another day.

Tina understood partly why the woman who was now standing outside of the limo had hated her. One fateful evening, she had been abandoned by everyone she loved.

She knew exactly how she felt but could never tell her that. Could never tell her the family secrets; those were wretched gifts she would keep all to herself.

As she carried the small suitcase to her niece, Tina understood her need for revenge, but she knew firsthand that avenging rarely cured the inflicted injury, and revenge wasn't sweet. That was why Tina never returned to avenge the damage her niece had inflicted on her. She had dreamt about it but knew it would never be worth it.

Tina had come to see Essie after she had called, remorseful after cancer ravished her body. As Tina approached, she was ready to hand off Nana's gift. Essie had found it in their mother's things after she died and kept it to herself.

As her final wish, Essie asked Tina to give it to their niece and tell her she was sorry for everything she had done.

Upon seeing her mother's gifts, Tina wanted to keep them but couldn't as her mother had stated who they were for. Ultimately, she hoped it would give the angry woman what she needed most—closure and comfort.

Just past Tina, Savannah could see them taunting her; Essie's body in the casket, Tina's irk, Mya's smirk, and Essie's husband and son who molested her. She wished she had a rocket launcher to blow them all to pieces.

As Tina walked towards Savannah, a million thoughts and emotions ran through her. First, she wanted to tear her apart, limb by limb. Then she wanted to barrage her with curtains of fire that would incinerate her.

The closer Tina got, the more rage mingled with terror, and suddenly, her body became frozen. She felt Will's grip tighten on her arm and then realized she was shaking so badly she was swaying. Tina's steely eyes met hers, holding the glare.

Savannah suddenly felt lightheaded, and as nausea swept through her, she fought back the urge to vomit. Just as she felt her knees begin to buckle, she felt Will's arm wrap around her waist, steadying her.

"Are you okay?" He asked, concerned, but she tried to push his arm away. She couldn't move him; his arm held her strongly. The two bodyguards, also seeing her discomfort, moved closer, but their presence couldn't stop the trembling snaking through her body.

She could see Essie's coffin as it was lowered into the ground. The wicked witch was finally dead. All the nights she had wished for it, and now she was gone. The only thing that would have made it more perfect was if Essie's husband and son shared her grave.

"How long have you known Nana left this for me?" Savannah asked bitterly, looking at the suitcase in Tina's hand.

Tina just stared at her for a long moment.

"I hope you are next to join Essie!" Savannah screamed, flailing her arms, trying to reach for Tina. Will held her tight as the bodyguards stepped up between her and Tina.

"Life hasn't been easy for any of us," Tina paused. "But we can't get better until we look in the mirror and take responsibility for what our life is or isn't."

"Fuck you, bitch!" Savannah raged and spat at her. "You fucked up my life."

"And you, mine," Tina said calmly.

Tina held out the suitcase to one of the bodyguards, and he took it. She looked at Will, then back to Savannah. "I guess since Tanzi left, you had to find your next victim."

"Bitch, you don't know anything about me," Savannah yelled, trying to break free from Will. He swung her body back away from Tina.

"No matter what your life was, it is still your life. The sooner you stop blaming everyone else and fix what is broken, the better off you will be." Tina said and walked away and then suddenly stopped and turned.

"My Momma was the wisest woman I've ever known. She said when she first looked into your eyes, she knew you were 'the one.' Tina lifted her finger, pointing it at her.

"Whatever she meant by that," Tina gripped Mya's hand, "I hope you find out who you really are just so she won't have been wrong." Mya held onto Tina, and they both walked away.

"What you need to be concerned with is yourself," Savannah yelled as Will moved her to the limo.

"You both better watch your back!" Savannah said as Will put her in the limo and closed the door.

Will intensely eyed Savannah as she glanced around the small, crowded restaurant, looking for someone. Her unconscious gaze made Will look around too. He wasn't a paranoid person, but he was an observant one, and his eagle eyes scanned for any threats.

He saw none, just a mix of multiethnic, multigenerational locals and adventurous foodies enjoying their southern fare, easily chatting about politics, sports, and the latest police shooting of an unarmed local teen.

Savannah had instructed the driver to bring them to this diner in an unassuming area of Oakland. Will had protested; he didn't want to go anywhere else with Ms. Hothead.

When they had pulled up to *Lois the Pie Queen*, at the confluence of 60th, Adeline, and Genoa Streets, Will couldn't believe she wanted to eat inside the sparse building. It was nestled in a corner in the shape of a slice of pie amid rows of houses and a small business, but the amazing smell that wafted through the cramped spot made him overlook the surroundings.

Will hadn't smelled fried chicken this good since visiting Willie Mae's Scotch House in New Orleans, known for having "the world's best-fried chicken." He was ready to wrap his lips around a crunchy, golden piece. The waitress greeted them quickly and then went to take another order.

As she was otherwise distracted, Will surveyed Savannah St. Clair and concluded he knew two things about her. One, she and pain were intimate bedfellows, and two, one day, she would really let her pent-up fury loose, and everyone in her path would face a world of hurt.

The bandages on her wrist and the scene at the cemetery told Will not to get involved, and he was determined to stay clear of the blast zone. He glanced at his watch; in ten minutes, he would call the senator again to find out if he could drop her off to him instead of taking her to Napa.

Will's stomach growled loudly; he was hungry and tired, a bad combination, and he looked around for their waitress. He had already reviewed the menu and was ready for the Chicken and Waffles Combo. She was still taking the order of the four patrons a few tables over, and he willed her to hurry.

An answer to prayer, their waitress headed to them, smiling as she reached their table. She did what most women did when they saw him in his uniform; she gawked and beamed. At one time, it had been what he lived for;

female attention and adoration. Not now. It was an annoyance.

"Hello, welcome to Lois the Pie Queen," the woman whose name tag identified her as Gladys said, gazing into Will's eyes. "What can I get for you? Will looked over at Savannah and saw her eyes, cold and steely, turn to the waitress and then see the waitress's smile disappear.

"I'll have the Reggie Jackson Special, no gravy, eggs scrambled hard, with three biscuits," Savannah said, not taking her eyes off the woman, "and he'll have the Chicken and Waffles, with three eggs scrambled soft, two coffees and no phone number."

The waitress wrote the order, smiled fakely at Savannah, then left.

"Desperate bitches!" Savannah said, her eyes now focused on him. The moment became a tense staring match.

"How do you know what I want?" Will asked, annoyed.

"Because I know you!" She said angrily.

"All of you are just alike," Savannah said, folding her arms and daring him to speak.

"I don't know who you think you are, but this bullshit needs to stop!" He said, nostrils flaring.

"So fucking what!" Her eyes focused on him.

His masculine frame leaned into the table as he said, "I've had it with your antics."

She glared at him, measuring her words. "Why are you even here?"

Her eyes began to tear up again, and he dropped his head into his hands.

Why was he here? He thought. From the moment he saw her walk out of the terminal, he should have backed his jet out without letting her board, but he hadn't. The only reason was that the senator was such a big part of the plans for his business he couldn't afford to piss him off.

"Why am I here? Why don't you ask your fucking boyfriend," he said and angrily got up.

Savannah watched as Will headed out of the diner and could have cared less if he was pissed off or left. She had only called Richard because she needed to get out of that fucking hospital, and she knew he had the connections. Richard had insisted that he was sending a plane for her.

She had no idea this crazy bastard would be the one flying her or that Richard had, without her knowledge, asked him to keep an eye on her. She only wanted to get what Nana left her and leave Oakland.

Suddenly, a sickening feeling wrapped itself around her midsection. A warm sensation went up the right side of her neck, and Savannah grabbed the sides of the table as weakness took over, and she fell into the darkness of night...

She sat beside her sister, their chairs tightly pushed together, sharing pancakes and a bowl of grits. Across from them sat their mother, Lolita, and this man they had rarely seen, whose name was Gary. He said he was the "twin's" father to the lady who had brought their food. She wouldn't call him Daddy as he kept telling them to do. On the other hand, her sister was dutifully smiling and worshipping the monster.

Gary had traveled from Los Angeles to Oakland to beg Lolita to come back. He promised to do right, but she could tell her mother didn't believe him. She didn't believe him either. She and the girls had been living in Oakland for months with their Aunt Essie after Nana had died while she tried to get clean.

"Daddy, can I get some pie from over there?" her sister had asked, pointing her syrupy fingers to the old counter.

"Only if your sweet, fine momma comes back with me," he said, smiling, trying to kiss their mother. She smiled and playfully pushed him away.

"I don't have money for pie," her mother said as the waitress walked up.

"Can I get you anything else?" the waitress asked, smiling at her and her sister. "I would like a piece of pie, please," her sister asked, smiling back.

"I don't have money for pie," their mother scolded them.

"Please!" her sister begged.

"Didn't your momma say no, little girl?" the monster said, frowning at her sister.

"I'll tell you what," the smiling waitress whispered, "We'll be closing soon, and I've got two slices left of Lois the Pie Queen's famous Lemon Ice Box pie for two sweet little girls, at no charge. How's that?" she said looking at their mother.

"Okay, that will be fine," their mother said as she sipped her tea. Gary frowned at both of them.

"You sound just like your momma, spoiling these kids," the monster fumed.

"It can't hurt to....," their mother was interrupted by his banging on the table.

"You need to let me take care of them so I can get their minds right," he said, smacking her sister's hand as she played with the syrup on the plate.

She hated him already and didn't want to be anywhere he was. She listened as he told their mother his plan. They could sell Nana's small house, get a bigger house, and finally have a fresh start.

As the waitress brought the pie and sat it before each of them, the monster took a big spoonful of hers.

"I don't want to live with Auntie Essie anymore; I want to be with my Daddy," her sister said with a hopeful smile.

If only you could see what I see, baby girl, you wouldn't be smiling, she thought. "Okay, let's do it," her mother hesitantly agreed.

Three months after they left, they were back in Los Angeles, living in a two-bedroom apartment. The filthy walls were caked with dirt, graffiti, and urine. Lolita promised as soon as they sold Nana's house, she would get them a nice place.

Most nights, she lay awake thinking how different their lives were when Nana was alive. Now, she and her sister slept on the dirty floor, covered in old, smelly blankets. As tears ran down her face, she had wished so many nights that her mother would have said no to him that day in Lois the Pie Queen's diner.

Will stood outside the limo and cursed loudly, "Dammit!"

He'd hung up with the senator, who would be "unavailable" for the next few days! He was "gravely concerned" for her physical and emotional health and still wanted Will to take her to Napa. He had strongly implied that if Will did this for him, he would be richly rewarded, and if not, well…

The senator knew Will didn't need money; the favors he needed money couldn't buy. His business dealings required access to the exclusive powers of the prestigious body the senator belonged to, but Will didn't think he could do this.

He didn't want to be with her for one second, much less two days! He hit his assistant's number. "Hey Margie, how's it going?" Will said, rubbing his brow.

"All is well, Mr. Dozier; how is Napa?" she asked.

"I haven't made it there yet; I had a change in plans," Will said, sighing deeply. "Listen, reserve the Penthouse Suite at The Fairmont for one night and have my car delivered there. I'll be going to Napa tomorrow."

"I'll get it done, sir," Margie said confidently.

Will steeled himself, preparing to go back in and join her. "Don't fall for any of her bullshit," he said loudly, warning himself as he placed his phone in his pocket and headed towards the diner.

When Will reached the table, Savannah looked up at him like she had just fought a battalion of ghosts and lost. Her face was tear-stained, and she was trembling. "Here *we go*," he said as he grabbed a handkerchief from his pocket, passed it to her, and sat down.

She looked up at him and took it. Just then, the waitress came up and sat their food down. The woman looked back and forth between them as if she had interrupted a lover's quarrel.

"Can I get you anything else?" the waitress asked kindly. "No, thank you," Will said smiling, "that will be it for now."

Will was quiet except for the slightest sounds he made while eating. The food was delicious, just as he had hoped.

"How did you know I liked my eggs scrambled soft?" he said, trying to lighten the moment. She looked at him and let out a little giggle.

"That's easy," Savannah said, cutting into one of her pork chops. "You appear to be hard to the world," she took a bite and chewed. "But inside, you are soft."

"What is that supposed to mean?" Will asked, preparing for an insult.

Savannah stared at him as if seeing deeply into him. It made Will uncomfortable, and he looked away.

"I'm sorry I've been mean to you," she said, tears flowing down her face. "This has been a really difficult time for me."

"I can tell," Will said quickly. "So why don't we call a temporary cease-fire in this war we are waging?"

"Okay, but it's only temporary!" Savannah said, smiling. "I like it being me against the world," she added.

Will wanted to ask what happened in his absence but thought he was better off not knowing. He wanted to steer clear of the emotional waterworks, so he chose a safe topic.

"This is really good food," Will said as he ate heartily.

"Good is not the word," Savannah swooned.

"I concur," Will said, cutting his waffles and pouring lots of maple syrup. Savannah speared a piece of waffle with her fork and smiled at him.

"Why didn't you order some waffles?" Will said, pulling his plate closer to him. "Cause they taste better off of your plate!" Savannah said jovially.

Will reached over and took a big helping of grits off her plate. He put them in his mouth and smiled back. “You’re right!”

As the limo merged onto I-580 W, leaving Oakland behind on their way to San Francisco, Savannah suddenly realized nothing seemed familiar. When she was a child growing up in Oakland, she hated everything about it. As a teenager and young woman, she couldn’t wait to leave.

Savannah glanced down at Nana’s suitcase. She had wanted to open it but was afraid. Nana was the only one she was sure had loved her besides her sister. Would what she read to change that? What if Nana revealed some things she didn’t want to know? She was holding on by a very thin thread and couldn’t take anything else.

Savannah glanced over at Will, who was reading an Oakland Tribune. She knew he wasn’t interested in the paper but was using it to distance himself from her, and that was fine; she didn’t need his pity or help. He was just Richard’s flunky anyway.

Savannah knew she shouldn’t have told Richard she was hospitalized, but she needed his connections to escape and come to get what Nana left her. She had wanted to return immediately to New York, but his brief call confirmed a plan change. He was worried about something he couldn't discuss on the phone.

Was it her suicide attempt, or was the hospital trying to reinstate the commitment? Whatever it was, having Will and his two bodyguards watching her had to be serious. She knew all of the Senator's secrets. Maybe he was just trying to protect his interests. Or perhaps he would try to make her disappear. If that was the case, she would have to remind him what would happen to him if she went missing.

"Where are we staying tonight?" Savannah asked Will.

He casually looked up from the paper, "The Fairmont," he said.

"I want my own room, a non-connecting room," she said aloofly, looking out as they went over the water on the San Francisco-Oakland Bay Bridge.

"Too late," Will said, returning to reading his paper.

"Why is it too late?" She asked angrily. She wasn't used to being told where she could and couldn't go.

"Look, I don't like this any more than you do," Will said civilly. "but we will be together three more days."

She looked at him like he had some nerve telling her what she would do.

"What if I don't want to be in San Francisco for three days?" She said, folding her hands over her chest.

“You won’t be,” he said as he continued to read.

“And who the hell made you the itinerary king?” She said, slapping his paper hard. His temples flexed, and she could tell he wanted to say something rude but thought better.

“Why don’t you sit back and kill the prima donna act,” Will said scoldingly. Savannah stared at him, waiting for an answer.

“Look, I had planned on spending the weekend in Napa Valley before I knew you were coming along,” he said matter-of-factly.

“I have some business I need to handle there,” Will paused, choosing his words carefully.

“Besides, it’s really beautiful and quiet. I figured you could use some alone time,” he said, looking at the suitcase and then back at her.

Savannah remained quiet, not sure what to make of this development.

“Then I’ll personally deliver you to your boyfriend and take you back to your wonderful life in New York,” he said, smiling weakly as he lifted her bandaged arm. She yanked her arm away.

“He’d better hope he lives to see three more days,” Savannah thought, rolling her eyes at him.

When the limo turned onto Mason Street and stopped under the regal black awning Porte-cochere of the world-renowned Fairmont San Francisco, Will's tired body came alive. It wasn't just because they had arrived at the elegantly crowned grand dame of Nob Hill. It was because it brought back heartwarming memories of the first time he had walked through the prestigious doors.

The majestic entrance, with more than seventy multicolored international flags waving in the afternoon breeze, still had the same awe-inspiring effect on Will as it had when he was six. He had sat in a limo similar to this one as his kingly man of a father, Wilson Fairmont Dozier, Sr., Esq., had regaled him with stories of the hotel's history and legendary guests.

Will had most been enthralled with the story about his grandfather, Booth Dozier, a legal expert in trusteeship matters and worked alongside Dr. Ralph Bunche and other African Americans who participated in the writing of the United Nations charter, which had largely been completed in the Fairmont Hotel.

Booth had spent much time in the Fairmont with the others drafting the documents, but he couldn't stay there. Mostly because he was an African American and wasn't afford the benefits of his white counterparts, but also because he couldn't afford it. Instead, he had been taken by an acquaintance to Hunter's Point to get a rented room. There he had met the owner of the home, Gladys, "a colored lady who was passing for white."

Will's grandfather had been so taken with her intellect and wit that they married later the following year. A colleague had booked and paid for two nights at the Fairmont as a honeymoon gift. While there, Will's father was conceived. So, as his father had so eloquently stated, *"This is literally the place of my creation."*

The driver held the door open as Will exited the vehicle and turned to offer his hand in assistance to Savannah. She obstinately slapped it away, pulled herself and her suitcases from the car, and headed through the doors. Will just shook his head as he followed her in.

Will stepped off the private elevator into the opulence of the Penthouse Suite foyer and was thoroughly impressed. The suite's earlier flamboyance had given way to a sophisticated and distinctive blend of East meeting West with rich, purple walls, black and white checkered marble floors, and stately gold accent furnishings.

Will hadn't been here in years. Every inch of the 6,000-square-foot Penthouse Suite was luxurious, and he was looking forward to a hot bath and a good night's sleep.

"Welcome to the Fairmont, ma'am," their butler said to Savannah as he escorted her into the massive living room.

"Welcome back to you, Mr. Dozier; I hope everything is in order?" the butler asked as they walked in.

"Yes, everything is fine. Put me down for a 7:00 a.m. wake-up call," Will said, heading towards the main bedroom.

"Yes sir," he nodded and exited quietly.

"Richard must have paid a small fortune for this," Savannah said as she walked onto the balcony and looked at the spectacular view of the Bay and the San Francisco skyline.

Hearing her words, Will stopped and watched her for a moment but was too tired to set her straight. She thought he was just a measly, poor pilot. He would let her keep on thinking that.

Chapter Twelve

"I have been in Sorrow's kitchen and licked all the pots."

—Zora Neale Hurston

Will awoke with a start; the racing of his heart and the fact that he couldn't breathe only added to his intense anxiety. The darkness consumed him, and he could only feel wetness beneath him. *Breathe.* He ordered, but his body ignored the command.

As his hands fell around blindly, Will was sure the heavy wateriness under him was her blood. But his trembling fingers soon discovered that the sheets he laid were soaked, not with her blood but with his fear and sweat.

As Will struggled to recall where he was, his eyes slowly adjusted to the darkness, and he could make out the bedroom at the Fairmont. But the recognition didn't relieve him; the dream had been real. So was the pain and regret snaking through his wrenching, naked body.

Will had dreamt about Sophia again, only this time, he was standing in a phone booth on a dark, unrecognizable street. He struggled to remember his home phone number to call her.

But then the phone rang, and he quickly picked it up. It was Sophia calling him. *How had she known where he was?*

"Will," she had said calmly.

"I've been trying to reach you!" Will screamed frantically into the phone.

"Why? Did someone tell you the news?" Sophia had asked, concerned.

"What news?" Will yelled as it dawned on him that she was dead.

"I'm pregnant!" Sophia had said, a smile in her voice.

Will saw movement on the dark street and focused his attention. He could see Sophia's mangled Mercedes sitting eerily under a dim street light. He dropped the phone and ran as fast as he could, screaming her name into the foggy night. But as he reached the car, he saw her stiff, pregnant body slumped in the driver's seat. She was already dead.

"No, no!" Will screamed as he took her cold, lifeless body in his arms and rocked her, sobbing uncontrollably as her blood covered him.

As Will struggled to sit in the bed, the sweat on his brows and the tears in his eyes mingled in a bitter dance of guilt and shame. He hated these dreams; they were cruel mockings of what he had done and lost.

All these months later, her death haunted every fiber of his being. He had been just as guilty of killing her as the young men sitting behind bars, awaiting trial, but Will would never be that lucky. He would live out his sentence every day for the rest of his life, especially when he looked into the face of their beautiful daughter. Would he ever be able to tell Chloe the truth about her mother's death? Of course, he couldn't. She would never forgive him.

Will threw the covers back, swung his legs over the side of the bed, and sat in the eerie darkness, hoping the feeling would subside. He looked at the clock; 10:45 pm. Maybe he would head to the Tonga Room. A few drinks should help him forget the memory of death looming over him.

On Will's way out, he purposefully entered the living room and looked out to the terrace. He didn't owe Savannah any explanations of where he was going, but it would be extremely rude not to inform her he was leaving for a while.

The doors were open, but he couldn't see Savannah. *He thought she was probably sitting in one of the chairs enjoying the San Francisco night view.*

When Will walked out onto the terrace where Sean Connery had received his infamous shave in *The Rock* and looked around, he didn't see her. He walked over and looked down to ensure her body wasn't splattered on the ground below. It wasn't.

Maybe she had gone to bed for the night, Will thought. When he came to the luxuriously appointed bedroom suite, the door was open, and the light was on. Will investigated the bedroom; the towering master bed was empty. Except for Savannah's bag and the suitcase she had picked up.

Already pulsating from his nightmare about Sophia, Will's heart became a rapid beat. *Damn!* He said, cursing himself, as he walked towards the bathroom. He knew she had been too unstable to leave alone. He should have had the bodyguards stay in the suite.

The door to the bathroom was open, but the light was off. Will paused momentarily, not wanting to find her in a tub full of bloody water. *What would he ever be able to tell the senator?* Richard had entrusted her to his care.

Will pushed himself forward and turned on the light. The 24-karat gold fixtures of the tub held no blood-spatter. He was relieved at first, then grew increasingly annoyed. *Why the fuck couldn't she just behave herself?* He thought while urging himself to calm down.

Maybe she was just exploring the Presidential Suite as he had done the first time he stayed there. The suite included many expansive rooms, including a billiards room, a gourmet kitchen, and a two-story, domed library with a secret passageway concealed behind the bookshelves on the library's second floor.

"Dammit," Will screamed as he stood perplexed in the foyer. After going through the entire suite, his fear and anger were mounting.

Will took out his cell and dialed. He couldn't let anything happen to Savannah, not because he cared about her; he didn't. But because his reputation was on the line and in his business, that's all you had.

When the senator's bodyguard answered on the first ring, Will knew instantly there was trouble. By the end of the call, he knew he was in for a night that would try every ounce of his patience.

On any other occasion, Will would have been honored to step foot on the hallowed floor of the legendary Top of the Mark, the world-renowned sky bar on the 19th floor of the InterContinental Mark Hopkins Hotel. Few patrons enjoying a martini while gazing at the night sky, knew that the sky bar, the converted 11-room penthouse suite of the hotel's owner, saw over 30,000 service members per month at the height of World War II. US troops were either drinking what might have been their last drink before heading off to war in the Pacific or toasting their return from their tour of duty.

Will's paternal great-grandfather, Andrew Weeks, an Englishman who had married his great-grandmother, LouEllen Leden, a fair-skinned Negro woman, had sat in this very room before heading off to Okinawa, toasting with his squadron for good luck, praying to make it back to LouEllen and their daughter Gladys, who Will's grandfather, Booth Dozier had married. Andrew never made it back.

But tonight, as Will stepped from the elevator, he was indignant rather than reverent. The senator's bodyguard informed him that Savannah had visited several Nob Hill bars drinking inordinate amounts of alcohol before heading to Mark Hopkins. When the bodyguard had gently intimated before they entered the hotel that he was sure the senator would like her to be safe in her room at the Fairmont, she had slapped him hard, advising him to "*mind his fucking business.*"

His stride increased as he walked past the small crowd on the shiny wood dance floor to the small, mahogany, half-moon bar where Savannah was leaning against some strange man, obviously wasted. Will passed by several employees who tried to inform him that patrons were waiting ahead of him, but with one look, they had been silenced. Will frowned and waved both of the bodyguards down as they stood. He would handle this himself.

As Will approached, he could hear Savannah's incoherent babblings about the senator and could strongly smell her intoxication. He steeled his eyes, and his jaws clenched as the man she was leaning against opened his mouth to protest. Wisdom made the man in the dark blue business suit lift his hands as if to signal his surrender.

Will knew Savannah would protest coming with him, so he didn't even give her a chance to form an objection, sweeping her up over his broad shoulders. She tried kicking him, but he held her securely, and soon her inebriation silenced her outcry and movement. One of the bodyguards walked before him as they headed through the crowd, moving patrons aside. Will was sure the other had stayed behind to do damage control.

As they neared the elevator, hotel security stepped in front of the bodyguard, and he moved the two men aside, securing the elevator and stepping in after Will. Several onlookers eyed the bodyguard and then Will as if he were a modern-day Neanderthal. A few people rose to raise their objections, but he firmly conveyed to them the need to mind their own business.

As the elevator descended, Will wondered just how bad this fallout would be. *What had she told others about the senator?*

The senator was definitely not a saint, but his reputation had always been stellar, at least in the eyes of the public. He methodically went to great lengths to ensure his Republican; Judeo-Christian rhetoric was never questioned or suspected.

So why had the senator been willing to risk everything on letting this maniacal woman out of her lair in New York?

The bodyguard on the elevator with him was talking into his mouthpiece, and Will was sure that another team was now sweeping the crowd and assessing the damage. He was also sure the man in the dark blue suit that Savannah spoke with would never be seen or heard from again. A fate that had befallen others before him that were in the wrong place at the wrong time.

As they neared the lobby, Will moved the now dead weight of Savannah from his shoulder to cradle her in his arms. It would look better that way on the cameras in the lobby. But as they walked through the hotel doors, a crew of two dressed in electricians' uniforms nodded to the bodyguard. This meant that all proof of their presence would be erased.

Will started to momentarily relax, and then Savannah mumbled a few indistinct words, emptied her bladder and bowels, and vomited, all in a concert of putrid cacophony.

This bitch! Will screamed. *How the fuck did I get saddled with this?*

Savannah opened her eyes slowly, squinted, and then closed them. She grabbed her head as if that would make it stop, but it didn't. Nor did it silence the asshole inside her head, jackhammering her skull, nor did it stop the room from spinning?

This was the very worst part of drinking; the fucking morning after. The stomach pain, the headache, the need to vomit. Savannah knew the only thing that would make it better was another drink.

Struggling to push the covers back, she wondered how she had even reached the bed. The last thing she remembered was being in a bar telling some douchebag who thought the senator was a god how he liked pegging; on his stomach with his white ass in the air, as she rammed a 12" dildo in him.

“What the hell?” Savannah said angrily as she looked down at the white men's t-shirt she wore; it didn’t belong to her. *So, whose was it?*

Savannah was perplexed; did she return to the room with the douchebag? No... she didn’t think so. *But how?* Underneath the shirt, she was completely naked; *someone* had undressed her. There was a faint memory just beyond her grasp, but she fought to pull it forth.

All at once, the flashback came. It was his face, his haunting eyes seeing her, his hands touching her.

Will heard crashing glass, and it jarred him out of repose. Reflexively, his right hand came up, ready to defend himself, as he moved off the sofa. She was charging toward him like a raging bull. A vicious, echoing scream flowed from her that caused the hair on his naked arms to bristle.

“How dare you touch me!” Savannah railed, her long hair swinging just as furiously as her arms as she reached him. Will moved quickly, and she fell hard against the cream-colored sofa, the t-shirt revealing her shapely ass.

“How dare you go out and get drunk!” Will shouted back to her as she quickly got back on her feet, heading towards him again, a feral animal.

“What I do is my fucking business,” she raged as Will blocked the onslaught of her blows, moving backward as he did.

The huge living room was starting to feel smaller. He should have locked himself in his bedroom instead of sleeping out here to be sure she didn’t leave again.

“I will ...fucking...kill...you!” she spewed, landing blow after blow against him.

Hadn’t he known that this would be her response? Instead of being grateful, he’d cleaned her up; she would be livid with him. He should have followed his first mind, left her in the foul dress, and put her in bed. But he hadn’t; he had undressed her, washed her off, put her in his t-shirt, and then in bed.

“It’s not what you think!” Will yelled as he continued to back away from her blows. His foot slipped, and he landed on the floor, just missing the black grand piano leg. This gave her the upper hand, and she pounced on him before he could scramble.

“All of you fucking men are the same,” Savannah said as Will blocked his face and took her blows. He forced himself to refrain from striking her. It wouldn’t go well for him if they found her dead body on the penthouse suite floor.

"Stop it!" Will yelled.

"Fuck you!" she yelled back, out of breath.

Realizing that she had no plans to relent, He grabbed her hands and restrained her. She was straddling him, and the thick nipples of her full breasts strained against the tee. Her hot nakedness pressed hard into him. Without his consent, an intense desire coursed through his body, creating a beastly thickness in his sweats. He fought to control it, but her movements made it worse,

"Let me go...dammit," she said between jagged breaths.

Will flipped her over, attempting to get up, but her legs gripped him, and he fell awkwardly on top of her, their mouths inches apart, a heat escaping their lips. The lingering moment was tense and silent until she headbutted him just above the bridge of his nose. Both of his nostrils began to bleed, dripping onto her t-shirt.

"Goddammit!" Will screamed, his anger mounting as he wiped his nose.

"Calm your ass down!" Will said as he pinned her arms against the floor.

"Don't you ever fucking touch me again, you bastard!" Savannah said, trying to break free of his grip.

"Why because I'm not paying your whoring ass, or I'm not a lesbian? Which one?" he said, wanting to hurt her bad.

"Because you are a punk-ass bitch, that's why!" Savannah said defyingly.

Will saw an intense red and wanted to wrap his hands around her throat and squeeze until the life left her.

"You're going to find out; I'm not one to play with," Will said quietly, pushing her hands away as he got up and walked away.

Savannah knew when Will walked out of his bedroom and tossed his bag by the door, he was still pissed. He wore a smart, navy blue jogging suit with a crisp white polo shirt and white suede sneakers. His physique was...well, arresting. The same heat she had felt earlier when they had warred was surging through her now. *Bitch get a hold of yourself!*

Savannah was sitting on the veranda in front of an elaborate breakfast prepared by their butler, who had gently offered his suggestions based on '*Mr. Dozier's* previous stay.' Not because she liked Will; she didn't. Simply because it was her way of apologizing. Although she had taken the butler's advice and ordered the Fisherman's

Wharf Crab Benedict with a side of Grilled Pacific Salmon, Savannah had also ordered various other foods, including Brioche French Toast with a platter of fresh berries and Moet & Chandon Champagne Mimosas.

After fighting with Will, Savannah entered her bathroom suite and found her soiled clothes neatly folded inside a plastic bag. As she pulled her clothes out and saw the stains, she realized he hadn't undressed her to be sexual but rather to clean her up. She had also inquired of the bodyguards who revealed all of her antics.

It was kind for him to do, but Savannah wasn't used to kindness. She wasn't in the habit of saying sorry either, so breakfast would have to say it for her.

Yes, going out last night had been destructive, but drinking was the only thing to take the pain away, even temporarily.

His eyes met hers, and immediately, she felt judged. As if he was some infallible example of moral integrity. *Smug bastard!* He wore his arrogance like he wore his captain's uniform, tailored and sharp, making her want to curse him again.

But she didn't. Even though it was hard to admit, she felt protected by him. And right now, she needed that.

Savannah stood, pulled out a chair for him, and beckoned him to come. He stood for an eternity, staring at her and the food. She was nervous, not knowing whether he would sit down or throw her over the balcony.

Will stood there eyeing this woman who had been a ravenous lioness hours ago. Now, she acted like she was a calm doe. He had contemplated leaving her there, driving to his estate in Napa, and letting his business with the senator be damned. He couldn't for two reasons; he had been preparing for this moment with his business for a long time. Secondly, because he saw through her act. He knew she was both afraid and alone.

Although he shouldn't have one bit of empathy for her, he did. He knew exactly what she was experiencing. He had felt the same way when Sophia died. No matter what he felt about her personally, he felt obligated to protect her.

As Will took in the backdrop of the beautiful San Francisco morning, he had to admit it paled in comparison to Savannah. She looked stunning and dressed in a plain pink sweatshirt and white jeans. Her skin was flawless; her long mane was pulled back in a simple ponytail, and a few wisps of goldenness fell over her face. She wore no makeup except for a touch of frosted lipstick.

Suddenly, a glimmer of an ethereal vision addled his mind. He saw a smiling Sophia standing in the form of Savannah. Just as quickly as the vision had come, it disappeared. At that moment, the recognition that had eluded him became crystal clear. Sophia and Savannah could have been sisters. *Was that why he had felt a need to protect her?*

Will couldn't face the revelation just yet and averted his attention from Savannah to the spread before him. It looked like she had ordered everything on the menu. Her way of apologizing for beating him like a rag doll. She must have found her clothes just as he had purposed.

Savannah smiled innocently, tilting her head as if she had done nothing wrong. Typical female, creating chaos, then standing back, assessing the damage with naivety. Will shook his head, walked to the veranda, and sat down.

Smooth jazz played in the background as Savannah poured coffee for him and then sat down and played with a small bowl of fruit. He was paying royally for this spread, so he might as well enjoy it. He ate quietly, ignoring her.

“I figured you'd be hungry after all that exercising you were doing,” she said, looking out at the San Francisco skyline while she sipped her mimosa.

Will was determined not to let her bait him. He was already distracted and off schedule, two things he hated.

“I had planned to leave early for Napa,” he said and took a bite of salmon. “I have work to do, and like it or not, you will be with me,” he said stoically.

Savannah looked intently at Will, then looked out again at the skyline. The fog was a cottony blanket, slowly moving away.

“I was asked to look out for you,” Will said, sipping his coffee. “I complete my assignments.”

“So I’m an assignment to you?” Savannah asked, looking vulnerable.

Will looked out at the city for moments and then looked back at her.

“I have a lot going on right now, and I’m just asking you to make this easier,” Will said.

Savannah grabbed a muffin and threw it at him, barely missing his head. Tears fell down her face.

“Why did you do that?” Will said, laughing easily.

"Because it was *easier* for me to do that rather than toss this table over on you!" Savannah said, narrowing her eyes at him.

"I left New York against the advice of my doctors," Savannah said, lifting her arms.

"I'm on the verge of a nervous breakdown I might not come back from," she said, pushing strands of hair behind her ear.

Will listened intently, knowing the gravity of the moment.

"When I got that call saying my Nana had left something for me, it gave me a reason to make it one more day."

Will nodded his head, understanding exactly how she felt. Chloe had been that reason for him.

"I just want you to know I resent very much being your assignment," she said, wrapping her arms around herself and looking away.

Will looked at her face, his eyes focusing on her lips, delicious lips he had been inches away from tasting. Heat began to rise again, and immediately, he felt discomfited. This was going to be his hardest assignment ever. *Literally.*

Chapter Thirteen

"There is a condition worse than blindness,

and that is, seeing something that isn't there."

—Thomas Hardy

As he and Savannah headed out of San Francisco, Will smiled inside; he loved this 80-minute drive to Napa. He had been worldwide, but this road trip did something for him that only a few things could. It centered him, put his priorities in perspective, and linked him to his father. To Will, it was a priceless connection.

Will had vowed no matter what was going on with Savannah, he wouldn't let her ruin the next several days. So as soon as they had exited the hotel and climbed into his Dark Sapphire Jaguar XJR, he issued her a warning.

"The next several days *will* be free of your drama. Are we clear?"

Will could tell by how Savannah rolled her eyes and said, "Whatever," that she didn't take him seriously. He knew how to get her attention. He recklessly pulled into traffic, swerving around cars with the precision of a professional stunt driver. Before she could fasten her seatbelt, he peeled away from the hotel, and every one of the 550 horse powers of the supercharged engine screamed.

“Are you fucking crazy?” Savannah screamed as she reached out with one hand to hold onto the dashboard. With the other, she fumbled with the seat belt.

Will made a sharp turn, and the car drifted sideways and straightened under his skilled hands. He purposely took his eyes off the road as his speed increased, watching the terror on her face.

“Are we clear?” Will asked calmly as Savannah finally got her seat belt fastened while shrilling.

“You fucking bastard, are you trying to kill me?”

Will smiled, still eyeing her. “Well?”

“Alright, you sadistic asshole!” Savannah said, holding onto the dashboard and breaking with her feet.

“Thank you,” Will said as he slowed, straightening his rearview mirror and focused on the road again. She sat silent, her chest still heaving. He knew some foul shit was running through her head, but she knew it was better to leave it there.

Will chuckled, but Savannah wasn’t amused in the least. She looked at him hard and then flipped him a bird. Will laughed loudly, his head leaning against the headrest as they sped through the northbound toll booth and soon traveled over the Golden Gate Bridge.

Although leaving later than Will had planned, they missed the notorious San Francisco fog. Will rarely rode with the windows down, but he made an exception today. He lowered all four, and Savannah's ponytail whipped in the crisp autumn air.

The Golden Gate Bridge's lofty International Orange suspension towers still amazed Will. To their left were the Marin Headlands and the glimmering blue Pacific Ocean. San Francisco, the Bay, Tiburon, and Angel Island were to the right.

Will could still hear his father's voice, strong and gusty, as he described the miracle of The Bridge. Will had been an impressionable young boy sitting beside his father as they drove to Napa over the 4,200-foot-long engineering wonder.

"Will, we are riding over what many said couldn't be built," his father had said with great definition.

"So, the fact that we are riding over it tells you that *nothing* is impossible!" Will Sr. had said, waving his strong hand as a magician would.

Will's dad had always been a motivator of men; although he was physically dead, he lived on in every fiber of him. His dream of being a captain and owning his own jet company was set in concrete as he and his dad conversed on the way to Napa, where his father met a client.

His dream had been 27 years in the making, and although it had been stalled by so many things, he was finally bringing it to fruition. He wanted to cross this bridge in honor of his father, who, to his last breath, had done all to honor his son.

"Do you know how many people have committed suicide here?" Savannah asked, looking out the window as many people; some walking, some jogging, some riding bikes, flew by.

Will wondered if she was just making small talk or wanted to tell him what she had recently gone through.

"There is no way to know the exact amount because many jumps weren't witnessed," Will said quietly. "But they say it is around 2,000 or more. It's one of the most popular places to commit suicide worldwide."

Savannah continued looking out the window, but Will could tell she was a million miles away.

"Wonder how it feels?" Savannah asked, more musing than questioning.

\

"When my Aunt Essie, the bitch buried yesterday, was mad at me, she would throw a dollar at me and say, "Why don't you catch the bus, hop off the Bridge and do us all a favor!" Savannah said, chilled.

"What kind of person says that to a child?" Will said angrily.

Savannah looked sadly at him. "Oh, that was one of the nicer things she said."

There was a heavy silence between them for minutes, and then Will, against his better judgment, looked intently at Savannah and asked what had been rolling around in his mind since he had seen her bandages.

"So why that road for you?" Will asked, looking at her.

"The truth is that attempted suicide and I are long-time friends. I remember the first time I really wanted to die; I was six years old." She said, looking out at the ocean.

Will twisted his head around, his eyes wide. He thought no other child could want to die that young. For her, it had been six; for him, it had been eight. He wondered what had happened to her to make her want to leave this life. But he wasn't ready to hear the answer, so they rode silently.

As they continued on Highway 101 north toward Santa Rosa, Savannah fought to keep despair at bay. She thought she could easily slip back into the Bay area and exit unscathed, but it hadn't been so.

Every piece of her that she thought was long dead since being in New York had come back to life. She couldn't shake the memories of her traumatic childhood, the years of pain and loss she had suffered being with Michael.

Savannah screamed silently. *Why did life have to be so fucking difficult!* It would have been so much easier if she had died on the floor of her apartment. Then she wouldn't be riding with this crazy man, wondering what was inside her Nana's beat-up suitcase.

Savannah kneaded her temples hard in the hopes of arresting the pounding headache. But ever since she had gotten the suitcase in her possession, she had been terrified to know what was in it. The very thought of getting her Nana's gift had given her the courage to get off her deathbed. Yet now, it seemed like a tormenting curse.

She had wanted to open it but couldn't. Life had played so many cruel tricks on her; she wouldn't survive one more.

Will had been speculating as he drove about what had happened to her at such a young age that had pushed her to thoughts of suicide. *Why had she been raised by her aunt? What had happened to her parents? What had happened to her grandmother?*

As they turned onto Mark West Springs Road, Will shook the concern off and let the scenic country road become an enchanting distraction. He remembered the first time he and his father descended into the Napa Valley; his father told him about the original people, the First Nations of Wappo, who called this place “the land of plenty.”

The fertile, small piece of grape-strewn real estate was only 35 miles long and 5 miles wide, but it was considered the country's most extensive playground for wine and luxury aficionados. As an adult, Will understood why; the ambiance of privilege, the abandonment of indulgence, and the harmony that went with it.

A few miles later, having driven through the most exquisite autumn hues of red, orange, and yellow foliage, they were winding up the private road to Will’s estate. He had bought this magical haven a decade ago, and although he didn't get to visit much, it was still his favorite sanctuary.

As he brought the car to a stop in front of the main house, Will realized he had never brought anyone here, not even Sophia.

“Wow,” Savannah exclaimed as she stepped from the car turning in a full circle and taking in the magnificence of it all. Will had done the same thing the first time his realtor had shown it to him.

Chateaux Val d'Orcia, as Will affectionately called his estate, had been given her name in homage to the sweeping, majestic views in Val d'Orcia, that timeless and magnificent region in Southern Tuscany, where Will had once traveled. Gazing over the endearing valley, Will instantly understood why it had been called the most perfect part of Italy.

Likewise, the views from Will's estate were just as breathtaking. The southern part of Napa Valley, including San Pablo Bay and Mount Diablo, seemed to wrap you in an extravagant, bewitching embrace.

Will opened the trunk and extracted Savannah's bags. He had lost enough time fooling around with her.

"Let me show you where you'll be staying," Will said quickly as he headed towards the sprawling, grapevine-covered, two-story Tuscan-style guest house before she could make any demands.

The first thing Savannah had thought to do was strenuously object as Will headed towards the guest house. The nerve of him! She wanted to throw a tantrum in the middle of the palatial driveway but thought better of it. She should be staying in the main house after the senator arranged all this place.

Although she wasn't in the habit of obeying any man, she knew he had been serious when he had issued her a warning.

He reached the front door and opened it, setting her bags down. She had heard him close the door behind him but was too enraptured to speak. So instead, she walked around the first floor of the exquisite Mediterranean guest house in disbelief. She was inundated with the fragrant smell of nostalgia as she walked in.

It was as if someone had gone inside Savannah's mind and captured a snapshot of what she had enjoyed most as a child; the smell of flowers, baked bread, and strawberry jam. She lifted items, smelling them deeply, embracing each while listening to the smooth jazz playing. It was a bittersweet reminder of the special times spent with her sister and Nana.

Savannah braced herself expecting to see her Nana emerge wearing her blue apron and a wide grin. When she entered the master bedroom and saw the bouquets of blue hydrangeas, she stopped suddenly, grabbing the wall to keep from falling over. These were her grandmother's favorite flowers.

Several moments of eerie silence passed, and her joy was replaced with a dark sadness. She sat on the bed and stroked her Nana's suitcase that she'd carried upstairs.

"Nana," she whispered, echoing throughout the simple yet elegantly appointed room.

Will hurried away from the guest house, smiling as he passed the fragrant olive trees and cypresses that lined the driveway. He'd gotten her inside without one complaint.

He hoped she would remain cooperative as he climbed the sweep of Italian stone stairs leading to the palatial main house.

"Good afternoon, Sir," Will's butler said as he opened the massive, double doors. Every detail of his Italianate *palazzo* was perfect.

"Thank you, Henri. It's good to be back."

As Will crossed the threshold, he stepped on the opulent Pietra Dorata Italian marble floors. He stood momentarily, taking in the calm Val d'Orcia offered him; she was such a welcoming lover. *Finally, he could unwind in her embrace and get some work done.*

Chapter Fourteen

"... joy and sorrow are inseparable. . . together they come and when one sits alone with you . . . remember that the other is asleep upon your bed."

—Kahlil Gibran

Although their mother, Lolita, had prepared their favorites for their birthday dinner, they ate guardedly. On any other day, they would have barely stopped between bites of crispy golden fried chicken, the cheesiest macaroni, and the sweet cornbread, but not now. They were waiting for the other shoe to drop.

She couldn't believe that hours earlier, she and her twin had held hands, lying on the grass in their backyard, looking up at the beautiful sky and thinking everything would be alright. Thinking the horrors of the past were over. As always, someone had to mess things up; this time, it was their father. He had made many promises for their birthday. The one they wanted most was their treehouse.

Their father, Gary St. Clair, had apologized for his past failings, swearing, "This time, I will keep my word," through tears the night before. She had, against her better judgment, believed their father. But it was dark now, and the empty tree in the backyard still didn't have a house.

She had heard her mother admit to her sisters that Gary had taken the cash she had stashed away from her portion of the sale of Nana's house. All of it was gone. Tina had tried to comfort Lolita, but Essie had berated her sister for leaving her house in Oakland and returning to L.A. with that "heathen."

She now understood that things would never change. Men couldn't be trusted. That realization made her angrier by the second.

Their mother told Tina and Essie she would figure it out later. She wanted to ensure the girls had a good birthday at that moment. The women were oblivious to her rage. When Lolita put candles on the chocolate Cinderella cake, and the ladies sang, she rolled her eyes at them.

"What's wrong with her?" Essie said, pointing at her niece.

"She's mad at her daddy...disappointing them as usual," Tina replied, shaking her head at Lolita.

"He's just an infidel," Essie said, pointing at her sister. "I told you to leave him alone!"

"Will you please shut the hell up?!" Lolita screamed at Essie. "These girls have been through enough heartache without you worsening it."

Her sister turned and looked out the window hopefully. Still expect the liar to keep his word. Never, ever will I trust a man again!

Her mother set a huge piece of cake and ice cream in front of her. She felt hot tears rising, but she was determined not to cry. She just stared at the happy princess whose smile taunted her.

"Why don't you eat some of your cake," her Aunt Tina said, leaning over to kiss her cheek. "It's really good." She looked at her sister, who was spooning ice cream in her mouth like she didn't have a care in the world.

By the time they had opened their presents, the fury in her had a life all its own. Her sister quietly said, "Thank you," as she opened her gifts, but she remained wordless, tearing paper and tossing it to the floor, barely looking at the gifts that previously would have made her jump with glee. When she got to the last one, a heavy gold box with a pink ribbon, her mother told her it was from her father.

She stared at her mother, her eyes daggers, seeking a release from the overwhelming hate she felt. Suddenly, she stood and forcibly threw the unwrapped present so hard it crashed through the window of the small living room, leaving shattered glass everywhere.

"I hate him!" she yelled as her tiny body trembled violently.

The three women looked at each other in stunned silence, mouths agape, gazing out the paneless window. Jagged edges were all that remained.

Savannah tried to shake herself free of the memory that still, after all these years, caused her tremendous rage and agony, but it didn't work. She remembered each detail, each emotion vividly.

"Let it go," she ordered as she walked to the French doors, which opened to a magnificent terrace with a breathtaking valley view. Savannah took a deep breath as if the peacefulness surrounding her could infiltrate her by osmosis. She desperately needed it too.

Savannah, who had been a master at controlling her feelings, now seemed like a faucet, permanently stuck in the "emotionally unstable" position. She had worn an armor-plated bodysuit for so long that it stopped serving its purpose. There had been a chink; Tanzi.

Savannah wondered how Tina knew she and Tanzi weren't together. Tanzi had promised to always be there no matter what happened, but she was a liar, just like the rest. Eventually, Tanzi would come crawling, begging Savannah to take her back, and she would, just long enough, to torture her to death.

As Savannah looked out at the estates and homes dotting the valley, she imagined the hustle and bustle of families enjoying their weekends together. She had desperately wanted that life. To be the wife of one husband, with a beautiful bunch of happy children, but the goddamn fate genies had cursed her, and the only thing she could count on was being utterly alone in this world.

Stop your sorry-ass whining Bitch! Do you know who we are? We don't give a fuck about being alone!" her alter ego's venom spewed. Normally, those chiding words would be enough for her to ward off the sadness, but not now. Truthfully, it didn't matter how desirable or sexy she thought she was or how much men would spend just to be with her. Nor did it matter how many of the world's movers and shakers she had on speed dial. *She had no one and nothing in the end.*

A light breeze blew around and then through her, causing her to shiver. Savannah thought about going inside, getting a cup of tea, and listening to Al Green while she went through Nana's suitcase, but as soon as she stepped back inside and looked at it, she realized she wasn't ready.

Savannah had often wished she could talk with her Nana again. Her Grandmother was the warmest, kindest woman she had ever known. The one who had made her sister, brother, and herself know they were completely and unconditionally loved. *And then she was gone.*

Nana's suitcase held something important; she was sure of it, but she had the overwhelming feeling that the "something" would utterly undo her. So Savannah walked past the tattered suitcase, down the stairs, and into the kitchen. She looked through cabinets and closets and then moved to other rooms, searching for alcohol but found nothing, not even cooking sherry. Goddammit!

She picked up the Napa Sonoma Magazine lying on the marble counter and searched for a place that would deliver spirits to her. But the more she thought about it, she was sure Will's smart ass would be watching and blocking her from getting her drink on. He had told her as much as they had turned into the estate. She had the run of the property, the sauna, the spa, the pool, and the staff, but she couldn't drink or leave the property. *Like she was some goddamn prisoner!*

An article caught Savannah's eye, and she saw a way to outsmart him. She headed towards the door and remembered his outright threats about interrupting his *work.* She wondered what the hell was so important that he had to be held up in the main house anyway.

Savannah had met many men in her life, but none like him. Will made her feel afraid and protected at the same time. *The bastard!* But she needed to set him straight if he thought she would stay in the guesthouse while he jacked off in the palatial mansion one of the Senator's friends owned.

Will had finally settled in to get some work done, but his mind wouldn't cooperate. Manifold thoughts, like the unkindness of ravens, assailed him. Maybe it was speaking with his mother about preparing for Chloe's first birthday party. It was supposed to be a joyous occasion, but all it did was dredge up memories he would rather forget.

He could feel the tears welling in his eyes as he remembered lying in bed with Sophia and hearing Virginia's words. "With her last breath, she called your name, and no matter what happened that night, Sophia's heart was grateful for you."

Those words had played in his head many times, but he still couldn't fully come to terms with the guilt, shame, or blame that was his. He had buried Sophia but knew he could never entomb the pain or sorrow, not just for what he had done to Sophia but also for what he had done to his daughter. He had robbed Chloe of the greatest gift; a mother that had loved and wanted her more than life itself.

With Rosaria and the teenagers, Will had tried desperately to lay the blame elsewhere, but it didn't work. It had been him. *He* had been the one that had used Rosaria, and *he* had been the one that broke his wife's heart.

The pain subsided as he thought of Chloe. A huge smile spread across Will's face. He remembered the awe-consuming love that his daughter had given him. Her confidence in him had made him a better man.

A man who, throughout the last year, had refused, despite his enormous cravings, to ever use a woman again. *Even Savannah St. Clair.*

She still caused a fire to surge through him, just as she had the first time he laid eyes on her. But he was determined to avoid her at all costs. She needed to keep her ass at the guesthouse, and he needed to get busy with his project.

As Will opened his laptop, he felt an eerie pressure on his neck. He instantly knew it was Savannah; she was plotting something. He shook his head and rubbed his neck to relieve the pressure, but it didn't work. Damn!

Savannah angrily walked the olive-flanked stairway, ignoring the rugged mountain landscape to her left, covered in oaks, chaparrals, and manzanitas. The main house sat far off, but something about it was so inviting. It blended into the landscape like it had been a part of the planning of the valley, just as much as the hills and the sky. *It was breathtaking.*

As Savannah walked the hand-carved stone risers, she was pissed at his nerve. This place belonged to one of the Senator's friends, meaning she was entitled to the best it could offer. As she neared the two-story main house and mounted its grand steps, she opened the massive entry doors like she was the owner.

A sturdily built, Euro-aristocratic-looking butler quickly greeted her, bowing as he spoke.

"Hello, Madam. May I help you?"

She quickly eyed him; black tailcoat, smoke gray pinstripe pants, gray vest over a stark white shirt with a wing-tip collar, long black tie, perfectly shined black shoes, and white gloves. Piercing blue eyes that seemed to hold a thousand secrets.

"I've got this," Savannah said, patting his chest and strolling past him over the stunning marble entryway.

Savannah's keen senses were guiding her through the massive home. Will's scent was strong, a lingering maleness that momentarily interrupted her anger. She blocked the rising memories of him on top of her and took in her surroundings.

The home was an architectural delight with a mix of contemporary and traditional accents with a bold Italian flair. The furnishings and walls were a warm white with beige and dark brown. The brightly shining chandeliers were supplemented by warm built-in lighting. The bay window she passed offered a pleasing view of old cypresses, overhanging grape leaves, mature olive trees, and distant peaks.

This house was very strange, like it was a breathing organism. It had an ambiance of determined peace and graceful fortitude. Like it was a wise, old soul that had lived thousands of lifetimes.

"Don't get side-tracked," Savannah said sternly, rebuking herself. "Find his ass."

Savannah's intuition guided her through several hallways until she arrived at a slightly open door. She hesitated, wondering what she would find if she looked in. For some reason, her knees were weak, and her heart beat wildly in her chest.

When she garnered the courage to look in, the sight riveted her. It wasn't just the beauty and sensuality of the room that was so captivating; yes, the ivory walls, tan accents, and dark wood furnishings were exquisite, but it was *him.*

An eerie feeling of familiarity swept over Savannah causing her mind to teeter between the present moment and the past, a past where she knew him intimately. She had stood in this very place at another time and place, taking in the vision that was Wilson Fairmont Dozier. And then, just as quickly as it had come, the moment of knowing was gone.

Will sat shirtless in the middle of the king-size bed. His attention was on his laptop; only casual white shorts hid his nakedness. A pair of expensive earbuds made him oblivious to her presence. The moment had unsettled her, and Savannah tried but couldn't find the anger that had brought her here.

His presence evoked such intensity in her now, just as it had done the first time she looked at him. She remembered the feeling of him atop her earlier, his manliness between her legs. She felt him there, pressing into her, causing a quivering heat to expand into an electrifying inferno of desire.

Looking over his CFO's reports, Will had just settled into a good rhythm. The numbers looked great and were on schedule with many of their projections. Suddenly, Will felt something beckoning him and looked up, surprised to see Savannah standing at his door.

She wore a plain pink jogging suit with a see-through, white tank top that exposed every detail of her taut nipples. Will felt a familiar stirring in his groin and instantly moved his leg to hide it. He couldn't take a chance on her seeing the way she affected him. But she did affect him *deeply*.

Savannah's feminine wiles were so artful; she made it a game playing with the intricacies of his sexual predilections. She was so stunning standing there exposed that he wanted to do things to her that he hadn't done in a long time. But he wouldn't. He took the earbuds out and looked at her, waiting.

"I saw the French Laundry restaurant in one of the magazines in the guesthouse, and I want to eat there tonight," she said demandingly.

"First of all, don't you know how to knock?" Will said, irritated, setting his laptop aside. "Secondly, it takes months to get a reservation."

"I did knock, and if you can't get us in, then call the Senator," Savannah said, pouting as she folded her arms.

Will felt a recognizable fury surging through his body. He had wasted enough of his precious time on her bullshit. He rose quickly, moving towards her with a purpose. He was going to nip this thing in the bud before his short vacation was over.

"Look, I don't know what games you are trying to play, but I told you I have work to do," Will spoke angrily, stopping just inches from her.

"Aren't you being paid well by the senator to babysit me?" Savannah spoke, tossing her words at him like a wrinkled dress he needed to iron.

"Being Richard's bed partner may make you feel superior, but the shit makes you less than nothing in my eyes," he said.

"Fuck you," she yelled, raising her hand to strike him.

Will caught her arm in mid-air and held it tightly. "That's your married boyfriend's job," he said disgustingly.

Savannah yanked her arm free and stood looking at him defiantly. Will braced for venomous words to be launched in retaliation, but none came. Instead, it was her tears that hit him. *Dammit!* Will cursed silently.

Will hated when she cried; it disarmed him. He closed his eyes and dropped his head. He sighed deeply, knowing he wouldn't get any work done tonight.

"I'll get us in, but we must buy you something to wear. They won't let you in the place wearing that."

Chapter Fifteen

"Pain is inevitable. Suffering is optional."

—Haruki Murakami

As they sat across from each other, Savannah was amazed at how stunning Will looked. Yes, he wore his Captain's uniform well, but she saw another side of him tonight. The dark blue suit was bespoke. The light blue tailored shirt, with its white cuffs and collar, and richly embroidered initials, was held together by white gold diamond cufflinks with Blue Sapphire. It revealed a man of impeccable taste and class.

"You clean up well," Savannah said, smiling brightly. He smiled back, his dimples deep.

"So, is this what you expected?" Will asked, already knowing the answer.

"Not exactly," Savannah intoned. When the car had pulled up to the old, rustic two-story building built in the early 1900s, she had been completely surprised that this stone house had ever held the distinction of "*Best Restaurant in the World.*"

Will had told her some of the rich histories of the building, that it had originally been a saloon, a brothel, and then a French steam laundry before becoming the ultimate dining destination of the brilliant chef Thomas Keller.

Savannah had tried to summon the sommelier to order from their extensive list of alcohol, but Will nixed the idea, ordering her to *behave*. Instead, he poured her more sparkling water as their first course of the Chef's Tasting Menu arrived. Will had ordered "Royal Kaluga Caviar" for her and "Oyster and Pearls" for himself. Savannah looked down at the elegant yet small dish before her and then at Will.

"Act like you can eat more than chicken and waffles!" Will whispered.

Savannah kicked him hard under the table, and he almost dropped his silverware. She smirked, then winked at him.

"So, may I ask what it is that I'm keeping you from?" Savannah asked casually.

Will hesitated, and she could tell it was either too embarrassing or too personal for him to talk about, but slowly he stopped eating and spoke.

"Just a business proposal I'm working on," he said, diverting his eyes.

"Well, does it have to do with you being a pilot?" She questioned, not willing to let it go.

Will looked at her strangely for a moment. “I’m a captain,” he said, frowning. “There’s a big difference between the two.”

“And that would be?” Savannah snapped.

“About the same difference between being a streetwalker and a senator’s prostitute,” Will quipped.

Will could tell she was both angry and hurt by his retort. He could vividly see the words she tossed around in her head, but her face seemed to soften. She let out a barely audible sigh as if she was surrendering, too exhausted for any arguments or fighting.

“Can we take the gloves off for just a little while?” Savannah asked sincerely. Moments passed before Will nodded his head in agreement.

“The main difference is one of responsibility,” Will said as he straightened his back and leaned in as if sharing a huge secret.

“A pilot’s main responsibility is flying from point A to point B. The captain is responsible not only for the craft but also for the crew and every other thing involved in the process,” he continued.

“So, when did you realize you wanted to fly?” Savannah asked, noticing the excitement in his eyes.

“The first time I drew a breath!” Will laughed lightly and continued, “No, really, I was almost six. My father had taken me to the Tuskegee Airmen Museum.”

“I’ve heard of them but don’t know much about their experiences,” Savannah stated, taking a sip of water and realizing just how delicious her caviar dish was.

“One of my first memories was of my father telling me great stories about them,” Will said, wiping his mouth gently with his linen napkin. “They were his heroes.”

“And yours too, I can tell,” Savannah added.

“My favorite story happened on April 19, 1941. Eleanor Roosevelt visited Tuskegee and asked Charles "Chief" Anderson, can Negroes really fly airplanes?"

He told her, "Certainly we can; as a matter of fact, would you like to take an airplane ride?" Will laughed loudly.

“After Chief Anderson had flown Mrs. Roosevelt around for a half hour, she said to him, ‘"I guess Negroes can fly." Shortly after, it was announced that the first Negro Air Corps pilots would be trained at Tuskegee.”

Savannah listened attentively to Will as she savored the ELevages Perigord Moulard Duck, wondering details about him. His words and eyes stroked her, causing a desire between her legs. He was so striking hot to look at; her body responded with a heat that grew from a spark to a wildfire of need.

Throughout the next two hours, as the other seven courses of their tasting menu arrived, Will shared his accomplishments throughout his career; the U.S. Naval Academy in Annapolis, Maryland, and the Naval Air Station in Pensacola, Florida, where he was always top of his class. Then on to advanced flight training at NAS Whiting Field, where he learned to fly the famed F/A-18E/F Super Hornet fighter jet. He regaled in the memories of the first time he was shot off the U.S.S. Nimitz aircraft carrier; the massive steam-powered catapult successfully hurled his 36-ton aircraft so that he didn't "hit the water before catching sky."

Will detailed, sometimes with a distant, painful look, what it was like being at Aviation Officer Candidate School, always at the top of his class, and the overt and covert racism he dealt with because of it. It hadn't been easy, but he used jealousy and hate to improve himself.

Every movement of his lips was an invitation to partake in his intellect and masculinity. The ease with which Will spoke made each detail exciting. Savannah had underestimated everything about him; he had a brilliant mind, a sensitive heart, and infinite passion.

Previously, all she had wanted to do was tear him down, but just for tonight, she would enjoy this moment. And she had.

As they finished their last course, clinking glasses grabbed Savannah's attention. She looked towards the next table where a young couple was celebrating; a gold box with a pink ribbon sat between them. It was like the box her mother had given her on her birthday. The same box she had hurled through the window.

The memory caused deep pain to drill its way up to the surface of her mind, taking away the happiness she had experienced tonight. It was a wretched reminder of the indelible markings of all the losses of her life etched on her soul. Savannah could never escape it; like the Hound of the Baskervilles, it tracked her, determined to take away any ounce of hope she had of living. When she turned away from the couple and looked back at Will, he eyed her suspiciously.

Savannah had felt almost normal tonight for the first time in a long while. But now it was over. Any thought that she and Will could be anything other than enemies was gone too. That reality deepened the pain, and again Savannah knew she would forever be alone.

Will watched Savannah slide silently into the black leather seat of the limo just as soon as the driver opened the door. He got in and sat across from her, trying to figure it out. Her behavior was enigmatic; he had wanted to say something but hadn't. *Had he imagined the connection they had experienced throughout dinner?* No, it had been there; she had been enthusiastic and interested in everything he had shared, but she had crawled back into her cold, impenetrable shell as soon as dinner was over.

Now, Savannah sat stoically, looking out the window as they drove through Yountville, an eerie silence dancing between them. Will wondered what he had done or said that had caused her emotional retreat and replayed their entire conversation in his head, searching for a clue. He could find none and could draw only one conclusion: *the bitch really was crazy.*

The limo pulled up the estate's winding driveway and stopped in front of the main house. The lamp lights shone into the darkness of the car, and Will could see tears falling down Savannah's face. Not just tears of sadness but tears born of great pain. The agony that he had known on many occasions in his life.

Will exited the limo feeling sorry for her, and that realization made him uncomfortable. He extended his hand to Savannah, and she looked at it as though it was a rickety bridge over a 1,000-foot ravine. Hesitantly, she moved toward him and placed her hand in his as she got closer.

Will looked deeply at the fragile woman wearing the sophisticated, champagne sleeveless cocktail dress with small pearl earrings and necklace. Her hair was in an updo, with one gentle curl falling down the right side, showing off the beauty and softness of her face. The dress was a chic and timeless look for her, and the gold strappy heels added to the perfection of her shapely legs.

As Savannah exited the limo, Will held her hand tightly, supporting her. They were inches apart, and he could see the tears still falling. She tried to remove her hand from his, but he held it securely. She looked into his eyes, then turned her face away from him.

"What can I do to help you?" Will whispered, turning her face back to meet his. Her lips trembled, and it seemed she was on the verge of bawling, and then she smiled.

"What I really need is a drink," Savannah said impishly. "And I promise, you won't have to clean me up."

"You're an adult," Will said, still holding her face. "So, I can't stop you from drinking, but drinking never solves anything."

"No, but it helps me to stop feeling, and that's what I need right now."

"I understand," Will said, removing his hand from her face. "There was a time I needed to deaden myself too, but it only had tragic consequences."

Savannah looked at him for a long time, searching for the meaning of what he said.

"But you don't understand," she said, looking away again. "My reasons to die are stronger than my reasons to live."

"Come with me," Will said, leading her up the stairs to the main house.

Will's estate was more than just a beautiful dwelling place; she was "sacred ground," just like Uluru-Kata Tjuta in Australia or Mount Kailas in Tibet. She was said to have been a portal where communion with the spirit world was open. The myth was a Yukian elder's wife of the Wappo tribe used this land as a sweat lodge, a ceremonial sauna, and a place for healing.

Will wasn't much of a religious or spiritual man, but he knew that the land on which his estate was built had supernatural, healing powers. He had spent two weeks here after the funeral, soul-searching and ridding himself of the demons that had dogged his life. By the time he had left, he knew that his insides had been changed.

Will hoped that the woman standing next to him in the darkness, lit only by the moon and two massive fire bowls on either end of the 70-foot sweeping infinity pool, would experience it too.

"This place is unbelievable," Savannah said with deep reverence as she gazed over the Napa Valley, glimmering like a sea of diamonds.

Will quietly stepped back over the glass and marble floor to let Savannah experience it on her own. Moving towards his favorite chaise lounge, he took his jacket off, placing it neatly on the back of the chair. As he sat, he kicked off his shoes, undid his tie, then unbuttoned his shirt as he laid back.

As if summoned by Venus, the goddess of sexuality, Savannah removed her shoes, slipped out of her dress, and let her hair down. She tousled the thick mane as it cascaded around her shoulders and down her back. She was completely naked except for the pearls. The sight was so visually stunning it brought tears to Will's eyes.

The moonlight in front of her cast a perfect circle around her form and then seemed to light her from the inside out. The darkness upon her had faded, and now she was aglow.

Sure, he had witnessed an optical illusion, Will blinked several times, but the sight remained. It was as if the woman he had known as Savannah had disappeared, and an angel had emerged.

As she slipped into the pool, Will experienced something he never had before; a bone-chilling presentiment, a knowing that their paths hadn't crossed by accident. He had been placed strategically in her life to protect her. *But from what or whom?*

Will awoke with the bright morning sun resting on his face and a faint recollection of the night before. He opened his eyes, blinking as the light hit him, realizing he was still on the lounger. As he tried to sit up, he felt something heavy on him and looked down to see Savannah curled up in his lap, still naked.

The unforgettable experience of watching her last night had been so profound. Will still felt tangible awe covering his skin. It wasn't just that she was the most beautiful woman he had ever seen, nor that her sensuality was so exotic it made his eyes prisoners to her. It was because he had watched the unfolding of something preternatural, an undeniable change.

The woman he had first seen at the bachelor party, the one that had boarded his craft bandaged and that he had carried drunk from the Top of the Mark, was gone. In her place, nestled upon him, was lying a radiate angel.

Will wanted to push her locks away from her face to see her more clearly, but he didn't want to stir her.

"I'm awake," she said as if sensing his desire. Her face turned up, and her hazel eyes fixed on him. Will ran his finger over her cheek.

"For the first time in my life, I watched the sunrise," she said, smiling widely.

For moments, they just looked at one another deeply. Desire being a slow, intense waltz between them. Will's heart and manhood beat in unison, a wildfire raging out of control. His lust escaped the head of his penis, wetting him, making him want to put his fingers between her legs to see if she was wet too.

Will lifted her, embracing her as her full breast pressed hard into him. A salacious moan escaped her lips as he locked his hands in her hair, pulling her closer. Her sensuous lips reached for him, biting his lip softly, then kissing him fully. Their tongues were hot and wanting as they explored each other as if they were old lovers.

Tasting her had been better than Will had imagined, and he wanted more. As her hands moved towards his belt buckle, his hand slid down her back, gripping the fullness of her round ass. Her breast moved easily into his mouth, her nipple hard on his tongue. He sucked her in as she moaned. Finally, she released the buckle, unzipped his pants, and gripped his manhood. He shuttered, lifting her up into his arms.

He held her in his arms as they gazed deeply into each other's eyes.

"Don't hurt me," she asked as tears pooled in her mesmerizing eyes, calling forth a promise; he knew he would keep. He could make her his, sweep her away from all she had done and been. He knew more clearly than he had known anything else. They were meant to be together. Their destinies were tied; she was what he had always wanted and needed.

"I won't. I promise," Will spoke, tears welling in his own.

Minutes passed as he held her, his lust giving way to something he had never known. A profound connection fused them in that intimate embrace, transcending their physical desires. It was as if time stood still, and at that moment, their hearts aligned, beating in perfect harmony.

As their bodies pressed against each other, a gentle tenderness replaced the urgency that had consumed him moments ago. The remnants of lust melted away, leaving only a deep longing to explore the depths of this love he felt. He could tell she felt it too. *Love.*

For a man who had guarded his heart so fiercely, hesitant to love another woman beyond his mother and young daughter, this newfound love stirred within Will a tender vulnerability. It was a delicate emotion that both comforted and challenged him, filling the void he had unknowingly carried for so long. It was a love he yearned for but had denied himself out of fear.

In this tender journey of love, he realized that his fear had been a self-imposed prison, preventing him from experiencing the profound joy and connection that love could bring. As he opened himself up to her, he discovered that vulnerability was not a weakness to be feared but a gateway to a tender and transformative love.

He buried his head in her neck and let rivers of tears flow. Years of pain and grief evaporated in her healing arms as her hands gently stroked his back. He felt a safety he had never experienced in the warmth of her embrace. Her presence, like a soothing balm, eased his anxieties and insecurities. With each passing moment, his heart opened wider, embracing the possibility of a love that could heal his wounded soul.

Will looked into her eyes and marveled at the tenderness emanating from her, which shattered the remaining barriers he had erected around his heart. He saw compassion and understanding in her eyes, a reflection of the love he had longed for but had been too afraid to embrace. In her presence, he found solace, knowing that he could be his truest self without judgment or reproach. He could tell she was experiencing the same gifts of healing too.

Will easily caressed her cheek with trembling hands, whispering reassurance and devotion. His voice, once filled with desire, now quivered with a newfound sincerity. "I want to know you, all of you," he murmured softly, his words carrying the weight of a thousand promises. "Not just your body, but your hopes, dreams, and fears. I want to cherish you, protect you, and be there for you in every way I can."

Tears of joy mingled with the remnants of their earlier tears, painting a canvas of raw emotion on their faces. In that sacred moment, they recognized that their connection was far greater than mere physical attraction. It was a profound meeting of souls, recognizing that their paths had led them to this transformative encounter.

Their lips met in a tender kiss, conveying the depth of their emotions more eloquently than words ever could. As they melted into each other, their bodies danced in sync, fueled by passion and an unyielding desire to connect on a deeper soul level. With each caress and whispered declaration of love, they embarked on a journey of intimacy that would forever bind their spirits.

Savannah slowly lay on the grass, opening herself to him. He removed his shirt, then his pants. She waved him down to her, and he obliged. Pushing her legs back, his tongue explored and ravished every part of her body. First, the honey between her legs, as she screamed with delight and went over the edge. Then slowly moving up her body, planting kisses, relishing every part of her. As he hovered over her, she took him in.

As they moved slowly, his penis explored her; it was a homecoming. If asked to explain this moment in words, they would fail him. He only knew what he *felt*.

"I love you, Savannah St. Clair," he whispered.

She smiled from deep within. "I love you too, Wilson Fairmont Dozier."

For the next hour, they made passionate love. Will came within her easily, depositing his seed and heart. At that moment, they became more than lovers; they became partners in love, bound together by an unbreakable bond. Laying completely satiated, they talked about what they wanted to be to and for each other. He felt a new chapter beginning. Just as he was about to tell her about Chloe, his cell phone rang.

Time stood still for several seconds. He didn't want to break the magic that was happening, *but what if it was his mother and something had happened to Chloe?* He got up quickly, fished into his jacket, and retrieved his cell.

In a torrent of anger and betrayal, Will's heart shattered into a million pieces. The realization of her married boyfriend, and worse yet, his ties to the senator, collided with his dreams of a shared future, leaving him feeling foolish and deceived. How could he have allowed himself to believe they could have genuine love, to build a life together?

With clenched fists and seething rage, he contemplated ignoring the impending arrival of the senator and his bodyguards. But deep down, he knew that the reality was closing in on him, suffocating his expectations and drowning his hopes. At that moment, his illusions were mercilessly shattered.

A surge of resentment coursed through his veins as he remembered that the woman he had so passionately pledged his life and love to belonged to another man. There was no way she could walk away from the senator. The bitter taste of betrayal filled his mouth, mingling with his anger. Without a word, he forcefully thrust the phone into her hands, embodying his rage and disappointment.

"It's your boyfriend," he spat, his voice dripping with venom and disdain. Every syllable dripped with the weight of his shattered trust and the realization that he had been nothing more than a naive pawn in this deceitful game. The woman before him was a painful reminder of the illusion he had allowed himself to believe.

As he looked into her eyes, he saw the depth of her betrayal, which further fueled his anger. The flames of fury danced in his gaze, consuming any remnants of tenderness that had once resided there. The dreams they had woven together now lay tattered and broken, casualties of her treachery. She had played him all along.

At that moment, his anger burned brighter than any love he had ever felt. It ignited a fire within him, fueled by righteous indignation at the lies that had ensnared him. He would no longer be a pawn in their wicked charade, a disposable plaything in their twisted game of power and control.

With a heavy heart and a smoldering fury, he turned away from her, his back rigid with resentment. The air crackled with unspoken words; the silence punctuated only by the weight of their shattered dreams. He vowed never to be a fool for love again, to guard his heart against those who would exploit his vulnerability.

Savannah took it and answered.

"Hey," she said, looking perplexingly at Will as he pulled on his pants and buttoned his shirt.

"Alright," he heard her say as he picked up his shoes and jacket. He snatched his phone from her and headed to the house to pack his bag. *What the fuck had he been thinking?*

Chapter Sixteen

"Stronger than lover's love is lover's hate. Incurable, in each, the wounds they make."

— Euripides.

Eric rose from his desk and stretched, admiring the new watch his mother had given him. A smile lit up as he read the gift card, signing, "With all my Love, Big Mama." He finally understood why everyone, including family and friends, referred to the petite woman adored as "Big Mama." Despite her small stature, her heart and wisdom were immense, making her a giant among women. After all these years, he was grateful that he had been blessed to be her son.

The midnight skyline of Manhattan was a mesmerizing display of twinkling lights. Time didn't matter to him anymore. He could stay up as long as he wanted, working on his manuscript without fear of guards banging on his cell. The feeling of freedom was still surreal, yet oh so sweet.

He went to the kitchen, craving another slice of his mother's delicious Lemon Pound Cake. Walking through his older brother's luxurious penthouse, he still couldn't believe he was there. After spending the last twenty-five years locked up in the Mississippi State Penitentiary, everyone had told him there was no way the Parole Board would allow him to leave the state, let alone travel to New York. But they didn't know his mother or brother, who had fought tirelessly to bring him home. A week ago, he was finally granted parole, and now, he was relishing every moment of his newfound freedom.

As he carefully sliced a huge piece of his mother's irresistible cake, he couldn't help but shake his head in disbelief and let out a hearty laugh. How long and lonely days had he spent dreaming about his mother's delicious cooking? About the warm and loving embrace that only she could provide. He had made countless promises to himself that if he ever got the chance to be with her again, he would cherish every moment, never taking her or her love for granted.

Reimagining his life now, he couldn't help but think how misguided he was in his younger days. Anger and resentment had consumed him, blinding him to the love and support that had always surrounded him. He hated God, his parents, brothers, and everyone else around him and felt justified. Back then, he felt life had screwed him over royally. How do you go from having the best the world offers: parents who love and adore you, brothers who protect and spoil you, a comfortable home, and happiness in life to losing it all?

In a moment that shattered his childhood innocence, Eric's beloved father, Henry Jones, was killed during a routine traffic stop. The authorities, aided by a complicit press, smeared his father's reputation, trying to justify the cops' brutal actions. The tight-knit Hattiesburg community and their church stood by the Jones family, though justice remained elusive. The police chief ruled it justified, and the police were never charged.

Eric was only eight years old and with his father that fateful night returning from a T-ball game. Despite his young age, nothing could ease the overwhelming emotions he was experiencing. Within a week, he spiraled into deep despair, unable to shake off the trauma that had gripped him. As he lashed out at former friends, the school became a battleground, now reduced to mere targets for his pent-up rage. The allure of gangs and drugs beckoned to him, promising an escape from the pain he felt. Eric was at the helm of his city's streets in his teenage years. By his early twenties, the clanging of cell doors marked the end of his reign as a botched drug deal resulting in the accidental death of his closest ally and confidante. He was left with nothing but the bitter taste of regret and a life sentence.

In the aftermath of his father's murder, Eric had convinced himself that he was entitled to wreak havoc on the world. But the moment he watched the light flicker out of his friend's eyes, he realized the true cost of his actions. In his fifth year of imprisonment, he met a compassionate counselor, and his world began to shift. The last two decades had been a slow and steady transformation as he worked tirelessly to rebuild his shattered soul. Today, he stood as an honorable man, ready to embrace the next chapter of his life with open arms.

As he savored the cake, Eric couldn't help but feel grateful for the second chance he had been given. His family had stood by him even when he had pushed them away, and he realized now that they had never given up on him. He vowed to never take their love for granted again.

As he lost himself in thought, the sound of movement in the hallway jolted him back to reality. His mother had warned him to keep an eye out for the return of their neighbor, Savannah. He had heard stories about her from his mother and brother, tales of her profession, her brush with death, her hospitalization, her daring escape, and about the senator. Though he had never met her, he felt a strange kinship. He understood her in a way few others could, recognizing the raw pain, simmering anger, and desperate need to hurt others. It was a melody that had played in the background of his life, a tune that he knew all too well.

He felt he had something valuable to offer - the lessons he had learned about love, forgiveness, and redemption. He knew firsthand the transformative power of change and believed that Savannah could change too. His mother shared this conviction and felt a calling to be a part of her journey.

As he peered through the peephole, he saw a team of stern-faced men clad in black entering Savannah's apartment. But the sight of their weapons, drawn and ready, sent a chill down his spine.

Savannah stowed her bags in the overhead compartment slipping into the seat beside a man who looked like he had just rolled out of bed. He yawned, his bleary eyes sizing her as if she were the in-flight meal. She kept her gaze averted, subtly turning her body away from the stranger and sinking into her seat.

"Looks like someone needs their beauty sleep," the man quipped as the flight attendant came around to check seat belts.

Savannah fastened her seat belt and tuned out the ogre-like man beside her. Clasping her hands under her chin, she gazed out the window, lost in thought.

"I'm coming to Napa. We've got to talk," the senator's voice had been low and menacing over the phone. He had never been one for conversation, and his sudden interest in her made her skin crawl. After Will had stormed off, she refused to stay in Napa. He had warned her about the men who had picked her up in New York - they were the senator's hired goons. Though she couldn't remember much, she knew she had let slip some of the senator's secrets at the Top of the Mark. At the time, she hadn't cared; Will was with her, and she had felt invincible. But with his departure, she knew she had to protect herself.

There was a looming threat of war that made Savannah take precautions. She had left the estate in a cab and then hired a private car to drive her to Medford, Oregon, a journey over five grueling hours. She sent a message to the senator, claiming that she was headed to Dallas for treatment and would be back in Manhattan in a month. But she had other plans. Her destination was the Westchester County Airport in White Plains, New York. From there, she planned to hire a car to take her to Manhattan, where she could retrieve some belongings from her apartment, including the crucial DNA evidence. After that, she must find a safe place to lay low.

The sudden ringing of Savannah's cell phone made her heart skip a beat. Please let it be Will, she silently prayed.

As she dug into her pocket, Savannah's hands shook uncontrollably. An *unknown number*. Could it be the senator's goons? She quickly turned off her phone and removed the SIM card and the battery. She knew she had to stay one step ahead of them.

As the plane powered up, Savannah tried to distract herself from the memories of Will. But they flooded her mind, overwhelming her senses. She couldn't help but remember the touch of his lips on hers, the warmth of his tongue, and the intensifying pleasure of his body moving against hers. Even though he had stormed off, she knew the love he had professed to her was real. She clung to the memories, knowing they were all she had left of him.

A small bump jarred the plane as it headed down the runway, bringing her back to the moment. As it picked up speed, Savannah grimaced. The interior panel she'd been resting on began to vibrate, and she closed her eyes. Leaning forward, she placed her trembling hands on her knees. As the nose of the craft tilted up and the force moved her back against the seat, she wished that Will was in the cockpit! This was one of the reasons she hated flying commercials.

"Isn't this fun?" the Shrek lookalike beamed.

Will tiptoed into the extravagantly designed pink and white nursery with Chloe peacefully asleep. The musical mobile gently spun above her crib, the soft lullaby filling the room. Sophia had created a magical and enchanting space for their little angel, complete with a Jack and Jill Canopy Crib fit for a princess. He laid her down, gently patting her back as she stirred. She relaxed and went back into a peaceful sleep. As he turned down the lights, Will couldn't help but feel grateful.

As he headed down the hallway to the master suite, he thought about Sophia. Every inch of their exclusive Todt Hill estate was a testament to her love and care. Before marrying her, Will had never thought about living on Staten Island but had granted her wish because her family had lived there for over 30 years. Since her death, he had thought about moving away many times. But he felt it was the least he could do for Chloe; to allow her to be in the presence of the people, places, and things her mother loved most.

Will felt a pang in his chest. Sophia and Savannah had depended on him, and he had let them both down.

“Don’t even go there,” he chided himself. He refused to allow guilt to gnaw at his conscience any longer. Sophia and any thoughts of a relationship with Savannah were dead. With a purposeful determination, Will had left her behind in Napa. Even though the echoes of his undying pledge of faithfulness had consumed him on his flight back from Oakland, he understood exactly why he had left. They could never be.

A sharp stab pierced his chest at an intrusive vision of Savannah lying on the grass in his sprawling estate. He fought it, but it pushed past his defenses, seeping into his consciousness and besieging him with memories he dared not entertain. They tempted him, pulling him back into their unfinished story. He couldn't allow himself to be entrapped in the labyrinth of his own emotions. He shook his head vigorously as if physically attempting to dislodge the unwelcome images.

"No," he whispered, his voice firm and unwavering. "I can't go there. Not now."

He had to get focused. The debacle in Napa had set him back on his plans. Tonight, he was going to get through the paperwork from his legal team.

As he walked into his master bedroom and saw his mother, Sarah setting up his dinner on the balcony, he forcefully pushed the vivid memories aside. Smooth jazz filled the room.

"Did our sweetheart put up much of a fuss?" she asked as Will shook his head, smiling broadly. "Not really. After her favorite story, Chloe was as good as gold," he said.

Sarah beamed, placing the grilled Mahi-mahi and steamed veggies before him. "She always loves spending time with you, son," she said, tucking a strand of hair behind her ear.

"Yes, but there's never enough time," Will sighed, taking a bite of the flaky fish.

"I know it's been a tough year, but you're doing a great job, Will. Sophia would be proud," his mother reassured.

"How's everything going with the business?" she inquired, resting her hands on his shoulders.

"It's going. I didn't get much accomplished in Napa," Will said as he poured a glass of Sauvignon Blanc. A momentary silence sat between them.

"Well, I'll let you enjoy your dinner and work," she stated, turning towards the stairs leading to the lower master suite.

"Thanks, Mom," Will said, staring into the night sky.

"Son, mind if I make an inquiry?" Sarah said with a hint of hesitation.

"Of course not, Mom." Will gazed at her, sensing the worry in her tone.

"I don't intend to meddle, but it seems that since you returned from Napa, you've been preoccupied," she expressed, hoping to understand the cause.

Will paused briefly, reflecting on his innermost musings and trying to fathom what his mother had detected.

"No, just the usual stuff," Will replied, spearing a stalk of steamed asparagus with his fork. For a moment, there was quietness again. She returned and sat beside him and spoke.

"Is there anything you'd like to share about her?" Sarah asked, taking a sip of Will's wine. He stared at her perplexed before bursting into laughter. "Mom, did you resort to reading tarot cards on my behalf, or did Uncle Lenny come back from the other side to whisper something in your ear?"

"I don't need to do readings or talk to anyone here or there," Sarah exclaimed, taking another sip. "I know things."

Will mulled over his thoughts. Unfortunately, his mother had always possessed a keen intuition about him. However, he wasn't ready to confide in her or anyone else about Savannah.

Sarah rose to her feet and embraced her son, saying, "I just want to remind you that you're a gifted young man with your whole life ahead of you."

Sarah leaned in close and whispered softly in his ear, "When you're ready, set aside guilt and fear and open your heart to her."

Will watched as his mother descended the stairs and disappeared. If only she knew Savannah St. Clair, she might not be quick to offer such advice. Especially if she had witnessed her actions in San Francisco. She would never have allowed her near Chloe. She could never escape who she was and what she did.

Savannah would never be the conventional "wife" or "mother." Even though she had mentioned briefly at the French Laundry about her desire for a family when she was younger, that dream was long over. He didn't know what kind of delusion had bewitched him in Napa, but she could never be his wife.

"If that's the case, why did you promise her your heart?" A flood of sentimental memories engulfed Will's mind, the weight of their shared moments becoming almost too much to bear. He extended his hand and guided her toward that fateful night's tranquil pool. In that simple act, he had offered her an escape from the burdens of a painful existence, an invitation to find solace and healing. And she accepted.

As he reminisced, his heart overflowed with a profound sense of awe. In the depths of his gaze, he had witnessed the beautiful transformation that had unfolded within her soul. Her burdens were momentarily lifted, replaced by a delicate vulnerability and a newfound radiance that had taken his breath away.

The memories played out like a tender melody in his mind, each moment etched in his heart with the utmost clarity. The vision of her naked body radiating in the darkness spoke volumes in the silence. It was a night that transcended time, a sanctuary where her soul had bathed in the same starlit healing flow he had experienced months before.

Will had become a witness to her metamorphosis, an accomplice in her journey toward healing and self-discovery. He had watched as the shadows of pain were replaced by a newfound lightness of being, and in turn, it had stirred something within him, igniting a fire that burned with an intensity he had never known. No matter how much he wanted to relegate her to the person she had been to deflect his cowardice, he knew she had changed.

The sentimentality of their connection as he had awakened with her resting safely in his lap overwhelmed him, flooding his senses with a tender longing. He yearned to relive those precious moments, to recapture the essence of their shared intimacy. The bond between them was electric and undeniable.

The weight of poignant regret settled heavily upon Will's heart as he revisited the memories of that special day. In the tender moments they had shared, he had made a solemn vow, promising to shelter her in his loving embrace, to fight for their connection with unwavering ferocity, and to shield her from the encroaching darkness that threatened to consume her very being. She had searched his eyes, seeking solace and honesty in his words, desperately pleading, "Don't hurt me."

But tragically, that is precisely what he had done. He had betrayed his sacred promise, shattering the fragile trust she had placed in him. In his own thoughtless actions, he had left her bewildered and vulnerable, abandoned to face the senator and his men without the refuge of his once-assured protection.

A poignant ache coursed through his veins as he confronted the magnitude of his betrayal. She had not deserved it. Regret haunts him with the knowledge that he had failed her, that he had become the source of the pain he had promised to shield her from. He yearned to turn back time and rewrite his departure script. But the stark reality of his actions remained a painful reminder of his fallibility and the irreversible damage he had inflicted upon her.

Amid the wreckage surrounding him, a familiar and solemn realization settled deep within him. His reoccurring self-destructive path when it came to personal relationships was not solely his burden to bear. At the tender age of eight, the very essence of who he had been and his future had been irreparably shattered.

The culprit behind the unforgivable acts of sexual molestation he had endured was his piano teacher, Mr. Phil Deighton. A despicable figure who had been a trusted family friend and a pillar in their community.

Deighton's actions had caused a long trail of catastrophic deaths. The first casualty was the death of Will's innocence and the joy of being a rambunctious boy. The next casualty was his father, whose life was tragically cut short when he, driven by a fierce determination to confront Deighton, set out on a fateful journey. In anguish and determination to seek justice for his son, he raced recklessly, oblivious to the curve ahead. The unforgiving consequences of that ill-fated moment resulted in his untimely death, leaving behind a void that could never be filled for Will or his mother.

Another casualty was Sophia. His infidelity, a product of his shattered innocence and fractured sense of self led to her untimely demise. In his desperate quest to prove his sexual identity, "that he wasn't gay," and erase the haunting doubts that plagued him, he'd engaged with countless women, using them as mere pawns in a futile attempt to deny his own past. Their lives, too, were casualties in this tumultuous journey, their hearts left broken and their souls wounded by his misguided actions.

Lastly, Savannah was the casualty that tore at the very fabric of a hopeful future of love. She was the one person who, for a fleeting moment, had held the promise of liberation from his demons.

Will's forehead furrowed with frustration as he muttered a string of curses. He strode over to the bar, the sound of ice clinking in his glass as he poured himself a stiff scotch. He lifted the tumbler to his lips, savoring the burn of the alcohol as it seared down his throat.

His gaze drifted to the beveled mirror behind the bar, and he caught a glimpse of his reflection staring back at him with a watery-eyed stare. He heaved a heavy sigh, the weight of his guilt pressing down like a huge boulder.

As Sade's "By Your Side" haunting melody filled the air, the lyrics struck him like a blow to the gut. He lowered his chin, unable to meet the gaze of the coward staring back at him in the mirror. He knew he had to confront the truth and face the consequences of his actions.

It had been easier to blame Savannah and storm off. But the truth was that Will was afraid to confront the senator, who had called his phone, not hers. He had been a coward to thrust the device into her hands, forcing her to take the call. *What kind of man did that make him?* What had he expected her to do when he couldn't even summon the nerve to answer the call himself?

"Shit!" Will shouted, his voice hoarse with anger as he punched the air with his fists, his breath coming in quick, ragged gasps. He knew he had let her down, had abandoned her when she needed him most. He had fled from the scene, grabbing his belongings and racing out of the door without so much as a backward glance.

On his way back to Oakland, he had his assistant call the senator, making an excuse. There was an emergency back home, and he needed to leave immediately. He had promised to send another flight crew to retrieve the senator and Savannah.

Now, as Will stood alone in his bedroom, the gravity of the situation he had left her in dawned on him. The fact that the senators' henchmen had accompanied Savannah from New York spoke volumes about Richard's intentions. Additionally, Savannah's revelation about the senators' secrets had placed her in even greater danger. The senator wouldn't hesitate to kill her if he thought she was a liability.

Frantically, Will ran his fingers over his hair, his mind racing as he reached for his phone. His hand trembled with fear and anticipation, sweat beading his forehead and trickling into his eyes. His face grew angry as he punched the buttons on his phone, dialing Savannah's number.

His heart sank as the line rang once, twice, and then clicked to voicemail.

"Dammit!" he cursed, slamming his phone on the table. He had to think of a new plan to save her and take down the senator. With a determined look, he headed out of his bedroom, his mind racing. He would do whatever it took to keep Savannah safe, no matter the cost.

As Savannah reclined in the car's back seat, her gaze fixed on the passing landscape between White Plains and Manhattan, a profound sense of tragedy and loss overwhelmed her. The burdens she had carried since childhood, marked by the untimely death of her grandmother and brother, weighed heavily on her heart. If her Nana was alive, her life would have been so very different. The haunting disappearance of her twin sister, Elisha, added to the deep-rooted sorrow that seemed to follow her at every step.

The once vibrant dreams of seeking vengeance against those she held responsible had turned into a bitter reality. Savannah had hoped to find solace and justice through her quest, but instead, it had only magnified her suffering. She had become the victim of her own pursuits, consumed by the anguish of her past. Memories intertwined like a tempest, echoing through her mind and soul.

Her mind wandered back to her childhood days, to the innocent moments shared with her beloved twin sister. The bond they once had, stolen away by an unknown force, left an emptiness that time had failed to fill. If she could have found Elisha, so much would have changed.

Then there was Michael, who she had trusted, and whose betrayal had caused her to become a detestable person. The pain intensified as she recalled the unbearable loss of her own children, a devastating blow that left her completely broken. She had been denied what she wanted most: a happy, loving family.

Savannah had tried to erase the feelings of anger and betrayal. Yes, she was heading into a life of uncertainty, but she knew she couldn't afford to let herself fall into the same pit of darkness and despair she had been in before. Her sanity was brittle. She might have trusted in the facade of dominance for years, but it had never been enough to keep her from the edge of madness. Her perfect ass had laid in vomit, shit, and Jack Daniel's. And people had died or moved on, leaving her alone with her pain.

Savannah's mind spun back to when she arrived in Oakland five days earlier. At the time, she had thought she was simply there to collect what her Nana had left her, with plans to quickly return to the familiar streets of New York. Little did she know, fate had far more in store for her than she could have imagined. Now she realized that her grandmother had been the guiding light behind all the unfolding events. And Will played a significant part in it.

Savannah found herself unable to confront the depths of what had transpired between her and Will. The pain it caused was still too raw, for she had discovered the love she had long yearned for in him. Their connection had felt genuine, and she had glimpsed a future brimming with hope and security within the sanctuary of his promises. Yet, as quickly as he had entered her life, he had vanished, leaving her adrift in a sea of unanswered questions.

Strangely, she couldn't summon anger towards him despite the ache that lingered within her. Instead, a bittersweet tenderness enveloped her heart, whispering of an unfinished chapter that awaited its final pages. Deep within her soul, an unwavering conviction took hold: they were not yet done.

There was an unspoken knowingness and a flicker of intuition that assured her their paths would converge again. Though circumstances may have led them astray for now, she harbored an unshakable faith that he would find his way back to her, drawn by an invisible thread that had woven their souls together in Napa.

In the moments when the weight of his absence felt unbearable, she sought solace in memories of their shared moments. His protection at the cemetery, their meal at Lois', the Fairmont, the road trip to Napa, the estate, and the French Laundry. She replayed their laughter, stolen glances, and how his touch had awakened a dormant fire within her. She had never had someone make love, not only to her body but to her soul. It was exactly how she imagined love could be. Each cherished memory was a lifeline, a beacon guiding her through the tempestuous sea of emotions.

As the car raced on, Savannah laughed out loud. Not too long ago, she considered putting Will in the top spot on her revenge list. However, she was done with that. Her longing for revenge had been misguided. The illusionary spoils she had fiercely pursued revealed themselves as empty and hollow. The fire that had burned within her, fueled by anger and desperation, now flickered, suffocated by the weight of her sorrow. Just as her laughter had erupted suddenly, so had her tears.

As Savannah rummaged through her bag in search of tissue, her eyes fell upon the books given to her by the lady who walked uninvited into her hospital room. Among them was a worn volume called The Prophet by Kahlil Gibran. Its presence sparked intrigue, drawing her to a card within its pages. The card bore the name "Sari," along with a contact number for a center.

Curiosity piqued, Savannah delicately flipped through the book's pages, her fingertips grazing the words penned by the poet. And there, like a hidden gem waiting to be discovered, she found the verses of a poem titled 'On Joy and Sorrow.'

"Your joy is your sorrow unmasked. And the selfsame well from which your laughter rises was oftentimes filled with your tears. And how else can it be? The deeper that sorrow carves into your being, the more joy you can contain...When you are sorrowful, look again in your heart, and you shall see that in truth you are weeping for that which has been your delight."

These profound words resonated within Savannah's soul, striking a chord that reverberated with pain and hope. In a not-so-distant past, before she immersed herself in the tranquil depths of the reflection pool nestled in Napa, Savannah would have cast aside this book without a second glance. But a transformative shift had stirred within her, altering the very fabric of her being. Though she struggled to articulate it, she knew it to be true. It was like a hidden stream of comprehension and connectedness had burst forth, breaching the barriers erected by years of anguish.

This newfound sensation mirrored the profound connection she once shared with her Nana. It felt familiar, like home.

Savannah and her beloved Nana had always had an intangible bond—a knowingness that transcended words. In those precious years, they had together, their souls danced harmoniously, entwined in a tapestry of understanding and love. And now, within the pages of this book, she felt that same current of familiarity coursing through her veins.

With trembling hands, she clutched the book to her chest, its weight a testament that somehow, and some way, her Nana was present with her. That she had not abandoned her. There was a profound shift unfolding within her. She marveled at how life had gently guided her towards this pivotal moment—the moment when Will led her to the edge of the reflection pool, and she dared to step in. There had been solace, healing, and clarity amidst the shimmering waters.

The barriers that had shielded her heart for far too long were now crumbling, revealing a profound depth of understanding that she had yearned for but had struggled to grasp. In this transformative embrace of her newfound awareness, Savannah felt a surge of gratitude for the journey that had led her here. The pain and trauma she endured were no longer burdens but profound catalysts for growth. They had led her to this juncture, this moment of awakening.

As she turned her gaze inward, she understood that the pain she had endured, the scars she carried, and the joy that had once filled her heart were not disparate fragments of her existence but intertwined strands of the tapestry that was her life. Now the only question was, where did she go from here?

Savannah needed time to figure it all out. She would return to Manhattan soon, and the senator was coming for her. Europe called to her, beckoning with the promise of a fresh start, a place where the senator's pursuit and the ghosts of her past might fade into the background. Or maybe she could escape to Seychelles, off the east African coast, a destination she had wanted to explore.

Wherever she landed, she was going to be alive and well. Her new self was powerful and enlightened. But her old self was there too, ready to destroy anyone who tried to harm her.

"Get it done; I don't care how," Betty Ann spoke sternly over the phone with a scowl. She had anonymously provided the committee with all the evidence necessary to bring an end to her husband, Senator Richard Effingham's career. The privileges of being a senator's wife were once a source of enjoyment, but that was about to end now.

Richard was clueless about her plans, making her wonder if his lack of intelligence or sheer hubris led to his downfall. Either way, he was on a downward trajectory. She was determined to see it through.

Rising with purpose, she returned the damning black dossier to the safety of her private vault. Several complications had surfaced in her plans, thanks to Richard's trollop, Savannah St. Clair. The whore spilled some of Richard's dirtiest secrets, forcing Betty Ann to accelerate her plans of disposing of her. She had ordered a team of mercenaries to break into her apartment while she was galivanting in Napa. Now that she was returning to Manhattan, plans had to be altered.

She needed to get her hands on the evidence that Savannah had squirreled away before she had her killed. Her men would torture it out of her if need be. Betty Ann couldn't risk mentioning Richard's depraved sexual behavior in the press. With kids and grandkids to think of, she had to ensure, at least in that regard, a pristine legacy for her family name.

With the dossier by her side, she carefully arranged a pouch overflowing with $10 million worth of glittering diamonds, gleaming gold coins, and crisp cash before swiftly shutting the lid. This was just a pit stop on her path to executing her ultimate plan. Her destination was her villa in the South of France after stopping off at the private haven at Luxembourg Freeport, where she had amassed a jaw-dropping fortune of $50 million over 15 years, all in anticipation of this very moment.

Over 40 years ago, Betty Ann had worn her pride like a crown when she married Richard, a war hero, a loving family man, and a bright spark in the Republican party. He was a staunch conservative and devout Christian whose father, William Effingham, had prophesied that he would one day ascend to the presidency of the United States. However, the seeds of doubt had been sown in Betty Ann's mind shortly after their honeymoon. Richard's reluctance to be intimate with her and his penchant for expensive call girls had left her feeling broken. Like many women of her time, she had suffered in silence, resigned to the fate of a passionless marriage, while channeling her energy into raising their three children.

For 15 years, Betty had dutifully played the role of a politician's wife, only showing up when it was expected of her. It wasn't until a fundraiser for her husband's potential presidential run that she had an encounter that shattered her world. One of her husband's right-wing allies had sidled up to her and shared a damning secret about why Richard would never make it to the Oval Office. It was a secret involving criminal conspiracies, bribery, and other heinous crimes against democracy that only a privileged few knew. Learning of these dark deeds had transformed Betty in every way possible - as a woman, a wife, and a mother. She had been repulsed by Richard ever since and biding her time, plotting her escape.

With masterful skill, she had concealed her inner turmoil, nodding along as dinner guests were captivated by the former Congressman turned Senator's hollow diatribes on the decline of democracy and morality in America. He preached against progressive policies on gay rights, immigration, and abortion, all while championing conservative values. Secretly, she couldn't help but chuckle as she watched him on TV, hypocritically chastising his fellow politicians embroiled in scandal.

Betty would play her part, standing stoically beside "her man" on the stage, just like Silda Wall Spitzer and Suzanne Thompson had done during their husbands' scandals. But as soon as the shit hit the fan, she would swiftly exit into her new life without him. From a distance, she would revel in the joy of watching Senator Richard Effingham's life crumble around him. He deserved every ounce of the devastation that was coming his way. It was a fitting end for a husband who had brought so much pain and misery into her life.

As the car cruised towards the bustling city, the familiar chaos of the New York streets washed over Savannah, leaving her with a bittersweet sensation. Although she knew she would soon depart from this place, she couldn't help but feel a deep reverence and awe for the city that had become her home.

On the drive into Manhattan, Savannah had finally summoned the courage to look inside Nana's worn suitcase. She gently cradled one of Nana's journals in her hands. Seven volumes were numbered and filled with her grandmother's precious words. Tears streamed down her face as she read the first page, blurring the familiar script.

"As I set these words down on paper, a warm chuckle escapes as I watch you and your sister twirl and sway to the rhythm of Al Green's "Let's Stay Together." The lyrics of that song carry such depth that they compel me to pen this message to you, my beloved granddaughter. How I wish we could remain together, intertwined in an unbreakable bond, forever. But deep in my heart, I know that I will have embarked on my eternal journey before you fully bloom into the incredible woman I know you will become. Nevertheless, know this, my dear one—I will forever be by your side, even when I am no longer physically here.

Life won't always be smooth sailing for you, my precious girl. There will be obstacles to overcome and hardships to face. And so, there are truths that I need you to hold close to your heart. To truly understand the remarkable woman you are destined to become, you must delve into your past experiences. Our stories are intricately woven into the fabric of our existence—the lessons learned during our childhood, our relationships, and most importantly, the lineage from which we come. I will share the narrative of our family, your parents, and your ancestors, for it can connect all the dots, illuminating the path that lies before you.

Painful experiences often tempt us to barricade our hearts, locking away the capacity to love, fearing that such vulnerability will only bring forth more anguish. This is especially true when those dearest to us wound us, causing the deepest scars. We instinctively run away from such pain, resolving to never let it pierce our souls again. But my dear one, love, in all its profound essence, rarely arrives in perfect packages. Instead, it is a precious gift, often hidden within the depths of our fears and the shadows of our tragedies.

Earlier today, as you cradled a photograph of your late grandfather and asked, "Where is Papa?" I pointed gently to my heart. You see, my sweet one, his presence lives on within me, his love forever etched upon my soul, changed me. I must let you know; I wasn't always your sweet, kind grandmother! I raised plenty of hell in my day and enjoyed getting back at people who did me wrong. These hands that bake all your favorite pies once nearly strangled a man to death. Yes, I did. But I'll get to all that."

Savannah laughed out loud and said, "Okay, that's where I get my crazy from!" She read on.

"I want to tell you about when your grandfather, Edward, entered my life—when bitterness and anger consumed my spirit, and I didn't want any parts of love. To me, love only meant sacrifice and a painful surrender that only invited abuse and heartache in return. I pushed him away, time and again, my heart filled with doubt. Until one fateful day, as frustration spilled from my lips, I yelled, "Why don't you just leave? You're going anyway!" In response, he looked deep into my eyes and spoke words that would forever change my life. He said, "Woman, I am not your daddy or no-good husband. I see the extraordinary gift that you are, and I vow to treat you right and never let you slip away. With every fiber of my being, I will love you unconditionally for all the days of my life." And true to his word, he did just that.

Too many souls journey through life like I did before Edward, held captive by fear, never allowing themselves the chance to experience true love. My dear one, I know that you will embark on your own path of love, encountering its many lessons. Every twist, turn, triumph, and setback is a cherished part of love's grand design. Embrace the unknown with courage, my precious child, and do not shy away from love's embrace. Even when you find yourself doubting its existence, trust that love can find you when you least expect it."

Savannah's thoughts drifted to Will. He had hovered over her, his body and words speaking of his devotion. As he had cum inside her, he gazed deep into her eyes. "You are mine, forever."

"We're here, Ms. St. Clair," the driver said as the car parked in front of her building.

"Thank you," she said as she exited the car, holding the place in Nana's journal. The driver gathered both of her suitcases. The night air was brisk and refreshing; she felt safe for the first time. Her doorman greeted her holding the door open, and inquired if he could assist with her bags.

"I've got it, thank you," she said, smiling. As she strolled through the lobby, she opened to where she had stopped reading and continued. "As I reflect upon our journey, from the moment I first held you, my heart swelled with gratitude and love. I see in you the strength and resilience passed down through generations.

And though I may not be physically present as you navigate the complexities of life, always remember that my love, guidance, and unwavering belief in you will forever reside within your heart. You are destined for greatness, my beloved granddaughter, and with each step you take on your own path to love, may you be guided by the wisdom of God's spirit and our shared journey."

Savannah stepped into the elevator feeling her grandmother's love and wisdom guiding her. She pushed her code for the penthouse floor and continued reading.

"God will be there with you and in you. That's why I named you Elisha, which means *Woman of God*."

A chilling presence closed around her, stifling her cries as an unknown force yanked her mercilessly away.

About the Author

L.D. Jackson, a native of Los Angeles, California, is the master weaver of soul-stirring tales, spinning narratives that resonate deep within the hearts of readers. Through her profound trilogy, "Who I Am," she deftly threads together stories that honor the rich tapestry of human existence, exploring the intricate melodies of love, pain, and redemption. Her pen dances upon the pages with a bold and sensuous imagination, conjuring worlds where passion and intrigue intertwine, leaving readers spellbound and yearning for more. She lives in Maui, Hawai'i with her brown Lab, Hoku.

www.ldjackson.com

www.facebook.com/ldjacksonwrites.com

www.instagram/ldjacksonwrites.com

Correspondence for the author should be sent to:

l.d.jacksonwrites@gmail.com

Visit Ldjackson.com

and sign up for L.D.'s newsletter!

Front Cover design: DLR Designs

Back Cover & Spine design:

Andrade Hendricks (quiettsunamirising@gmail.com)

Coming Soon!

Book Two in the Who I Am Trilogy

Unquenchable: Something Better Than Vengeance

Cover design credit: @maroohpublisher

In the electrifying second installment of the captivating Who I Am trilogy, "*Unquenchable: Something Better Than Vengeance,*" the flames of passion and intrigue burn brighter than ever. Picking up where "Obsessable" left off, we reunite with Savannah, the indomitable protagonist who has narrowly escaped a harrowing assault on her life.

Amidst the turquoise waters and breathtaking beauty of Seychelles, Savannah seeks solace and safety. But this tropical paradise holds more than mere tranquility. In a twist of fate, she stumbles upon a staggering revelation that will shatter her world, unveiling secrets that will reshape every aspect of her existence.

Meanwhile, Will, the lover who once vowed eternal devotion, battles against insurmountable odds in a race to find Savannah and seek redemption. Faced with formidable adversaries who will stop at nothing to thwart his mission, Will's determination becomes a beacon of hope amidst the darkness that threatens to consume them both.

As Savannah's life hangs in the balance, torn between the pursuit of vengeance and the yearning for fulfillment, the stakes have never been higher. Will she find the strength to transcend her thirst for retribution and embrace a brighter future? Or will the chains of her past continue to deny her the realization of her deepest desires?

Unveiling a tapestry of passion, suspense, and unexpected twists, "Unquenchable" propels readers on an enthralling voyage, delving into the depths of human emotion and the resilient spirit that drives us all. Join Savannah as she confronts her inner demons and discovers that sometimes, something better than vengeance can pave the way to an extraordinary destiny.

Made in the USA
Las Vegas, NV
08 November 2023

80134203R00197